BIRTHRIGHT

The Legacy Series
Book One

Jessica Ruddick

Cover design by Paper and Sage Design

Edited by Judy Roth

ISBN 978-1-946164-01-8

CHAPTER 1

MY MOM LOOKED AROUND MY room at the haphazard tower of boxes and pile of unzipped suitcases spewing clothes. She pursed her lips in that disapproving way moms have. "Aren't you going to unpack?"

I spared her a glance before returning to the book I was reading. "Why?"

"It'll be nicer for you if you unpack."

I flipped over to my stomach without missing a word on the page. "There's no point. We'll be moving soon anyway."

"Yes, but we're here now."

"Not for long," I muttered. Just long enough to ruin some lives, then we'd be on our way again.

She sat down on the edge of my bed, pursed lips replaced by the concerned mom brow furrow. "Can we talk about this?"

"Nope," I said, not looking up.

"I know the last assignment was hard on you. I've found—"

My knuckles whitened on the edges of my book. "I already said I'm not going to talk about it."

She sighed. "Do you want to go to the movies today or something? I don't have to work until tonight."

"No."

She sat quietly for a few moments, looking down at her hands, which were folded in her lap. I didn't know why. My tone clearly did not invite quality mother-daughter bonding time. She finally left, shutting the door behind her.

Maybe it was petty, because it technically wasn't her fault, but I wasn't ready to forgive her for last year's birthday present—my sweet sixteen. A car would have been nice. More realistically, I would have settled for an iPhone. Earrings, a t-shirt, a book. Hell, I would have settled for socks.

Coming into my birthright of being the Grim Reaper's seeker was not what I'd had in mind.

You see, I now worked for the Grim Reaper. Yup, at seventeen, I was a lackey for the bringer of death. It wasn't a job I would wish on anyone. And it didn't even pay anything.

We'd always moved around a lot, but I never really gave it much thought since it had been that way for as long as I could remember. I'd always figured my mom was just restless. I didn't mind. *Much.*

But lately we'd been moving more and more often, and I couldn't help thinking it had something to do with the increased number of assignments.

I still couldn't believe my mom had kept this from me my whole life. A little advance warning would have been nice. You know, something like, *"Ava, Uncle Xavier isn't really your uncle. He's the middleman between us and the Grim Reaper. And did I mention we have to identify the next platoon of angels?"*

I slammed my book shut and threw it against the wall. I had just read the same paragraph three times and couldn't tell you the first thing about it. Reading was usually my escape, but I was too agitated.

Thanks again, Mom.

I shrugged into a hoodie and slipped on my knock-off Vans. I didn't bother to tell my mom I was going out, instead I just slammed the apartment door loudly behind me. She'd get the idea.

I trotted down the flights of stairs and took a left out of the apartment complex. A right would take me to a town center, complete with shops, restaurants, and a park. Left took me into the ghetto.

I shoved my hands into my pockets and walked purposefully. After about a mile, I was in the thick of the projects. Men and some not-yet-men congregated outside a convenience store, clutching bottles covered in brown paper bags. Across the street on an abandoned stoop, a drug dealer palmed twenties and handed the goods over to a woman in dirty clothes with wild disheveled hair. Even from twenty feet away, I could see her twitching.

I could read the drug dealer's aura, which meant he couldn't be much older than me since my aura reading range was limited to people in my relative age bracket. His aura was black with a tinge of red. No surprise there. In this part of town, that was typical. It was one of the reasons I liked coming here. There was no danger of running into any pure white auras.

I kicked a plastic cup into the gutter and crossed the street to enter the park. I sat on the one remaining swing, which was surrounded by chains that no longer had swings attached. The metal links swayed in the breeze like metal skeletons hanging from nooses. Some kids—two girls and a boy—ran into the park soon after. My best guess put their ages around eight. They were no older than ten at any rate, too young to be without adult supervision.

They climbed the jungle gym for a few minutes before moving to the slide.

None of them were wearing coats. The smaller of the two girls was only wearing a thin t-shirt with leggings. She had to be cold. I was beneath my long-sleeve shirt and hoodie.

I wondered if they realized how down-trodden their lives were by society's standards. I never thought my mother and I were rich by any means, but it wasn't until I got a little older that I realized how old our car was, that our furniture was secondhand, and that my mom's clothes were often threadbare so that I could have new ones. Our apartment was always clean and I never had to worry about having food to eat, but we certainly weren't living the high life.

Judging by the state of those children's clothes, I doubted they could say the same.

Screams and shrieks caught my attention. A shoving match had started at the top of the slide. A long ago buried instinct surfaced, and I had to stop myself from intervening.

In the last year, I'd learned that detachment was the best policy.

The boy suddenly shoved the little girl so hard she fell five feet down from the top of the slide. She let out a cry and curled into a ball, her little body shaking with sobs while the bigger kids laughed and ran away, leaving her there.

I watched for a few minutes before closing my eyes and groaning. I hated breaking my own rules.

I walked over and knelt beside her. Now that I was close, I could see eight was an overestimate. Her age was probably closer to six.

I touched her shoulder gently. "Are you okay?"

She jerked up and scooted away from me, her big brown eyes wide and frightened. She used her arm to wipe the tears from her face. Her hands were filthy, dirt caked under her nails.

"Are you okay?" I asked again, keeping my hands to myself.

She nodded.

The sun was setting, taking any remaining warmth with it and leaving a chill in the air. She shivered.

"Do you live around here?"

She hesitated. Maybe in school they had taught her

not to speak to strangers. Stranger danger and all that.

There was nothing I could do to improve her life situation, but I could at least make her walk home more bearable.

I unzipped my hoodie and held it out to her. "Here."

She hesitated again, her little hands clasped in front of her, each one stopping the other from snatching the garment.

I shook it a little. "Take it. I know you're cold. I have another one at home. It's a little big for you, but it should be warm."

She didn't take it from me, so I put it down and walked away.

When I got to the corner, I looked over my shoulder to see her running in the opposite direction, her little body nearly swallowed whole by my hoodie.

AS DARKNESS OVERTOOK THE WANING rays of sunlight on my walk home, goose bumps formed on my arms, and I regretted having given away my hoodie. Just a little.

My stomach growled, angrily reminding me I hadn't eaten lunch today. A meal of canned ravioli followed by a night alone in the apartment sounded fabulous about now. With any luck, my mom would be gone by the time I got home.

Luck was not on my side. Looking at our car in the parking lot, I frowned. She said she had work tonight. She didn't like to let on, but money was tight, and we needed the tips she'd get waitressing on a busy Saturday night. So why was she home?

As soon as I opened the front door, the hair on the back of my neck stood up and a tingle ran down my spine. The scent of cinnamon filled my nostrils. It was like having those little candy Red Hots shoved up my nose. Dread in the form of a knot settled in the base of my stomach.

Xavier.

Xavier was...I wasn't sure what he was. Was he the descendant of a fallen angel like me? Was he an angel himself? Or was he something else, something more sinister?

He certainly looked it. He certainly acted it. He exuded evil.

He was lounging on our couch, his arms spread out over the back of it and his right ankle propped on his left knee. His black hair was slicked back, and he'd grown a goatee since the last time I'd seen him. As usual, he was dressed in a black suit with a red tie, what I mentally referred to as his "villain suit."

I couldn't believe he was the same man who used to read me bedtime stories and tuck me in when my mom had to work nights.

A smile stretched across his face and his black beady eyes watched me enter the room. The only thing that could possibly make him more snakelike was if a thin red forked tongue flitted out of his mouth.

I'd be less surprised than if a hippo flounced around my living room in a pink tutu in true *Fantasia* style.

My mom sat stiffly on a chair across from him. It was our home, but Xavier was in control here. Her eyes met mine, and she shrugged her shoulders slightly. She had no idea why he was here either. We hadn't expected him for at least a couple more months.

"Welcome home, Ava," Xavier said. "Why don't you have a seat?"

"No, thanks. I'll stand."

He chuckled. "Suit yourself."

Xavier took a moment to inspect his cuticles, as if he weren't in the middle of our living room, as if we weren't waiting for him to say whatever it was he came to say so he would leave again. I'd say he was oblivious to the effect he had on us, but that wouldn't be true. He knew, and he relished it.

I crossed my arms over my chest. "What do you want?"

He raised his eyebrows. "Is that any way to treat a guest in your home?" He looked at my mother. "You should really teach her better manners."

I laughed bitterly. "Calling yourself a guest implies that you're wanted here."

"Ava," my mom said, her tone sharp.

Xavier just threw his head back and laughed. "No, Mary, let the little vixen spew her venom. I like it. It's honest. Honesty is underrated in society today, don't you agree?"

I glared at him.

"I have your next assignment."

My glare faltered as I fought to keep the air moving in and out of my lungs. An assignment from Xavier meant the blood of an innocent would be on my hands again.

When I said I worked for *the* Grim Reaper, that was oversimplifying it a bit. There's actually more than one. Think about it—with all the people who die every day in the world, how could there possibly be just one?

The particular Grim Reaper I worked for was special, though. He collected souls that were worthy of being angels. It was my job as a seeker to find those souls.

How's that for an after school job?

"Forgive me, Xavier, but isn't it a little soon?" my mom said quietly. "She hasn't even had a chance to get settled in her new school."

He glanced at her before returning his attention to me. "She can handle it. Besides, it's time."

"But her last assignment was just last month!" my mom protested. "Are you sure—"

"I'm very sure."

I closed my eyes and pinched the bridge of my nose. The knot of dread in my stomach exploded, seeping into the rest of my body. I breathed deeply, desperately trying to keep control. The last thing I wanted was to lose it in front of Xavier.

"How long do I have?"

"Two weeks."

Two weeks. I had two weeks to put a plan into motion that would change lives irrevocably.

My classmates' faces popped into my mind. I hadn't bothered getting to know anyone or even learning names. I told myself it was easier that way, easier being a relative term.

But did any of them have a white aura? When I was at school, I always blocked them out. Otherwise, the barrage of auras became a colorful assault on my senses. School was difficult enough as it was. I didn't need the added distraction. Moving around so much had left gaps in my education, so even though I was pretty smart, I perpetually struggled to maintain decent grades. Why I even bothered anymore was a mystery, though. I would probably end up a waitress just like my mother. It was hard to develop a career or even think about college with our transient lifestyle.

I squared my shoulders and looked Xavier in the eye, faking the bravado I lacked. "I guess I'll see you in two weeks."

He stroked his goatee with a manicured hand, considering me. "You're quite advanced for your age. One of the better seekers I've worked with."

My mom's head snapped up, her eyes wide. Xavier was too busy studying me to notice her alarmed expression.

I kept my mouth shut. I supposed he meant it as a compliment, but it didn't feel like one. I was efficient at ruining lives. This wasn't something I would list on my resume as a skill set.

Xavier stood. "Two weeks then." He looked over at my mom who was rooted to her chair. She avoided his gaze. He chuckled. "I'll just let myself out."

The click of our front door closing signaled his

leaving, but the wrenching in my gut remained. My mom immediately went to lock the deadbolt. She came back into the room with her arms crossed.

"I'm sorry." Her voice was quiet, her tone resigned.

"It's not your fault," I said automatically, my tone dull.

"I can't believe it's so soon. I thought for sure we'd have a little bit longer after Woodlawn." That was how we referred to our assignments, by the names of the towns. "This is the soonest he's ever come." Her expression was troubled.

"Did he have an assignment for you, too?" I asked.

She shook her head. "No." Then she said again, "I'm sorry."

I didn't know why she kept apologizing. It was a good thing she didn't get an assignment. That was one less person who died. "Don't apologize."

She sighed. "Sometimes I feel like you hate me. I wish things were different, too, but they're not."

I didn't hate my mom, but I wasn't ready to be chummy, either. She couldn't just snap her fingers and undo sixteen years of secrets. Even now, a year into this gig, I still didn't know everything. I'd been lied to and betrayed my whole life. That kind of behavior didn't exactly encourage trust or friendly feelings. So forgive me if I didn't want to have a mother-daughter tea party.

"I don't hate you." I sighed. "I just...can't. Not yet."

She wasn't the only one hurting. My whole life she'd been my best friend, my ally, my partner-in-crime, and now there was this void between us. Deceit was quicker and sharper than a knife, and it didn't leave a clean division. Our relationship had been severed by a hacksaw, and now all that was left were jagged edges and the shards of what was.

I stalked to the kitchen and grabbed a sleeve of saltines and a jar of peanut butter. Calling "good night" over my shoulder, I headed to my room. After my oh-sonutritious dinner, I was calling it a night.

A girl needed her beauty sleep when she had a life to ruin.

CHAPTER 2

I WAITED AT THE BUS stop with the freshmen who lived in my apartment complex. Upperclassmen generally didn't ride the bus. They either had cars or finagled a ride with someone who did. The bus suited me just fine.

I climbed the steps onto the bus and moved to sit at the seat behind the driver where I normally sat, but stopped. Instead, I chose a seat farther back, earning a dirty look from a freshman as she walked past. She chose a seat across the aisle, leaning back to talk to her friends sitting behind me. She huffed again and looked at me, her expression clearly indicating the anguish I had caused by separating her from her friends. Whatever.

If she only knew what I really could do. My best guess was that her aura wasn't white enough though.

I took a deep breath and lowered my guards, preparing myself for the onslaught of colors. Auras were like a glow that surrounded a person's whole body. The glow extended a foot or two, depending on the variety of colors. I'd seen them my whole life and had figured out over the years which combinations were good, which ones were bad, and which ones were pure evil. My mother had also taught me at an early age to hide this ability from others. She'd worked with me until blocking them became as second nature as breathing. Now it was letting the colors in that was difficult.

I squeezed my eyes shut as I was momentarily blinded by the colors. Gradually, I opened them, squinting until my eyes adjusted. My heart was racing, both from the exhilaration that came with such a density of colors and fear of what I'd see.

Fear that I wouldn't find what I was looking for and fear that I would. Would it be someone I knew? I kept to myself, but I was alive. There was no way to avoid all human interaction. Would it be Lissa, the girl who lived in the next building and walked the elderly woman's dog from downstairs every day? Or what about Tyler who helped his single mother carry the groceries up three flights of stairs every Sunday afternoon? As a seeker I was naturally attracted to the goodness in people, so I noticed it whether I wanted to or not.

The aura of the girl whose seat I stole was a mix of dark pink, purple, and green. That didn't surprise me. Immaturity mixed with jealousy and moodiness, a pretty typical combination for a teenage girl. She had some light yellow thrown in as well, signaling creativity. That didn't surprise me either. Her outfits were always well put together, even if the clothing itself wasn't high quality. The girl knew how to do a lot with a little.

Her friends' auras were similar.

I was relieved to see that while Lissa and Tyler's auras did contain some white, it was not enough white to warrant my attention—or the attention of others. They were safe from me. They could get hit by a bus tomorrow while crossing the street, but it wouldn't be on my conscience.

By lunch my head was pounding. After blocking out the auras for so long, I really should have taken it slow, but I was eager to get it over with. The sooner I gave Xavier a name, the sooner I could try to forget about it. It was the quick rip Band-Aid approach.

I stared at a quiz in my trig class and rubbed my

temples. The numbers were all blending together, and I couldn't remember the formulas for tangent and cosecant. I worked a problem for the fourth time, erasing my scribbling so fiercely I ripped a hole in the paper. I gave up at that point. What did it really matter in the grand scheme of things? After spending my morning seeking, I didn't have it in me to care if I failed a stupid quiz.

I walked up to Mr. Tolliver's desk to turn in my quiz just as the bell rang. Most of the students rushed out, but one girl lagged behind, biting her lip and shoving her hands in and out of her pockets, like she wasn't quite sure what to do with them. Her hair was dark brown, cut short in a pixie style, and she wore brown hipster style glasses. I took a deep breath and walked down the aisle to gather my belongings.

I smiled at her, a cordial smile, yet not one that invited conversation, and shoved my pencils and notebook into my backpack.

"Hi," she said, not taking the hint.

"Hi...Katie?"

"Kaley, actually."

"Sorry, I—"

"No, it's okay. I know you're new. Well, not super new. You've been here about a month, right?"

I nodded, slinging my backpack over my shoulder.

"I'm good at math." She blushed and a nervous little laugh slipped out. "I mean, I can help you if you want. I noticed you were struggling with your quiz."

"That's nice of you," I replied, "but I'll be fine."

"Really, I don't mind," she insisted with an eager smile. "I was the new girl last year, so I know how hard it is to switch schools."

"Thanks." I tried for a smile but was only half successful. "Can I let you know?"

She grinned, and I felt a pang, realizing how desperately Kaley wanted friends. But friendship was something a seeker didn't have to offer.

"Sure," she said. "I'm free most afternoons. Or at lunch. Or in the mornings. You know, whenever you're free."

As she walked away, I looked at her aura, and my gut churned. Her colors were almost perfectly balanced, so balanced that at first all I saw was white. My breath caught in my throat, and I took a few steps forward so I could still see her as she walked through the door out into the hallway. I squinted, scrutinizing.

Please, don't let it be her.

There—a touch of tan.

I collapsed into a desk, putting my head between my knees. *It wasn't her. She has tan—she's too conservative to be pure white.*

"Miss Parks?"

I pulled my head up and rested my elbows on my knees. Mr. Tolliver was staring at me with his brows furrowed.

"Are you okay?"

I took a shaky breath. "I'm fine. I just got light-headed."

He frowned. "Perhaps you should go to the nurse."

I stood, hoping he didn't notice my white knuckles gripping the desk. I pasted a smile on my face. "I'm fine. Forgot to eat lunch. Silly me."

Mr. Tolliver nodded slowly, still frowning, but said nothing as I left his classroom. I took a right, going away from my next class, and burst through the closest exit door. Once out in the parking lot, I ran. I had no idea what direction I went in, had no idea where I was going. I didn't care. I needed to get away.

After several blocks, I stopped running and leaned against a brick building, choking back a sob. I couldn't do it. I couldn't condemn another good person. It made no difference to me that the person I chose had the potential to become an angel.

The worst part was that I had condemned the first two

without even knowing I was doing it. My mom had asked me to find fated white auras, so I did, not thinking anything of it. Her request wasn't that unusual and was reminiscent of my childhood when we would play the "aura game" at the playground or the mall. She would search the adults, and I would search the kids. Whoever found a fated white aura first won a candy bar.

I ate a lot of chocolate as a kid.

It was through this game that I learned how to tell if an aura was fated. An aura's glow was usually translucent, like a mist. When an aura was fated though, it became less transparent, solidified. I worked hard to find those auras, to learn the difference. I wanted to make my mom proud.

And I wanted to win the stupid candy.

At the time, I just thought it was a special secret game between me and my mom that only we could play. Now that I knew the truth about our little *game*, it made me wonder what other parts of my childhood were lies, especially considering the most recent lie, the biggest one, the one I couldn't bring myself to forgive her for.

It didn't take long for me to figure things out. I came home early from a friend's house and interrupted her giving the second name to Xavier.

I was horrified, shocked, betrayed. There were no appropriate words to describe it.

That's when I learned the truth, that Xavier was our connection to the Grim Reaper, that our job was to find white fated souls to die and join the ranks of angels, that I'd already been inadvertently responsible for the deaths of at least two people.

Xavier couldn't even confirm whether or not the souls achieved angel status. Apparently it wasn't a certainty. Some would become angels. Others would simply die. It all depended on how well I did my job finding pure auras.

Grief of those left behind was the only certainty. I went to the funeral in Woodlawn. I sat in the back, but there was no mistaking the heart wrenching sobs of the girl's mother. The father whose voice broke in the middle of thanking everyone for coming to mourn his daughter. The weeping friends she'd left behind, the church so full there was standing room only. The ten-year-old little brother who insisted on being a pallbearer even though he physically couldn't carry the casket. His chin quivered as he stoically bore the emotional weight of his sister's death.

Her name was Ashley. Ashley Marie Middleton.

I liked to think she was an angel now.

I liked to think she was at peace.

I liked to think there was a higher purpose for what I'd done.

But I just didn't know.

Any faith I'd had started eroding when I learned my role in life. There was none left.

William Gurganis was the name of the boy from my first assignment. He'd collapsed on the track in gym class. I didn't go to that funeral. Of course, I'd had no idea I'd played a role in his death. But now I couldn't put my head in the sand about what I was doing like my mom did. And it was never going to end.

I couldn't do it again, especially now that I knew.

I started walking again, tears blinding my vision. I didn't know how far I walked. A mile, maybe two? I was in a busy section of town I didn't recognize, but that didn't mean anything. I'd only lived here a month, and I didn't get out much other than my walks through the projects.

I stood at the busy intersection and watched the light change to green, then back to red, then green again. The walk/don't walk sign flashed. Faded pink flowers were tied on the same pole. A cross that had seen better days was propped up.

Tears blurred my vision. I wiped at my eyes with the sleeves of my hoodie and stepped out into the intersection.

I smelled the burning rubber before I saw it, heard the squeal of breaks before I saw the silver bumper on a forest green car careening toward me.

As the headlights got closer, the most inane thoughts ran through my head.

I forgot to give my mom the message from the bank. Now she'll never know about the free checking account they offer.

My library books are due.

I hope the car doesn't ruin my shoes—they're my favorite pair.

The world slowed down to nearly standing still. I watched as the car crept toward me, the Ford emblem on the grill getting closer and closer.

Then the strangest thing happened.

The car slowed down. As it slowed, my world sped up.

The tires screeched, and the car veered to the right, hopping the curb. All I could see through the windshield were the whites of the driver's eyes.

I was no physics expert—in fact, I hadn't even taken the class—but that car shouldn't have been able to slow down enough to avoid hitting me.

Someone grabbed my arm and hauled me back onto the sidewalk.

"Are you okay?"

I looked up at my rescuer. He was tall, with dark hair and eyes—the quintessential tall, dark, and handsome.

I couldn't help myself. I swooned. Of course, that was probably mostly due to the near death experience. Now that I was safe, my mind reeled. *What the heck happened back there?* It was like I was possessed or something. It wasn't like me to step out into traffic. I'd been a junior crossing guard in fifth grade for goodness sake.

For the first time in a year, I worried about my appearance. I wished I had fixed my hair instead of letting it hang straight. I wished I had delved into the bag of makeup I'd shoved under the sink and forgotten about. I wished I'd chosen something other than scrubby jeans, a hoodie, and tennis shoes to wear this morning.

"What the hell were you thinking?"

I looked up, shocked. That comment brought me out of my swoon in a flash. That was no way to talk to someone who almost had her teeth flossed with the grill of a Ford. I opened my mouth to tell him so but was distracted by the commotion of the car reversing and speeding off down the street.

The guy cursed. "I didn't get the full license plate number."

"That's okay. I'm not going to report it."

He let me go and took a step back, putting his hands on his hips. He was wearing grease-covered faded jeans and a green t-shirt with *Bill's Auto Repair* printed on it. "What the hell were you thinking?" he said again.

"It was an accident."

"Bullshit. I saw you step right in that car's path. Do you have a date with death or something?"

I almost laughed at that. If he only knew.

I looked up at him, now able to focus since my racing heart had slowed from I-think-I'm-going-die speed to OMG-he's-hot speed. Yup, he was a looker. His skin was tan, and I'd bet he had Latino somewhere in his lineage. His lashes were long, unfairly long for a guy. Girls shelled out big bucks to make their eyelashes look like his.

In my former life, I would have hated him for that. In my current life, I hated him for the way he made my skin tingle with his presence.

"Well, thanks," I said, taking a few steps back the way I came.

He grabbed my arm, stopping me.

Okay, so now my skin was tingling for a different reason.

I pointedly looked at his hand on my arm, then looked up at him with venom in my gaze. "Do you mind?"

"I don't trust you to walk home."

"Excuse me?"

"You obviously don't know how to safely walk in traffic."

"What do you care?"

"I don't." He dropped my arm, then cursed. "But I'll be damned if you hurt yourself and it's on my conscience."

"You don't have to worry about me."

Annoyance flared in his eyes. "If someone gets hit right in front of the shop, it'll be bad for business." He jerked his thumb at the automotive repair shop behind him.

I opened my mouth to fire off a snappy retort, but my phone chimed, signaling an incoming text. My mom and I didn't have much money, but she insisted I have a cell phone so we could always stay in touch with one another. I pulled it out of my back pocket.

Come home now.

I frowned. My mom didn't usually issue directives like that. I didn't recognize the number, but she was the only one who had my cell number. My calling circle was more like a straight line.

I glared at my rescuer. "What's your name?"

"Cole." His voice was full of caution at my sudden lack of resistance.

"Nice to meet you, Cole," I said. "Do you have a car?"

"Yeah." He eyed me warily, as one might eye an unruly puppy.

"Can you drive me home?"

He waited a beat. "Let's go." He turned and walked toward the shop, not bothering to make sure I followed. Funny—a minute ago he was preventing me from walking away. Now he didn't care?

I stalked behind him, following him into the shop. One car was up on the lift with most of its guts spewed onto the floor. A pudgy balding man wearing overalls had his hands all up in the car's nether regions.

"Bill, I've got to take off," Cole said, pulling a faded black hooded sweatshirt over his head.

Bill spared him a glance. "Same time tomorrow."

"Yeah," Cole said, then jerked his head toward the

back door. I followed him out to where a rusty sedan was parked. I balked at the sight of it.

"I don't know if I'll be any safer in this." It didn't look like it would make it out of the parking lot, much less several miles to my house.

Cole stroked the rusty hood. "She might not look pretty, but she runs like a champ."

"If you say so."

Cole affectionately patted the hood one last time before opening the passenger's side door. "Get in."

My eyes went back and forth between him and the car as he walked around to get behind the wheel of the driver's side. I looked skyward for a moment and then sighed before walking over to the car. I wrinkled my nose at the sight of the front seat. It was a bench seat—how old was this car? I didn't think they'd made any cars with bench seats in the past ten or twenty years. A blue towel covered the passenger side. I lifted it up and peered underneath to see yellowed foam spilling out of ripped upholstery.

The engine started with a cough, so I slid into the seat and reached for the seatbelt.

"Where do you live?" He pulled a pair of sunglasses off the visor and put them on. They were aviator style with mirrored lenses. They worked for him.

My skin tingled again.

I hesitated only momentarily before giving him my address. I wondered what my mom would think of me being brought home in the middle of a school day by a strange guy. Hopefully, she would be at work, making it a non-issue.

But honestly? My cutting school should be the least of her worries.

Cole was silent on the ride. He was a very conscientious driver, almost to the point of driving like an old man. A glance at the speedometer confirmed he drove exactly the speed limit.

When we pulled in front of my apartment building, he

frowned, looking at the digital clock on the car's dash. "Wait, shouldn't you be in school?"

I shrugged. "Probably. Thanks for the ride."

I pulled on the door's lever and pushed the door, but it didn't open. I pulled it again and pressed against the door with my shoulder.

"There's a trick to it." Cole leaned across me, and I caught a whiff of motor oil, which was oddly appealing. I quickly shook my head a few times to clear that thought. That close call with the car had me all out of sorts.

That's all it was. Nothing more.

Yeah, keep telling yourself that.

He yanked down on the lever, then pulled it out, and pushed the door open.

"Thanks, again." I hopped out.

He nodded and pulled away from the curb, leaving behind the faint smell of exhaust. It wasn't until I had trudged up the first flight of stairs that the exhaust smell faded.

Then it hit me—cinnamon.

What was Xavier doing here?

He must have been the one to send me the text. That was why I didn't recognize the number. How did he get mine, though? My mom wouldn't have given it to him. Ever since he dropped the nice uncle act, she'd kept him as far away from me as possible.

I looked back out at the parking lot, hoping to see my mom's car. Its absence told me she must be at work. *Damn.*

Be careful what you wish for, I thought bitterly.

My first thought was to turn around and go back the way I came, but I couldn't run. He would know. I still didn't know exactly what Xavier was, but he had uncanny senses. I'm sure he knew I was here the minute Cole pulled into the parking lot.

I sent my mom a simple text. *Xavier's here.*

Breathing deeply, I slowly climbed the remaining

steps. I unlocked the door, dropped my backpack on the floor, and peeked around the corner into the kitchen.

"I'm in the living room."

I jumped at the sound of Xavier's voice and slowly entered the living room, my head down like a guilty child about to be reprimanded. That was how Xavier made me feel—like I wanted to run to my mommy and hide behind her legs.

But she wasn't here now.

And I wasn't the hiding type.

Xavier was sitting on our couch with one arm stretched over the back of it, a cigar in his hand. His right ankle was propped up on his left knee.

He blew out smoke in O-shaped circles. "Have a seat."

"I'll stand, thanks." I rubbed my arms, trying to smooth down the hairs that were standing on end.

"Tell me about your day."

I blinked. "It was, um, fine, I guess."

"Really?" He put the cigar out on the bottom of his shoe. Ashes fell onto our carpet, but he didn't notice, or in any event, he didn't care. "You're home early."

"I got sick."

He chuckled and smiled a Cheshire smile, showing the black nicotine stains on his teeth. "Ava, now you're just lying to me." He looked at me expectantly, but I remained silent. I didn't know where this conversation was heading, and I was afraid that whatever I said would only dig my hole deeper.

"What was the deal with the car?"

"Car?"

His expression shifted once again. The Cheshire was gone. In its place was something much more sinister. "The car you stepped in front of."

Oh, that car.

"There's no deal," I said. "It was an accident."

"Accident. So you didn't want it to hit you?"

I frowned, thinking back to being paralyzed on the

road, watching as the headlights of the car rushed toward me. Part of me didn't want to be saved. I would be lying if I said I didn't want it to hit me, to end it all. It would have been so easy.

"It doesn't work that way, Ava." *Did he read my mind?* Xavier paced the room, his agitation evident. "*You* don't get to choose. It's not up to you to decide."

"What? What don't I get to choose?" My eyes stayed glued to him, ping ponging back and forth as he paced.

"Your life, my dear. Your death."

I have no control.

I closed my eyes, letting it sink in. I knew Xavier had power over me, but I hadn't realized the extent of that power.

My life was not my own.

I choked down the maniacal laugher that threatened to escape.

I opened my eyes and realized Xavier was staring at me, waiting for a response.

"I didn't choose to almost get hit by a car."

"Then I guess you'd better be more careful. It's rather inconvenient when the Reapers have to save a seeker. They detest it, you know. It goes against their nature."

I hadn't seen a Reaper. If one saved me, then why didn't I see it? I'd *never* seen one. I thought back to the strange slowing of time when I was standing in the street. Perhaps that wasn't just in my mind. Could that have been the act of a Reaper?

"I don't understand. Why would the Reapers save me? They kill people."

Xavier studied me for a moment, then sat on the arm of the couch, tsking and shaking his head. "My dear, how ignorant you are. And I thought you were merely being defiant. Teenage rebelliousness and all that." He waved his hand, showing how nonsensical he deemed teenagers. "Every year, I request them to raise the induction age for seekers, but sadly, no one ever listens."

He didn't answer my question, but I didn't let it go. "So, what? I can't die? *Ever?*"

"Not until we decide." He brought his cigar to his lips and smiled. "Do you have any idea how much pain can be inflicted on someone who can't die?"

Chills ran down my spine. I took a step back, instinctively wanting to put distance between me and Xavier.

The front door opened and shut. My mom rushed into the room still wearing her waitress apron, her hair coming loose from her bun. "Xavier, what are you doing here?"

"Schooling your daughter, Mary. It appears she doesn't know the rules."

"I'll teach her, Xavier. I'll teach her the rules."

I hated my mom right then. Even though she was handling Xavier for me, she wasn't doing it the way I wanted her to. I wanted her to play the knight in shining armor, slaying the dragon, not acting like a possum and playing dead until the predator passed her by.

As she looked up at Xavier, I saw weakness in her hazel eyes, eyes we shared along with our auburn hair. Although we could have been twins separated by twenty years, I hoped my eyes never mirrored the weakness in hers.

Xavier stood, straightening his jacket. "See that you do, Mary. It's been a while since I've had to teach them, and I'm afraid my teaching methods might be deemed unorthodox by modern standards."

At the sound of the slamming of our front door, I began to breathe a little easier.

"What...did...you...do?" My mom's expression was fierce, the dead possum gone.

I flopped down on the couch and crossed my arms. "Nothing." I knew I sounded like a sullen child, but I didn't care. I *felt* like a sullen child.

She paced in front of me. Glancing at her watch, she cursed. "Shit."

I raised my eyebrows. My mom very rarely cursed.

"I have to go back to work. I'm not supposed to be gone this long."

My sullenness faded away and I felt tinges of guilt. Despite the fact that my mom never stayed in one job for long, she did take pride in her work. Plus, it took her longer than normal to land this job, so we were already short on cash. I didn't know what we'd do if she got fired.

She sighed. The sunlight streaming through the window illuminated her face, and for the first time, I noticed small wrinkles around her eyes. How long had they been there?

"We'll talk about this when I get home. *Don't* go anywhere."

"Okay."

I had nowhere to go anyway.

CHAPTER 3

AS SOON AS MY MOM left, I flipped the deadbolt on the front
door and checked the window locks. It was silly. If Xavier
wanted in, he would get in no matter how many layers of
security I put between us. Still, the methodical security
check eased my nerves a little bit.

Xavier's words echoed in my mind, like an old record
that was skipping.

*"Do you have any idea how much pain can be
inflicted on someone who can't die?"*

The answer to that question was no. No, I didn't know
how much pain could be inflicted on a person who
couldn't die. It wasn't something I wanted to find out,
especially firsthand.

Xavier had always been obnoxious, for lack of a better
word. There'd always been something a little off about
him, but I'd never been afraid of him. Recently though,
he'd crossed that line and was firmly planted in menacing.
Years ago, my mom actually had him babysit me a few
times when she was in a bind, and he'd helped us move on
more than one occasion. Now I realized he had a vested
interest in our lives. We were linked, for better—no, there
was no better. It was only worse and worst. When I gave
him the benefit of the doubt, which wasn't often, I figured
he and I were probably similar in a way—both stuck in a

crappy situation with crappy roles to play. I got the sense that Xavier wasn't in charge of his own destiny either.

I curled up on my bed under a blue and green afghan my grandmother had crocheted. It was my favorite blanket even though I'd never met her. My mom didn't talk about her much, just an errant comment here and there. I'd always had a natural curiosity about her, but even more so now that I understood she also must have been a seeker. I wondered what the dynamics were like between her and my mom. Probably not good since my mom rarely mentioned her. Now that I'd learned about the whole not dying thing, I was even more curious about her. She was dead—had been since I was three. What made the Reapers decide they were done with her?

I must have drifted off, and when I woke up, it was dark outside. The wind was blowing, making an eerie whistling sound as it rattled the screens on our windows. The click of our front door closing had me clutching the blanket to my chest and holding my breath.

The kitchen light flooded the hallway and danced at the edge of my doorway. I heard someone rooting around in the refrigerator.

I closed my eyes and blew out a breath. It was just my mom.

God, when did I turn into such a wimp?

I slunk down the hall and leaned against the door frame in the kitchen, like a kid waiting to be scolded.

That's kind of what I was.

"Did you get in trouble with your boss?"

"No." My mom spared me a glance from where she was scrubbing her hands at the kitchen sink. "Did you eat?" The faint smell of fried foods wafted off her. I could always tell how busy the restaurant was by how she smelled. Faint smell equaled slow day, which meant few tips.

"No, I haven't eaten yet."

"Good. There's takeout."

Two large Styrofoam boxes were sitting on the counter next to the fridge. How much had that cost?

As if she'd heard my thoughts, she said, "Don't worry. The assistant manager was there today, the nice one, and he sends us home with food if the kitchen is slow." She placed a box on the table and opened it, pushing it toward me. "Eat."

Grilled chicken, garlic mashed potatoes, and brown-sugar baby carrots. There was even a little roll, but I had to forgo the cinnamon butter, immediately tossing it in trash. Ugh. Cinnamon. I sat down and we ate in companionable silence.

The food was so good. I hadn't eaten that well in a while. That made it sound like my mom didn't provide for me, but it wasn't like that. We were poor, but I never went hungry. She worked odd hours though, so she wasn't always home at dinner time. That meant a lot of PB & J's and canned soup.

"What happened today?" she finally asked.

I sighed, and rested my elbows on the table, cradling my face in my hands. I told her the whole story, only leaving out little bits about Cole. I was used to telling my mom everything—well before the last year anyway—but the length of his eyelashes that framed deep chocolate eyes didn't seem relevant, even if I had noticed them.

My mom shook her head, blowing out an exasperated breath. "Ava, you can't do stuff like that."

"I wasn't trying to do anything," I protested lamely, staring down at the table and fiddling with the placemat.

"Aside from everything else, you were skipping school."

"I don't see why that matters," I muttered. "It's not like I can go to college."

She rose and crossed to the sink to refill her glass with water. "Skipping school is *not* okay, young lady. And about college—things are different now than when I was your age. There are lots of online options."

"How would we pay for something like that?" I snapped. She acted like I hadn't considered these things before. Aside from the finances, even if I did online school and got a degree, what then? What kind of profession would mesh with my seeking responsibilities? My options were mediocre at best.

Sadness and regret filled her eyes, and I wished I could take back the sharpness of my words. I needed to remember she didn't choose this life either. It just sucked, and there was no easy fix. It irritated me when she tried to slap a Band-Aid on it.

She crossed to the freezer and pulled out a small tub of ice cream. She tossed it to me. Mint chocolate chip, my favorite. She placed a carton of butter pecan in front of her space and fished two spoons out of the drawer.

This could not be good. Whenever anything bad happened, like when I got cut from the softball team in middle school, she soothed my woes with ice cream.

"I need to tell you some things." She sat and pried the lid off her ice cream.

I sighed and eyed the ice cream warily. She held a spoon out to me, and I took it reluctantly.

"Our situation is very...unique," she started.

This information was not new to me. If this was how she was easing into the conversation, it would be next week before she got around to telling me what I needed to know.

Xavier's words once again played in my mind. *"Do you have any idea how much pain can be inflicted on someone who can't die?"*

I took a quick breath and blurted out my question before I could chicken out. "Can we die? I mean, Grandma's dead, so we obviously won't live forever, right?"

Her spoon paused midway to her mouth, her eyes widening. Slowly, she brought the spoon the rest of the way to her mouth and licked off the ice cream. "That's complicated."

"How is it complicated?" I tried not to sound annoyed, but failed miserably. "It's a yes or no question."

"Yes and no."

I slammed my spoon on the table with a clatter. "There's no point in having this conversation if you aren't going to tell me anything. I can't believe you would keep something this important from me."

Actually, I could. She'd kept *everything* from me for sixteen years.

She met my gaze, then calmly slid her spoon into her ice cream, eating another spoonful before speaking. "If you're not going to eat your ice cream, then put it back in the freezer so it doesn't melt."

"Mom." This one syllable word carried the weight of all my questions.

She sighed. "We can die, just not until they're done with us."

"They?"

She waved her spoon in the air, toward the sky. "You know. The powers that be."

"So Xavier, then."

She shook her head. "Xavier is not as all powerful as he would like you to believe."

Some of the tension left my shoulders. "That's good to know."

"Oh, he's still powerful, but after all these years, I get the impression he's either a big fish in a little pond or a small fish in a big pond. I can't figure out which."

"Have you ever met anyone else like him?"

She chuckled. "There's no one like Xavier. To answer your question though, I haven't formally met anyone like him. I've seen others, but they didn't approach me, and I certainly didn't approach them."

She held her ice cream out to me, offering me a taste. I shook my head. "So what exactly does it mean that we can't die until they're done with us? I mean, accidents happen." I shifted uncomfortably. "What if that car had hit me?"

"You wouldn't have died," she said simply.

"What if it were a bus? How could I not die if I were creamed by a bus?"

She winced, no doubt imagining my gray matter splattered all over the windshield of a Greyhound. "You would be saved."

"How?" I pressed. I felt like I was Dorothy and she was the wizard, only showing me what was in front of the curtain. I wanted to see behind it.

She shrugged. "Reapers. Maybe angels. I don't know for sure."

I snorted. "That's rich." Angels saved seekers so that we could continue adding to their ranks. How twisted.

She smiled wryly. Yeah, she caught the irony in that. We actually had similar viewpoints and thought a lot alike, which was one reason why her deceit over the last year hurt so much.

"How do you know this?" I asked.

She hesitated. "I had a near death..." She paused, obviously wrestling with something inside herself. "...experience." She put the lid on her ice cream and put it in the freezer. The discussion was over.

I suddenly felt like a little kid again, like when my mom used to cover my eyes for the more mature parts of PG-13 movies. Just when it was about to get good? Hands over the eyes.

I stood abruptly, slamming the lid onto my ice cream container. "You know, I thought you were finally going to treat me like an equal here. Why are you still hiding things from me?"

Here I thought we were on the road to mending our relationship, and she had to ruin it by throwing up a huge roadblock.

"You're not an adult yet."

I stared at her. I couldn't believe she was still treating

me like a child when I held the balance of people's lives in my hands.

"Tell that to the kids who die because of me."

I strode to my room and slammed the door.

MY MOM DROPPED ME OFF at school the next morning. I think she wanted to make sure I got there. It wasn't getting there that was the problem though—it was staying there. By the end of the day, my stomach was churning from interacting with my classmates, knowing I was scouting them for reaping.

By my last class of the day, junior seminar, I was ready to bolt. My head was pounding from looking at auras for hours on end. I'd tried wearing sunglasses to ease the glare, but that made me look like I was hung over or something. I took them off after the third teacher graced me with an accusatory stare. The last thing I needed was to spend the afternoon in detention.

Junior seminar was a joke from what I could tell. It was a required class for all students, and it was supposed to prepare us for our senior year. My teacher was Ms. Green, who decorated her classroom walls with posters with cutesy sayings like "Warning! Your Future is Closer Than it Appears!" So far all I had to show for the class was a stack of SAT vocab word flashcards. I now knew that a dromedary was a one-humped camel.

I felt so enriched.

Ms. Green was unusually perky today, which didn't help my throbbing head. It felt like my brain was trying to pound its way out of my skull.

"Today is the best day of the year. Today..." she paused, looking around for dramatic emphasis to ensure we were all sufficiently excited. Seeing our droll expressions, she pursed her lips a little, then pasted on an even brighter smile as if her enthusiasm could make up for our lack of it. "Today you start your career projects!"

She walked down the front of the rows, distributing brightly colored handouts. Most other teachers relied on basic white paper. Not Ms. Green. Today's color selection was blue, and not even plain blue—electric blue.

I tuned her out and instead read over the handout. Huh. We had to do a project on a potential career. In addition to writing a paper, we also had to work with a partner to do a massive presentation at the end of the unit.

I looked around at my classmates who were already pairing up and sighed. Finding a partner was going to be a problem.

I raised my hand. Might as well get the embarrassment of having the teacher find me a partner out of the way.

Just as Ms. Green noticed my hand, the classroom door swung open.

I slowly pulled my hand down. *You have to be freaking kidding me.*

Cole filled the doorway. He was wearing faded jeans, a navy blue shirt, and a disinterested attitude. No oil stains. I guessed he saved those for the garage.

I ducked down, waiting for him to get what he needed from Ms. Green and leave. Instead, she announced to the class, "Everyone, this is Cole Fowler. He'll be joining us for this project."

A few of the girls perked up, flipping their hair over their shoulders and subtly giving him the once over. He stood at the front of the class with his hands shoved in his pockets, a backpack slung over one shoulder. His expression stopped just short of a scowl.

The ever-attentive teacher that she was, Ms. Green turned in my direction. "Did you have a question, Ava?"

I sat up in my chair. No use trying to hide now. I'd been outed. "Yeah, I, um, don't have a partner."

Ms. Green looked around the room. "Raise your hand if you need a partner."

No one raised their hand. There might as well have been crickets chirping.

She turned to Cole and smiled brightly. "Now I'm doubly happy you're joining us, Cole. You can partner with Ava."

He looked at me, and some sort of smile-*thing* crossed his face. Like half-smile, half-grimace. It was the kind of look I probably made when old men hit on me at my mom's job.

He took the handout Ms. Green gave him and sauntered down the aisle. Dropping his backpack on the floor, he slid into the desk next to me.

I twisted to face him. "What are you doing here?" I blurted out.

He eyed me warily. "Getting a diploma."

"Aren't you like twenty-five or something?"

"Nineteen."

"And you're a junior?"

"No, I'm a senior, but I transferred so I didn't do this project last year. They won't let me graduate without it." His tone expressed his annoyance. "Any other questions?"

I twisted back around in my desk and picked up the handout. I didn't read it. I just needed something to focus on other than him and all his...*Cole-ness.*

"My mom works at a restaurant." I spoke without looking up from my handout. "We could do something with that for this project."

"It says here we're not allowed to work with our parents."

"What? Where?" I looked over at where he was pointing. Sure enough it was right there in black and electric blue. That severely limited my options down to, oh, nothing since it also clearly stated that we were responsible for finding our businesses to volunteer with. I didn't know any other adults with jobs I could ask, and it was doubtful my mom did either.

"Let's do the repair shop."

I wrinkled my nose. My career options were limited at best, but I could safely say I would not end up a mechanic.

Cole noticed my reaction. "Is there something wrong with that?"

"We're supposed to choose a career we'd actually want to have, and I have *noooo* interest in working on cars."

He stared at me for half a beat. "Do you have a better idea?"

I shook my head.

"Good. Give me your phone."

"What?" I frowned. "Why?" He was crazy if he thought I letting an arrogant, bossy, know-it-all grease monkey put his paws all over my phone. I didn't care how hot he was.

I got that stare again, like I'd suddenly morphed into an ogre or something.

"So I can put my number it in," he said. "We might need to contact each other." When I didn't hand it over, he added, "For the project?"

"Oh." Of course. Duh. I leaned down to fumble through my backpack for my phone. And hide the massive blush that had started on my cheeks and spread to every other part of me. I was such an idiot.

After we'd put our numbers in each other's phones, he glanced at his watch.

"I've got to go. Come by the shop tomorrow afternoon." He stood and slung his backpack over one shoulder. He gave a short wave to Ms. Green and left.

My mouth hung open. What was that all about? The class didn't end for another forty-five minutes. I crossed my arms, fuming. Not only was I paired with someone I never wanted to see again, I was also going to be stuck hanging out in a dirty, smelly repair shop.

I should've chosen today to skip school.

CHAPTER 4

"I TRUST YOU MADE IT here without any near-death experiences."

My cheeks flushed as Cole looked back down into the car engine that appeared to have eaten his arms up to his elbows.

"Ha, ha," I said, pretending to go along with his little joke. Inside, I was fuming, but if I didn't make a big deal about it, then maybe he would drop it. I had little experience in this kind of garage, but the place looked typical to me. Red toolboxes, metal shelving holding a variety of motor oils, and an ancient radio.

I squinted at a poster of an eighties hair band hanging above the stereo. The boom box had probably been new when the glam rockers were at their peak. Inspecting the counter that ran along the wall next to where Cole was working, I looked for a clean spot to put down my bag.

Bill came out of a door on the other side of the shop. Wiping his hands on a rag, he puffed up his chest and said, "How can we help you, miss?"

"Bill, this is Ava," Cole said. "I told you about her."

Bill grunted and returned to his office, closing the door behind him.

"Nice to meet you too, Bill," I muttered to the closed door.

Cole slammed down the hood of the car and put his hands on his hips. "Watch your attitude with Bill. He's a good guy."

My first instinct was to correct him. It was not technically giving someone attitude if the person in question wasn't even in the same room.

Instead, I said, "Of course." The man was letting me intern in his shop. It was a bitch move to sass him behind his back.

Cole got in the car and started it, then backed out of the garage while I stood gaping. Was he leaving? And he called *me* rude?

After about a minute during which I considered both walking out and pounding on Bill's office door to find out what the heck was going on, a blue pick-up truck pulled into the spot vacated by the car, and I saw that Cole was behind the wheel. Now I felt stupid. He just had to switch out the cars. Of course. He could have said something though.

Cole got out of the car, and I cleared my throat. "How should we do this project?"

Cole grimaced, lifting the hood of the truck. "Read the requirements while I work." He pulled a long floppy stick thing out of the car and wiped it on a rag.

I huffed a little bit in reaction to his bossiness but settled on a stool and proceeded to read the instructions. We each had to intern for at least eighty hours and keep a journal about our experiences working in the career field. The journal part didn't sound too hard, but eighty hours? That was a lot. I had a mild freak-out until I read farther down on the page that we could be released from school early to do some of the internship. That made me breathe a little bit easier.

But why did I even care? If everything worked out the way it usually did, my mom and I would be moving on before the project was due. I hoped not, though. Our moving signaled the death of an innocent. I wanted to delay that as long as possible, even if it was inevitable.

Cole lay down on a flat board with wheels and pushed himself under the truck until only his feet hung out.

"What are you doing under there?" I asked.

"What does it look like I'm doing?" came the muffled reply.

"If I knew I wouldn't be asking," I snapped. "Plus, I can't even see you under there. How can I know what you're doing if I can't even see you?"

He rolled out and looked at me with one raised eyebrow. "You seriously don't know what I'm doing?"

I crossed my arms and rolled my eyes. Childish, I knew, but if he was going to talk down to me, then I shouldn't be blamed for playing the part. And only he could find a way to talk down to someone while lying flat on his back nearly on the ground.

He stood and walked over to the shelving unit against the wall. Using his foot, he nudged another wheeled board out from under the unit and kicked it over to me.

I stopped it with my foot before it slammed into my ankle.

"Lie down," he commanded.

He'd lost his mind.

"Uh, I don't think so."

"You're supposed to be interning."

"The internship hasn't officially started yet," I protested. "Besides, you're crazy if you think I'm going to lie down on your oversized skateboard and slide under that big truck."

He snorted. "It's a creeper."

"What?"

"The *skateboard* is called a creeper."

"Can't I just hand you tools or something?"

He crossed his arms, saying nothing. A standoff.

I crossed my arms to match him and gave him my best stare right back. He didn't move a muscle, barely even blinking. I wanted to look away and not get lost in the dark abyss of his eyes, but it was a matter of principle. A knot formed in my stomach, sending tingles down my arms and legs. The longer I stared into those eyes, the more tingly I got.

Finally, I looked away. "Fine," I grumbled, grabbing a stray rag off the counter. I crouched next to the creeper, the *creepy creeper*, and wiped it down.

And it was creepy, just a little piece of plastic to wheel me under a truck that weighed who knew how many tons.

Cole probably knew how much the truck weighed.

I was totally out of my element.

I wasn't even dressed right. I'd taken more care with my appearance this morning, wearing my nicest blouse with black pants and heels. I'd even smeared on a little lip gloss and mascara. I wanted to make a good impression on my new boss for the next few weeks. It had nothing to do with my new better-looking-than-he-had-any-right-to-be co-worker.

I gritted my teeth and lay down on the creeper face up, my knees bent.

Cole lay down on the creeper next to me and used the edge of the truck to pull himself under. The wheels whooshed on the concrete, and he slid effortlessly into place.

I took a deep breath. It would be okay. I would *make* it be okay.

I grabbed the edge of the truck in an attempt to do the same, but the wheels didn't whoosh as well for me, and I only made it partway under. My face was in line with Cole's crotch. I hurriedly looked away and used my toes to nudge myself the rest of the way under.

Once in place under the truck, I closed my eyes and tried to even out my breathing. It was a trick my mom had taught me when I had nightmares as a little girl. By focusing on my breathing, I was able to block out other thoughts.

Thoughts about being trapped in a tight, closed space.

No, no, don't think about that. You're under a car. Perfectly normal.

Think happy thoughts. Puppy dogs, ring pops, rainbows.

When I was sure I had control of myself, I opened my eyes.

Our creepers were nearly touching, putting us only inches apart. My foot accidentally bumped his leg. I jumped, pulling my foot back toward my body.

Cole and I were lying down together. No, not together. Just next to each other. There was a difference.

A different kind of bad thought filled my mind. Thoughts I would never admit to.

I closed my eyes for a moment.

Gummy bears, unicorns, kittens.

Yeah, I was going to need something stronger to get those thoughts under control.

"See that pan over there?" Cole asked.

I turned my head and indeed saw a black pan.

"Hand it to me." I could feel his breath on my face. It smelled like peppermint. Thank God it wasn't cinnamon. I might have vomited.

But I could certainly handle peppermint. Yummy.

I grabbed the pan, immediately dropping it. "Yuck!" My fingers came away covered in black grease and oil.

"You aren't supposed to put your fingers in it."

"That would have been nice to know *before* you told me to grab it."

He tossed a rag onto my stomach. His silence made me wonder if he was secretly enjoying this.

I let out an annoyed breath and used the rag to wipe the black oil off my hands. In the process, I managed to push it further under my fingernails. I cursed.

"Are you done?" He was getting impatient.

I threw the rag back, but of course it just bounced off him and landed harmlessly on the ground. "I guess so."

"Then give me the damn pan."

I grabbed it again, this time careful to keep my fingertips on the outside of it. He slid his creeper over a little, positioning the pan where he wanted it.

"This cap will release the used oil," he said, unscrewing said cap. Black liquid oozed into the pan. It was disgusting. It made me pity all those pelicans featured on the Discovery Channel's documentary on oil spills even more.

I stared straight up at the engine above me. At least, that's what I assumed I was staring at. I knew next to nothing about cars, never had any use for the knowledge before. After this more-than-slightly humiliating experience, I was definitely going to do some research so I wouldn't feel like such an idiot for the remaining seventy-nine hours in this internship. Not that I was counting.

I shifted on the creeper, trying to get more comfortable. I reached under my back and twisted to try to see under there as well. Something was poking me right in my spine.

When I looked back up, the engine above me began to grow somehow, getting bigger and closing in on me.

No, no, no. *Not now.*

I squeezed my eyes shut and started my breathing exercises again. The oil pan incident had caused me to forget my breathing. *Stupid.*

"Are you okay?" Cole asked.

I opened my eyes. The engine was on my chest. Cole was no longer next to me. I was surrounded by sooty pipes and mechanical pieces. They were closing in on me, encircling me.

My chest tightened. I couldn't breathe. I closed my eyes, succumbing to the darkness.

Suddenly, I felt a yank on my leg and my creeper jerked forward. Hands grabbed my arms.

"Ava. Breathe. You have to breathe."

I opened my mouth, choking on the sudden rush of

air that filled my lungs. My eyes sprang open. Cole was leaning over me, inches from my face.

He sat back. "Christ, why didn't you tell me you were claustrophobic?"

"Would you have believed me?" I whispered. He would have thought it an excuse not to do the work.

"Fair enough," he said.

My claustrophobia was a relatively new phenomenon. It started in Woodlawn after the funeral. Ashley's casket was black with a white satin interior. It took weeks after the funeral for the nightmares of being trapped in that casket to stop. The walls always closed in on me until the satin suffocated me.

"I guess I should take you home," Cole said, standing. I also quickly stood and brushed myself off, avoiding his gaze.

How humiliating. Twice now Cole had felt the need to drive me home as a result of my neurosis. As if my life needed more complications.

"I'll be fine." I straightened my blouse and smoothed my hair. "I just need a minute."

He hesitated, jingling his keys in his pocket. "Are you sure? You seem pretty freaked out."

"Yeah." Yeah, I was sure, and yeah, I was freaked out. It was all in my head, though. Going home wouldn't help me escape from that. Unfortunately, there was no escape.

"Can I get you a soda or some water or something?" Cole asked.

I cocked my head, studying him. His concern seemed genuine, and I could tell he was at a loss for what to do.

"A soda would be nice. Diet Coke, please."

He walked over to the dented soda machine in the corner of the shop. The lights behind the beverage choices flickered. I wouldn't risk putting any money in that machine.

Cole punched in a selection and then literally punched the machine, first in the middle of a dent at the top left, then in the middle of the biggest dent right in the middle.

That explained the dents.

The machine rattled and reluctantly spit out a can.

"Does your boss know you abuse the machine like that?"

He handed me the soda with a crooked grin. "Who do you think showed me the secret spots?"

I popped open the top and guzzled half the can. The cool fizzy bubbles were soothing as they slid down my throat.

Cole leaned against the counter next to me. "What else do we have to do besides the journal?"

I grabbed the assignment sheet from the counter and scanned over it, grateful for the distraction. "A twenty-to-thirty minute presentation."

He grimaced. "Ouch."

"Yeah, that's not going to be fun." I drained the rest of my soda.

He nodded toward the empty can in my hand. "You already done with that?"

I looked down at it sheepishly and nodded. He took it out of my hand and crushed it, tossing it basketball style into a recycle bin in the corner of the shop. It whooshed through the rim and clanged into the bottom of the metal bin.

I raised my eyebrows. "Nice shot."

He jerked his chin up in that way guys did. It was the universal guy language that meant a bevy of things like *what's up*, *hey*, or *later*. This time I was guessing it meant *thanks*.

"I've got to finish this oil change. There's three more lined up behind this one, so..."

"Right," I said. "You do what you need to do. I'll just sit and watch."

Cole slid back under the truck to complete the oil change. To my unknowing eyes, it seemed like he was good at it, efficient. He had all the cars finished and parked back out in the lot in about an hour.

Once during the hour, Bill wandered out of his office, rifled around in a few tool boxes, then shuffled back into his office, empty-handed. I'd honestly forgotten he was here. He didn't say a word to either me or Cole, even though I offered him a hesitant smile.

As Cole was parking the last of the cars, I packed up my backpack and slung it over my shoulder.

"Are you sure Bill doesn't mind I'm here?" I asked, following Cole out the back door to his car, which I'd mentally dubbed the Rustinator.

"Yeah, it's fine."

"He doesn't seem to like me that much."

"Why do you say that?"

"He won't even talk to me."

Cole opened the passenger door. How chivalrous. Since I hadn't ridden in Cole's car under normal circumstances, I couldn't help but wonder if he was usually so gentlemanly or if he was being extra nice because of my freak-outs.

"He's not good with women," Cole said.

I snorted. "Referring to me as a woman is a stretch."

I stepped past him to slide into the car. In doing so, my hip brushed against his leg. I blushed furiously. When I looked up, I found Cole looking at me with a funny expression on his face.

"Don't sell yourself short." He said it so quietly I wasn't sure if the comment was meant for my ears.

Cole shut the passenger door and crossed around to the driver's side. My cheeks flushed even more, and I willed them to return to normal. When Cole got in, he buckled his seatbelt and turned the key. Instead of shifting into drive, he looked at me expectantly.

"What?" I asked. His looking at me did nothing to calm my crimson cheeks. They had to be nearing stop sign shade.

"Seat belt."

"Oh." Now I felt really stupid. He just grinned and pulled out of the parking space.

Some people brought out the best in others. Cole brought out the awkward in me.

Not to mention the naughty thoughts and tingles that reverberated down to my toes.

It was going to be a long month.

CHAPTER 5

"HAVE YOU FOUND AN INTERNSHIP yet?" Kaley asked.

"Huh?" I turned my head toward her, squinting as I was assaulted by her blinding aura. I was searching for auras, and I'd almost forgotten she was sitting next to me. I was used to eating lunch alone, but ever since Kaley offered to help me with trig, she'd been sitting with me, helping me whether I liked it or not.

I closed my eyes briefly and put my guards back in place.

"You know, for the junior project," Kaley replied, ever-so-patient.

"Oh, yeah. Cole and I are working at a mechanic's shop. Bill's Auto." I returned my gaze to the students in the cafeteria. I'd chosen a seat in the corner with my back to the wall so I'd have a view of the whole room. I'd eaten in at least a dozen school cafeterias in my life, and this one was no different. Sticky tables that smelled faintly of disinfectant, hair-netted lunch workers, a cacophony of food smells, and the dull roar of student conversations.

So far there had been no pure white auras. Kaley's came the closest, and I was terrified I'd look at hers one day and see pure white. The streak of conservative tan was still preventing the aura from balancing into white. I prayed she'd stick to whatever uber-conservative views she had.

"Chelsea's mom's friend is a paralegal, so we might try to do that," Kaley was saying. "I don't know, though. That sounds kind of boring."

I shrugged. "It's no worse than a mechanic's shop. At least you don't have to worry about your clothes getting oil all over them."

Kaley laughed as if I'd actually said something funny. "I wish I had been paired up with Wyatt. His dad has a friend who works at the planetarium. Now that's a cool job."

I stopped myself before shaking my head at Kaley's version of cool. She was a science and math nerd through and through. She owned it, though. She was an awkward science and math obsessed nerd, but at least she knew who she was and was comfortable with it.

I would never be comfortable being a harbinger of death. If I ever did, well, I shuddered to think about the person I would be. Definitely not one I would want to see in the mirror staring back at me every day.

Kaley pulled out her trig homework, so I did the same and paid just enough attention not to hurt her feelings. She really was trying to help me, but knowing the various definitions of the Pythagorean theorem in all their sleep-inducing glory just wasn't at the top of my priority list.

It was taking longer than expected to find a pure soul. I never realized how rare they were until I needed to find one quickly.

The integrity of the student body at this school was questionable at best.

I drummed my fingertips on the table. Maybe all the good kids simply had a different lunch period. I could hope, right?

On the other side of the cafeteria, Cole slipped in and stood in the cold sandwich line. Wise decision. It was sloppy joe day in the hot line.

"So what's the value of the hypotenuse?" Kaley was

pointing to a diagram she'd written on my homework.

"Uh...four?"

She sighed. "Were you even listening to me?"

I guiltily shook my head. "Sorry, I was distracted."

"That's okay." Kaley pushed her glasses up on her nose, her expression patient. She wasn't lying when she said it was okay. The girl had the patience of a saint. I once again thanked my lucky stars for her overly conservative values.

"Here, let me explain it again," she said. "You know this line here is the hypotenuse..."

I nodded and tilted my head down toward the paper, but after a few seconds I focused my eyes back toward the lunch lines. People watching was much more interesting.

I jerked my face away and squeezed my eyes shut as blinding light beamed across the cafeteria.

"Are you okay?" Kaley asked.

I breathed deeply. This was it. I'd found one. I should be happy. I could start blocking out auras again, which meant saying good-bye to the frequent migraines. I could get Xavier off my back for a while. Once I turned in the name, I could pretend to live a normal life, at least for a few months. Even though I wanted those things, my conscience was screaming.

"Fine," I whispered. Kaley loosened the grip she had on my arm.

I forced my eyes open, simultaneously wanting and not wanting to know who the pure aura belonged to.

Holy freaking crap.

It was Cole.

He took his lunch with him out of the cafeteria, unaware he was in possession of something that marked him for death. Unease settled in my belly. Cole, my project partner and occasional knight in shining armor, was who I was looking for.

"I gotta go." I blindly stuffed my trig notebook in my backpack and stumbled out of the cafeteria, leaving Kaley gaping behind me.

How could it be Cole? I would have never expected him to have a pure white aura. I mean, yeah, he was a decent guy for the most part, but possible angel material? I didn't think so.

I'd never been wrong before, though. Auras didn't lie.

I could mix up similar aura colors, like certain shades of blues and purples, but the white aura was hard to miss. First of all, it was so blinding I could barely stand to look at it. It felt like the sun was shining directly into my eyeballs from five feet away. That's how bright it was. Second of all, it was pure white light with not a hint of color. That was the whole point—all of the other colors were perfectly balanced. There were no other colors to confuse it with.

The real question was if the aura was fated. I'd been so shocked I hadn't taken the time to determine if it was.

But maybe the aura wasn't his. I could have seen it wrong. Maybe it belonged to the guy standing next to him.

Except I knew it didn't.

I sat through my afternoon classes with anxiety taking up residence in every inch of my body. My mind was spinning out of control, but when I tried to stop it, visions of Cole took over, his tanned skin turned pale against the white satin of the coffin from my nightmares.

It was all I could do to listen to my English teacher drone on about the symbolism in Arthur Miller's plays. But skipping class was not an option since I didn't want to give Xavier another reason for a surprise visit, though it remained a mystery how he was always in tune with my actions. Plus I had promised my mom.

As soon as the final bell rang, I hightailed it out of the building without even stopping at my locker to pick up the books I needed for homework. I didn't have the energy to kid myself today. There was no way I could focus enough to read an act from *The Crucible*.

It would have been quicker to take the bus to Bill's

shop, but I didn't have the patience to wait for it. I wanted to be moving *now*, even if that meant it would actually take me longer. Screwy logic, but I couldn't sit still.

The reclusive Bill was in the shop talking to Cole when I swung open the door. One look at me had him scurrying under an old Cadillac. That man had issues.

"Hey," Cole said, sparing me a glance with raised eyebrows before returning to the toolbox he was organizing.

My hand was still outstretched on the door, my other hand on the doorway. My chest was heaving from the power walking I did to get here. Escapee strands of hair that had gotten loose from my ponytail were clinging to my face. My cheeks were probably red from both the exertion and the chill in the air.

I must have looked like a lunatic.

I fully entered the shop and closed the door behind me, doing my best to return my breathing to normal. I took a moment to smooth my hair before turning around.

"Hey." I slid onto the stool next to him, aiming for casual. My backpack that was still slung over my shoulder choose that moment to slide down my arm and get hooked on my elbow, the weight of it causing me to nearly fall off the stool.

So much for casual.

Or normal. Sheesh.

Normal. Everything is normal. Now I just needed to act like it until I could check his aura again.

I pulled some papers out of my backpack. "I brought the form we need Bill to sign to formalize our internship. You should probably give it to him."

Cole took the form from me and stuffed it into his back pocket. "Okay."

"I didn't see any cars out in the lot," I commented.

"Yeah, it's going to be a slow day, so I'm organizing the tools."

I looked down to all the shiny metal tools, some long,

some round. I had no idea what they were. They could be fancy toe nail clippers for all I knew.

I took out my journal. "I guess since Bill is afraid of ovaries or whatever, I'll have to ask you questions for my journal."

"Sure," Cole said. He hadn't been much of a conversationalist in the short time I'd known him. I hoped he was feeling more talkative today or my journal would only be about two sentences long. I was beginning to realize just how much I didn't know about him, despite having already spent hours with him at the shop.

"How long have you worked at the shop?"

"Since I moved here."

My pen remained poised over my journal as I waited for him to clarify. When he stayed silent, I prompted, "And that was?"

"Summer. About four months ago."

"Have you always wanted to be a mechanic?"

He shrugged. "I'm good at it."

"That doesn't answer the question."

"Fine, then, no. When I was four, I wanted to be Batman."

"Okay," I said, hissing the word under my breath. It was all well and good he'd had aspirations to be Batman, but that wasn't going in my journal. "Where did you live before here?"

He glanced at me before answering. "Just outside D.C."

So he'd only moved a few hours south. That was nothing compared to some of the moves I'd experienced.

"Why did you move here?"

He closed a drawer on the toolbox with a bang. "What does this have to do with the report?"

"I'm just trying to figure out how someone gets interested in the profession, that's all." I couldn't look at him as I gave him this lame answer. I didn't want to be looking at him when his bullshit meter started wailing.

But what was I supposed to tell him? The truth? *Yes, Cole, I want to know all about you because I want to know why your aura is white, why I may have to doom you to your death. Is that okay? Oh, and by the way, after you die, you might be an angel. Or go to hell. One or the other.*

"If you say so." Cole's voice said his bullshit meter was indeed wailing.

"Well, why do you want to be a mechanic?" I asked again.

"I'm good with cars."

"How did you get to be good with cars?"

He shrugged.

Geez, you'd think I was trying to pry the secret identity out of the real Batman. "Did you work on them with your dad or something?" I prodded.

"No," he said curtly. "Hand me that screwdriver."

I handed it over. "So what got you interested in cars?"

"They're fast. All guys like fast things."

While I didn't doubt the truth of that statement, his answer not being forthright only made me want to dig deeper. But given the hardness in Cole's eyes, I decided I didn't want to be the proverbial cat who got killed by its own curiosity.

"Do you have any brothers or sisters?" I asked. That seemed to be a safe subject.

Cole turned and leaned against the tool box, crossing his arms. His forearms were muscled and tanned, and his shoulders filled out the *Bill's Auto* t-shirt quite nicely. I licked my lips.

"Why do *you* want to work with cars?" he asked.

I wrinkled my nose. "I don't. I'm just here because of the project."

"Then what do you want to do?" His eyes bore into mine.

"I don't know," I muttered, looking down and doodling in my notebook.

"You're newer than me. Why did you move here?"

I clamped my mouth shut and narrowed my eyes.

He leaned closer, and I could smell the peppermint on his breath. "Here's the thing, sweetheart." His obnoxious use of the endearment made me cringe. "I thought we were on the same page here, but I guess not. We keep out of each other's business. If it doesn't involve the project, then don't ask."

I nodded, unable to speak. He crossed to the other side of the shop and busied himself with the equipment over there.

I started tapping my pen against my journal. Then I tapped my foot. The more I tapped, the angrier I got.

What was his problem? We had to work together for the next month. There was nothing wrong with wanting to know a little bit more about him.

Granted, my reasons for asking the questions weren't innocent, but he didn't know that.

I watched him, slowly letting down my guards.

I was blinded for my efforts, so I quickly threw my guards up again.

Fan-frigging-tastic.

Something must be wrong with my aura sensors, or whatever it was that allowed me to see auras. That was the only possible explanation. There was no way Mr. Bipolar over there could possibly be angel potential. One day he was all concerned about my claustrophobia and the next he was snarling at me for asking simple questions.

Batman over there needed to get over himself.

I jumped off my stool and stomped across the room to a toolbox. Yanking a drawer open, I pulled out a shiny metal tool.

As I whipped around, I caught sight of Bill slipping into his office and closing the door. I rolled my eyes.

These two were made for each other. This was a shop for social weirdos.

"Cole." When he turned, I held up the tool. "What's this?"

"A socket wrench."

I grabbed another one at random. "What's this one?"

"Another socket wrench." His tone was dry.

Huh. I looked at it. Yup, the same as the other one, maybe just slightly bigger.

"How about this one?"

"Spark plug socket."

"And this one?"

"Socket wrench."

Another one? How many socket wrenches did they need?

I slammed the wrenches back into the drawer and rummaged around looking for something that was *not* a socket wrench. I had the hang of those now.

Cole crossed the room, pulled my hand out of the drawer, and slammed it closed with a bang, barely missing my fingertips.

"You're fucking up the drawer. I just organized those."

I crossed my arms over my chest, flashing a defiant look. "I'm trying to *learn*, Cole. I'm asking questions relating to the project."

"You're just pissed because I told you to mind your own business when you tried nosing around my life."

My nostrils flared. I figured he would know why I was acting pissy, but I didn't expect him to call me out on it.

"You're an asshole." It wasn't the best comeback, but it was the best I could do at the moment. I grabbed my bag and stalked to the door.

I got two steps out before he grabbed my arm.

I pulled away and spun on my heel. "Don't touch me."

He didn't give an inch, putting us close together. Lucky for me, his foul attitude was trumping whatever it was about him that made my circuits fry or else I'd be short of breath.

"I'm driving you home." It was a command, but I had news for him. I wasn't playing Robin to his Batman.

"Like hell."

"This isn't the best neighborhood. You shouldn't be walking around at night."

"What's your deal, Cole?" His abrupt shifts from asshole to concerned humanitarian were giving me whiplash.

He spread his arms out with his hands palms up, with an *I don't know what you're talking about* look on his face.

"Whatever. I'm leaving."

"Ava."

I kept walking.

"Ava." He said it louder this time.

I looked back over my shoulder.

"Do you really want to walk home? It looks like it's going to rain." As if God himself were on Cole's side, an ominous roll of thunder sounded.

I looked up to the sky, finding dark clouds hovering above. Moisture was in the air. Cole was right. It was going to pour at any minute. Just my freaking luck.

I stomped back into the building and out to the back parking lot. I jerked on the handle of the Rustinator. Locked. Why did he bother? While he swore it ran perfectly well, and it had managed to get me home twice now, I had my doubts. It looked like a rusty piece of junk. There wasn't exactly a high likelihood of theft.

I stepped aside so he could unlock the door. And yeah, he opened it for me. I guess that was just his way.

It pissed me off.

We didn't speak the whole way to my apartment. About halfway there, huge raindrops began spattering the windshield. By the time he pulled in front of my building, the rain was steady. I got out of the car, slamming the door with a force that probably shook some rust free, and made a mad dash for the building.

Screw him. I'd have to deal with the white aura thing eventually, but for today, I was done.

My mom was sitting at the kitchen table clutching a mug of tea when I walked in. "You look like a drowned rat," she said before raising the mug to her lips.

"That comment is less than helpful," I spat. At her raised eyebrows, I sighed. "Sorry. I'm in a bad mood."

A foul mood. A Cole Fowler mood. God, that pun was terrible. He'd totally thrown me off my game. All the more reason to be pissed at him.

She stood. "I'll make you some hot chocolate. Chocolate makes everything better."

I stripped out of my damp clothes in my room and changed into yoga pants and a sweatshirt. When I returned to the kitchen, a steaming mug of hot chocolate overflowing with marshmallows was waiting for me.

I wrapped my hands around the warm ceramic. "Thanks."

My mom nodded and took a sip of her tea. She didn't have a magazine in front of her, she wasn't scrolling through her phone, and she didn't even have a radio on. She had been alone with a cup of tea and her thoughts.

What must those thoughts be? She'd been a seeker for twenty years now. I couldn't help but wonder how she lived with herself. Twenty years of souls—I didn't even want to think about how many people that was. I wondered how many of them had actually passed the test and become angels.

All white auras were not the same. Some were fated, which meant their time on Earth was up, that it was time for them to join the "holy fraternity of angels." Those were the names we gave to Xavier, and by doing that, we tipped the scales for those fated souls. This was the part that got me—what if we didn't tip the scales? Would those people get to live out more years with their families? If the souls were fated, then why should we have to do anything?

But that wasn't my biggest concern.

"Have you ever been wrong?" I asked.

She furrowed her brows. "How do you mean?"

"Have you ever been wrong about an aura? Like, seen the wrong color or something like that?"

"I don't think that's possible. But even if it were, I'd have no way of knowing. I've never considered that I might be wrong."

I chewed on my cuticle. "But what if you saw a white aura for someone who you knew couldn't possibly be an angel?"

"It's not for us to decide if those with white auras actually become angels. We just have to find the auras and determine if they're fated. After that, it's out of our hands." She got up and took her empty mug to the sink.

"What about white auras that aren't fated?"

"What about them?"

"Do they eventually become fated?"

She leaned against the sink and nodded. "As long as they stay white, they will eventually become fated."

"Have you ever been wrong about a fated aura? I mean, like whether or not it's really fated? They're so close in color. What if you turn in a non-fated aura?"

Wrinkle lines formed on her forehead. "I've only ever turned in fated auras."

I appreciated that she wasn't asking why I was asking these questions but I sensed I had reached the end of my grace period, so I shut my mouth, even though there was so much more I wanted to know. My mom swore she'd never turn in a name for me again, and even though I didn't know if Cole's aura was fated anyway, I didn't want to take the risk.

"I've got to get ready for work. Late night dessert shift," she said. "I went to the grocery store earlier, so there's mac and cheese and soup in the pantry."

"Thanks," I said. She leaned over and kissed the top of my head, wrapping her arms around me. I hesitated for a moment before placing my hand on her arm. Her sharp inhale was slight, but noticeable. Before I was forced into being a seeker, she and I had been very affectionate with each other. It'd been a while since I returned her affection.

As I lay in bed that night after gorging on mac & cheese, I watched some senseless reality TV show about "real life" teens. It was ridiculous. One girl was in tears because she had to wear last year's dress to prom and a boy declared war on his parents because they'd bought him a used Mercedes instead of a new one when he wrecked his BMW.

Woe is them.

I turned it off right as a girl puked in the bushes outside her prom venue. I snorted. What I wouldn't give to have their types of problems.

Several kids on that show were so despicable I'd bet my left earlobe their auras were black or at least close to it. And those imbeciles got to continue their meaningless, over-privileged, overexposed lives while pure souls were forced to die.

It just wasn't right. It was backwards.

Then I had a light bulb moment, sitting straight up in bed as the epiphany came over me.

Instead of dooming someone with a white aura to death, why didn't I choose someone with the blackest aura I could find? Xavier couldn't see auras. Otherwise, he wouldn't need us. He wouldn't know the difference.

Instead of choosing a good person, I could choose someone the world would be better without.

Excitement coursed through my veins.

When I'd asked Xavier about what happened to the people I'd chosen, if they'd become angels or not, he wouldn't tell me. Wouldn't or *couldn't*? The more I thought about it, the more I thought that Xavier probably didn't even know what happened to them. If he didn't know, then he wouldn't be suspicious when none of my chosen souls became angels.

The whole morality surrounding what I was considering was still wrong, because after all, I was still sentencing someone to death, but it was a kind of wrong I could live with, the kind of wrong that wouldn't result in screaming middle-of-the-night nightmares.

The world would have one less scumbag, and my conscience could rest easier. It was a win-win. Why hadn't I thought of this sooner?

I slept better that night than I had in months.

CHAPTER 6

I WAS LOOKING FOR AN asshole. Not just any asshole, but a grade-A top level asshole.

Then I was going to sentence him to die.

This was a lot trickier than I thought. Sure, high school had its share of assholes, but I wanted to find a pure black aura. Someone who was beyond redemption.

I searched all day at school and wasn't satisfied with what I'd found. Sure, there were the mean girls at the bus stop, the guy who bullied freshmen, and Cole. Of course, there was Cole.

He was definitely...something. Part-time asshole, part-time nice guy.

I hadn't forgotten about his aura being white. I avoided him at school, which wasn't hard considering he spent his mornings at the tech school for the auto mechanic program, and then he left early to go to his apprenticeship.

Cole *could* be a nice guy, but he wasn't white aura nice. And even though he could also be an asshole, he wasn't black aura evil. The guy was an enigma.

I needed to go to the really bad part of town. I'd walked there before, but I'd only skirted the edges and never got too deep. To find a black aura, I had to go into the trenches where little old ladies clutched their purses a little tighter and people needed alarms on their cars.

Learning the black aura's name was key. Simply seeing the black aura wasn't going to be enough. I had to be able to give Xavier enough information to identify him. Or her. I was not being sexist here. I was an equal opportunity life ruiner when it came to auras.

After school, I quickly texted Cole: *Sick. Not coming to shop today.* Not surprisingly, I didn't receive a response.

See? A classic asshole move.

I took off on foot in the direction of the shop, which was on the way. As I waited for the walk sign to illuminate at the traffic light right across from the shop, I stood behind the light pole, peeking around to spy on the shop. Cole was nowhere in sight, but I wasn't taking any chances. I put on my hood, and as soon as the light turned, I jogged across the street and kept jogging until I was out of sight.

The longer I walked, the browner the landscape. Even grass and trees refused to inhabit this wasteland. The paint peeling off the buildings reminded me of a snake shedding its skin. The only building showing signs of life was the local Quik In, except the sign was missing some letters, so it just read Q k I. Signs advertising low, low prices on cigarettes were plastered on the barred windows. Another sign promised the widest selection of 40s this side of the Mississippi. Granted, I didn't know much about 40s, but I was guessing that promise was exaggerated.

Since this appeared to be the local hot spot, I decided to do some surveillance. Diagonally across the street from the Quik In was a park with several basketball hoops and a meager playground with a cracked slide and swings with broken chains.

I leaned against an old tree hardened by years of existence, its roots spreading out like bony fingers clutching the ground. I stuck out like a neon light in a sea of grays, so I didn't bother to try to conceal myself. Looking like I was trying to hide would only make me more conspicuous.

I didn't have to wait long. A group of guys came walking up the street toward the Quik In. Their swaggered gait was enough to brandish their presence, and those in their path cleared out. In fact, where the store was bustling with activity just moments ago, it was now deserted except for a lone individual.

I took a few steps closer so I could see better. The group of guys had their backs to me, shielding the other guy. I cursed, but it wasn't like I could call over to them and ask them to step aside—*Excuse me? Can you step to the left a bit so I can watch your nefarious activities?*

I took the opportunity to check out their auras. All grays and blacks, exactly what I wanted to see. It saddened me that I was able to find black auras so quickly though. Why was it so hard to find a white aura, yet I found multiple black souls on the first try?

What did that say about us, about humanity?

Now was not the time to wax philosophical.

I chewed on my cuticle, pondering my next move. My grand plan was to find the black aura and turn the name in. I hadn't actually planned for how I was going to learn that name.

A little short sighted on my part, I knew.

Standing here wasn't getting me any closer to that name. I'd bet the clerk in the Quik In probably knew these guys. I doubted this was their first time loitering in front of the store, scaring potential customers away.

So all I had to do was cross the street, slip into the store, and ask the clerk their names. Simple, right?

It was only slightly complicated by the fact that they were blocking the entrance to the store. Sure, they were thugs, but they had no reason to bother me if all I wanted to do was go into the store, right?

Because I was sure their auras were black from *not*

bothering people.

Arg!

This was so stupid. I was so full of righteousness I'd charged into battle without a plan. *Stupid, stupid, stupid.* My aura was probably full of brown dogmatism right now.

One thing was certain, though. I did not want to have to come back tomorrow to try this again. I had to get a name soon, preferably today so I could be done with this. I didn't have a purse to clutch tighter, but I was definitely looking over my shoulder a little more.

I reached out to press the button at the crosswalk to find it was smashed. *Figures.*

A gap in traffic came, and I was about to dart out into the street when a familiar car zoomed up and stopped at the curb.

The Rustinator.

No. What was he doing here?

Cole rolled down the passenger window and leaned across the front seat. "Get in."

I frowned at him. "Go away."

"You shouldn't be here." His eyes were dark, his expression menacing, making me question whether I would be safer in his car or out here on the street.

"Go away, Cole," I hissed, desperately looking across the street. We were attracting the attention of the thugs, which was *not* in my hastily crafted plan.

Cole was not in my hastily crafted plan.

He opened the driver's door, unconcerned with the cars careening down the road.

And he thought I had unsafe habits on the road? He was crazy.

He crossed in front of the car and grabbed hold of my arm.

"Hey!" I protested, trying to jerk my arm away, but he held it fast. He yanked on the passenger door and shoved me into the car.

I could have jumped out and made a run for it while

he crossed in front of the car to get back to the driver's side. It was presumptuous of him to think I'd stay where he put me.

I did stay put though because there was no way I could slip into the Quik In after the display Cole put on.

So totally *not* inconspicuous.

Cole gripped the steering wheel with both hands, staring straight ahead. The muscle in his jaw clenched and unclenched. He acted like he was pissed, but why should he be? *I* was the one who should be pissed.

And I was.

"What's your problem?" I spat, crossing my arms.

"You," he said. "You're my problem."

"Me?" My jaw nearly fell into my lap. "You're the one who keeps getting into my business. What happened to the mind your own business stuff?"

He laughed softly, bitterly. "You really do have a death wish."

I looked out the window. "No, I don't," I muttered.

"Then what were you doing back there?"

"None of your business. And why do you care anyway?"

He avoided the question. "Do you know who those guys were?"

I sat up straighter. Maybe my time wasn't spent in vain. "No. Do you?"

He shook his head. "Not specifically, no."

My shoulders fell, and I sank back into the seat. "Oh."

He cursed. "You're clueless. Didn't you notice what they were wearing?"

"Um, clothes?"

"No shit, Sherlock. You don't pay attention to detail, do you?"

I huffed a little at that one, but stayed silent. I paid attention to detail. I had no freaking choice in that. I saw the effects of every accomplishment, every bad decision a person made in their aura. That was a lot of detail to take in.

I noticed how the ring leader's aura was the darkest. He was the most evil. Red and orange lines threaded through the black, signaling anger and ignorance. I noticed the bulge in his waistband, probably a gun. I noticed how the others walked a few steps behind him, deferring to him and his apparent authority.

So excuse me if I didn't notice the clothing he was wearing. I had become a master at reading people this last year, but that involved behaviors. Clothing wasn't even a blip on my radar. I glanced down at my uniform of jeans and a hoodie. Nope, clothing wasn't my thing.

Cole glanced over at me. "Gang colors. They were wearing gang colors."

"How so?"

"On their heads."

I tried to remember what they were wearing. "Black beanies?"

"They had bandanas on under the beanies."

I blinked. Yeah, maybe I saw a snatch of blue beneath the beanies. So what? So what if they were matching?

Then the *so what* dawned on me, and I felt like an idiot.

"So you're saying they're gang members?"

Cole maneuvered through traffic, just barely making it through an intersection on a yellow light. "Glad to see you've finally caught up."

I didn't know the implications of their being gang members. It was bad, obviously. But what kind of bad and how bad I had no clue. I was so pissed at Cole right now I could hardly see straight, much less think straight.

"You're an asshole, you know that?"

"I've heard that about me." There was no pride or sarcasm. He was simply matter-of-fact. It dawned on me that this was a person who truly didn't care what others thought of him.

That must be nice, freeing.

It made me hate him a little more.

"What were *you* doing in that part of town? Were you following me?" I accused.

His expression told me how ridiculous that accusation was.

"Don't flatter yourself."

His words stung. Okay, so maybe it was a ridiculous accusation, especially since I was pretty sure he didn't see me go by the shop. He didn't have to be an ass about it though.

"What *were* you doing there?" I asked again.

He pulled the car into the shop parking lot and remained silent.

I smirked. "Someone's got a secret. I'll tell you mine if you tell me yours."

He turned off the car and gave me a scathing look. "Just be glad I *was* there. You don't know what those guys are capable of."

I didn't *know* what they were capable of, but given their auras, I could make an educated guess. I had been scared back there. Part of me was relieved Cole whisked me away. The other part of me was angry. I'd gone there because I had a task to complete, not because I had a death wish as Cole liked to say. I was no closer to having a name for Xavier than I was this morning. Even if I went back tomorrow, who knew if my luck would be the same and I'd find a black aura so quickly? For my sake, I hoped it would be easy.

For humanity's sake, I hoped otherwise.

I unbuckled my seatbelt. "Your concern is touching, truly, but I can take care of myself."

He snorted and got out of the car. I did the same.

As I entered the building, I called out, "Bill! It's me, Ava! You may want to hide now!"

Cole slammed his keys down on the counter. "That's enough. I've told you before not to mess with Bill."

I crossed my arms and raised one eyebrow. "I'm doing

him the courtesy of announcing my presence." I was being a bitch. I knew it, but Cole brought it out in me.

"If you're going to hang around, then do something useful." He pulled two boxes off the shelf and shoved them into my arms. "Match these up."

I looked down into the boxes. One was full of bolts, the other nuts. They were various sizes and shapes.

I gave Cole one last dirty look before hopping up on my stool and starting on the task. Even though I knew I was acting like a bitch, I really wasn't one. I shouldn't tease Bill, and I wouldn't except it annoyed Cole. Bill was doing us a solid by letting us use his shop for our project. It could be much worse. One group was working at a dry cleaners. I overheard them talking about how awful it was and how the manager basically used them as slave labor.

So if it would help Bill for me to match up nuts and bolts, then I would, even if it was Cole who gave me the order.

Cole pulled a car into his work area. I recognized he was going through the routine of a basic oil change. I smiled a little, pleased with myself. A week ago I wouldn't have known that.

While Cole was busy with the oil, I took the opportunity to observe him. I didn't know why I let him get under my skin. I *let* him have that power over me.

I just...couldn't help it. There was something about him that drew me in, like that old *moth to the flame* saying. Except who was the moth and who was the flame? It could go both ways.

He was more...*competent* than most guys his age. Competent seemed like an odd word, but it was what popped into my mind as I watched him. He moved with purpose, like he knew what he was doing. He did because he'd probably changed the oil for hundreds of cars, but he was just like that in general. Everything he did had a purpose.

While I grudgingly admitted that being competent

was a worthy trait, it did not make him worthy of a white aura. I slowly let down my guards, bracing myself for the onslaught of brightness. I cringed as I was bathed in the pure white light. I had half expected (maybe not expected, but definitely *hoped*) the aura to be different this time, that last time was a fluke.

But despite my irritation with Cole, I knew somewhere in my gut he was good. I could see it in those rare moments he let his guard down.

Unfortunately for me, his method of keeping his guard up was acting like an asshole.

I forced myself to put aside my irritation and really study his aura.

It wasn't fated.

Thank God.

Still, it wasn't exactly *not* fated, either. I had never seen a white aura quite like his. It was odd. Instead of the white being consistently bright, it throbbed ever so slightly, so slight I almost missed it. But once I saw it, it was unmistakably throbbing.

It figured he'd have a difficult aura. I didn't know what to make of it. But now that I'd determined his aura wasn't fated, I could freely embrace my irritation with him.

The car he was currently working on was an older model. Still, he took the same amount of care with it as he did with the luxury car he had just finished, even taking the time to buff out a spot where it looked like another car's paint had rubbed off on it. He did a good job, worked hard, went the extra mile.

God, it pissed me off.

He would be a lot easier to deal with if he were a complete asshole. Then I could write off the knee jerk spine tingling that occurred whenever I looked at him as nothing but hormones, nothing but a reaction to his general hotness.

He choose that moment to look up at me. The spine

tingling turned into full on body tingling.

I blushed and looked down at the nut and bolt I held, my fingers fumbling when trying to fit them together.

He walked over and put his hands on his hips, surveying my pile of matches. "Not bad."

My blush deepened at the compliment. "I still have a lot more to match." I gestured to the still full boxes. "I hope Bill doesn't need them anytime soon," I added. If he could play nice, then so could I.

He grinned wickedly. "He doesn't."

I frowned. "Is there something I'm missing here?"

He rocked back on his heels. "These are junk nuts and bolts. Bill just throws them in these boxes whenever he finds them lying around."

I gaped at him. "So you're saying..."

"They're worthless."

I dropped the bolt I was holding like it'd burned me. "Worthless?" I growled the word.

He threw his head back and laughed.

COLE BOUGHT ME DINNER. NOTHING fancy, just fast food. Even though he didn't say so, I could tell he felt bad about the whole nuts and bolts thing. After I'd gotten over my initial anger, I had to admit it was kind of funny.

Cole had gotten up to get a drink refill, so I used the opportunity to check out his aura again. I took a few cleansing breaths and let down my guards. I squinted at the blinding flash of light but managed to keep my eyes open to inspect the aura.

I tilted my head, trying to get another angle. Every way I looked at it, it was white. No matter how hard I looked, how much I scrutinized the light surrounding him, I couldn't find any trace of color, just the strange throbbing. If I had to guess at Cole's aura, I'd say blue—he was definitely masculine—or red—he was a danger to girls everywhere. I *never* would have picked white. The more time I spent with him, the more I realized he was a nice guy, but I had a list of reasons why he shouldn't possess a white aura.

Starting with telling me it would be bad for business if I died in front of the shop.

Joking or not—and given his seriousness when he'd made that comment, I'd guess not—that was not a nice thing to say. Lucky for him, my grudges against my mom and Xavier didn't leave any room for any more.

Well, big grudges anyway.

He popped the lid on his cup and headed back to our table. I ducked my head and dragged my french fry through the blob of ketchup on my burger wrapper. When he sat down, the edges of his lips were curved up in a smirk.

Damn. He must have caught me staring at him. Heat rushed to my cheeks, so I kept my head down and focused on my food.

"So where did you move from?" he asked.

I waited a few seconds before raising my head to ensure the blush had faded. I raised one eyebrow, a cool trick I'd taught myself when I was nine by practicing for hours in front a mirror. "So we're those kind of friends, now, huh?"

He shrugged, then took a massive bite of his deluxe burger, his second one. The first one he'd polished off nearly before I could even get mine unwrapped. "If you don't want to be friends, that's cool."

"No," I said a little too quickly. I took a sip of soda, hoping it would cool the heat spreading to my cheeks again. "We can be friends."

I fidgeted, still not answering his original question. There was no way he'd connect the tragedy in Woodlawn with me. It didn't make the national news or anything, just the local news. He probably hadn't even heard of the place anyway.

"Woodlawn," I said. "I came from Woodlawn."

He looked at me with a blank expression, and my shoulders sank a little with relief. "It's a podunk little town in the middle of nowhere in southwest Virginia."

"Did you like it there?"

Sure, aside from being responsible for the death of the homecoming queen.

"It was okay." My mom had chosen it because it was small and unassuming. She thought it would be easier to find a white aura in a simpler environment, one where people hadn't been corrupted by the hustle of urban life. In a way, she was right. I spotted the white aura right away. But Ashley's death reverberated through that small town like an echo in a chasm. That had made it much harder.

"Why did you move?"

"My mom has a wandering spirit," I said. That had been her explanation for our moves my whole life. In the last year, that explanation had taken on new meaning. "What about you? Why did you move from D.C.?"

He hesitated, shoving a handful of fries in his mouth to buy time. I could tell he still didn't want to share personal details, despite his previous declaration that made us friends.

"I got an opportunity to go through the auto program here," he finally said.

There seemed to be more to it than that, but I didn't want to pry and ruin our little "Kumbaya" moment. His opening up to me, even this little bit, felt like a huge step.

"Did you like it there?" I asked, taking my cue from the questions he'd asked.

"It was okay." He took a sip of his soda. "There was always something going on."

"I've never been there."

"Really?" He looked surprised.

"Maybe I'll go some day, and you can show me around." I said it jokingly, but as soon as the words were out of my mouth, I wished I could suck them back in.

His expression was stricken. "I don't really go back there."

There was pain there. I suddenly wanted to reach across the table and hold his hand, but I knew it wouldn't be welcome.

And that would just open doors that were best kept shut.

"What do your parents do?"

The stricken expression was replaced by another one, this one hard. "My parents aren't a factor in my life."

Strike two for me. Not wanting to go for the trifecta, I munched on my fries.

Cole sighed, running his hands through his hair. A bunch of it stuck up in the front. I wanted to run my hands through it, to smooth it down, to soothe the obvious pain caused by his past.

Keep that door shut, remember? I chided myself. *Friendly. That's all you're going for here. Keep it simple.*

"I've never met my dad. He left my mom before I was born. And my mom—" he broke off suddenly, looking away.

"You don't have to tell me," I said quickly. If anyone understood about family secrets, it was me.

"I know," he said. "For some reason I want to. My mom was a drug addict. Probably still is. She wasn't the best mother, so I got used to fending for myself."

"That sucks," I said simply. Although I would love to coddle him, Cole wasn't the coddling type. A simply acknowledgment of his misfortune was enough.

"Thanks."

"I've never met my dad, either," I offered in solidarity. "He took off when I was a baby. I figure I probably don't want to have anything to do with the type of guy who would do that anyway. My mom and I are better off without him."

We sat in silence for a moment, Cole flicking his straw

with his finger and me folding up my burger wrapper into a tiny square.

Cole cleared his throat and grinned. "Are you going to do some real work at the shop tomorrow?"

I scowled but ruined it by laughing. "That bolt trick was mean."

He held up a soggy fry, offering it to me. "Do you forgive me?"

I looked at the fry skeptically before turning my gaze to him. "That limp fry is not going to win you forgiveness."

He looked at it, shrugged, and stuffed it in his mouth. "I'll tell you what. I'll teach you how to change a tire tomorrow. You don't have to go under the car for that."

"How do you know I don't already know how to change one?" It didn't escape my notice that he remembered my claustrophobia. I was pleased, even more pleased that he took it seriously, suggesting an activity that wouldn't set it off.

"Do you?" he asked pointedly.

I stuck out my chin. "No," I admitted.

"That's what I thought." He leaned back in his chair, observing me knowingly. "You're stubborn for the sake of being stubborn, you know that?"

I thought about that. Yes, I could be stubborn, but Cole brought that trait out in me like never before. My aura must be flooded with it right now.

If I could see my own aura, what other colors would I find? Would I have any pink for compassion? Or would I just find the steely blue that represents coldness? At what point would my aura become black? Surely it couldn't stay light. With every name I turned in it had to be getting darker and darker until one day it would be ebony.

But maybe, just maybe, if I could pull off turning in black auras instead of white ones, then I could slow down the blackening of my own aura.

"So what classes are you taking?" I asked in a lame attempt to keep the conversation going.

"Government and English," he replied. "Oh, and the junior seminar. Just for the project, though."

"You only have two full-time classes?" That was crazy. I had seven.

He shrugged. "I'm in the apprenticeship program, so working at the shop counts toward graduation."

"Geez, I wish I could do that."

"You can when you're a senior. What are your skills?" The smirk on his face was becoming a fixture.

I gave him a look, then opened my mouth to answer and promptly shut it.

I didn't have any skills.

I could write a decent essay and was scraping by in trig now, thanks to Kaley, but they weren't exactly skills. Did doing laundry count as a skill? Probably, but it wasn't an important or hard to learn skill.

I could see auras. That was a skill you didn't run into every day, but it wasn't exactly something I could share.

But it was the one that consumed most of my energy.

It shaped my world. The rest of my life was going to revolve around seeing auras and finding the white ones, being the Grim Reaper's seeker. It defined me.

The thought made me sick to my stomach.

CHAPTER 7

THE NEXT MORNING I SAT in gum on the bus. Bright pink bubble gum. It got all over the seat of my pants and the bottom of my backpack.

Awesome.

The worst part was that I realized it almost as soon as I did it, so I was forced to endure the rest of the bus ride with the knowledge that I had a wad of someone's spit filled gum becoming further enmeshed in the fabric of my jeans with every bump and turn.

I nearly ran off the bus in an effort to get to the restroom as fast as I could. The trouble was that I couldn't see the spot right below my left back pocket where the gum was smeared. I twisted and arched in front of the cracked full length mirror in the girls' bathroom, but it was just in that perfect blind spot.

So I could either ask a random girl to help scrub my ass, or I could take the jeans off and do it myself. Neither option was appealing, but at least one of them was less likely to start freaky rumors about me.

I moistened my paper towel again and took it into a stall. After carefully removing my tennis shoes, I stepped out of my jeans, careful only to step on my shoes. I did not have the most confidence in the custodian's diligence in sanitizing the tile floors in here, and I wasn't trying to get

Hepatitis or some other equally awful disease.

I had been fortunate in that no one else had come into the bathroom while I was contorting myself in front of the mirror trying to get a glimpse of my ass, but now several girls walked in, one of them sobbing. Her breath came out in gasps, and in between those gasps she tried to speak. Her friends shushed her, attempting to calm her down.

"He said—" another huge gasp and a wet sniffle "—he loved me."

"I told you he was a jerk."

"That's not helping, Brooke. Morgan, you'll find someone better than him."

I rolled my eyes. Girl problems. Some of the girls at this school wouldn't know real problems if they smacked them in their perfectly done-up faces.

"He...he—" Another fit of sobbing.

I stepped back into my jeans. There was a huge wet spot on my butt now, but at least I'd gotten most of the gum off. After tying my shoes and hefting my backpack onto my shoulder, I checked my watch. Five minutes until first bell. I wanted to avoid party crashing the sob fest outside the stall, but if the girls didn't clear out in the next two minutes, I would have no choice if I wanted to make it to class on time. I leaned against the side of the stall, eyes on my watch, to wait it out.

"He made me—" Sniffle, sniffle, sob, *snort*. That was new.

"He made you do what?" the nice friend asked, her tone gentle.

"He made me...he made me have sex with him." The words came out in a rush.

"Wait, what?"

I stopped staring at my watch and instead peeked through the crack of the stall.

Morgan, the girl who was crying, looked familiar. Maybe she was in one of my classes? No, that wasn't it. Then I remembered. When I transferred, she showed me around school as part of the New Pals transition program. She was the goody two shoes type, a preacher's daughter if I recalled.

"He took me back to his house to watch a movie. No one was home, but I didn't think anything of it. Then we started making out, and the next thing I knew I was naked. I said no. *I said no.*" Morgan's voice broke.

"Did you tell anyone?" Nice Friend asked, a concerned look on her face. I didn't recognize her at all.

"No, I don't want anyone to know." Morgan shook her head emphatically.

"You've got to tell someone," Nice Friend said. "Tell your mom."

"I can't. She'll tell my dad."

"You have to *do* something," Brooke said forcefully. "You can't let him get away with this."

Nice Friend put her arm around the sobbing Morgan. "She doesn't have to do anything. It's her decision."

"He's just going to do it again to someone else. Someone—and I mean *you*—has to stop him." Brooke crossed her arms and leaned against the sink, her disgust plainly displayed in her expression. "I can't believe you went out with him in the first place."

"Shut up, Brooke," Nice Friend said, with a not-so-nice expression on her face.

"It's true! We *all* know what his reputation is like."

"I can't believe you're saying those things right now. Come on, Morgan," Nice Friend said, leading her away from Brooke. "I'll take you to the nurse and you can go home sick."

Nice Friend and Morgan left the bathroom, but Brooke stayed behind, a disgruntled look on her face. I didn't really know her, but she was in one of my classes.

The stall door made a bang as I swung it open and stepped out.

Brooke stood up straight, her eyes widening. "Were you in there the whole time?"

That question didn't warrant a response. "Who were you guys talking about?"

She crossed her arms and popped out her hip. "That's none of your business."

I cocked my head and looked at her. "Why are you protecting him?"

"Wait, what?" she sputtered. "You think I'm protecting that asshole? I'm protecting my friend."

"I already know who she is."

The look on her face showed she knew I had a point. "I just don't want anyone spreading rumors about Morgan."

I didn't bother pointing out that technically it wouldn't be a rumor because it was true. "I just want to make sure no one I know ends up dating him," I said, hoping that would encourage her to share.

She hesitated briefly, then said, "His name is Joey Huslander."

"How many girls has he raped?"

She sucked in her breath, startled at the bluntness of my question. Then the room was silent, tension hanging off the end of the question. The only sound was a slow drip from a leaky faucet.

"At least three, I think, but probably more," Brooke finally said.

"Thanks." I turned on my heel and left the bathroom. The bell had long since rung and I was late for my first class, but I didn't care. I wasn't going to class.

I needed to locate a teenage serial rapist.

I SKIPPED SCHOOL AGAIN. MY mom was going to flip when she found out, but if I told her it was related to seeking, then hopefully her wrath would be kept to a minimum. She just didn't need to know what *kind* of seeking I was doing.

I went down the street to the public library and logged into a computer. The librarian gave me a scrutinizing glare, but I smiled innocently back at her. No doubt she was wondering why I wasn't in school. Before all this seeking stuff started, I would have cringed under her gaze. Now I didn't care. She could wonder all she wanted.

It was easy to pull up his Facebook and Twitter pages. Within minutes, I learned Joey Huslander had graduated last year. I also learned where he lived, who his friends were, where he usually hung out, and where he worked. I also learned he was working today.

Some people obviously did not pay attention to all the mandatory internet safety information they spoon fed us every year at school. He made himself all too easy to find. But I guessed because he wasn't a teenage girl, he wasn't as worried about his privacy. And why should he worry about predators stalking him on the internet? He *was* the predator.

I knew better than to believe gossip. Since I'd bounced around from school to school, I had been the subject of gossip my whole life. *Who is the new girl? Where is she from?* Most of the gossip was innocent, but that still didn't make me feel better knowing people were talking about me.

I believed Morgan, though. Her anguish was all too real, and she was a church girl if ever I saw one. Even if I didn't already know her father was a minister at one of the local churches, I still would have pegged her as being a good girl. I hadn't checked her aura, but like I said, I was good at reading people.

I left the library less than fifteen minutes after I'd arrived. Target acquired. Joey was working at a coffee shop just a few blocks away. A quick look at Google maps on my phone, and I hoofed it over there.

A bell chimed on the door of the shop, announcing my arrival. It was an indie shop, not one of the large chains. It was quaint, with worn comfortable-looking couches scattered about and bookshelves full of battered paperbacks. A fireplace that was not currently lit lined one wall. The lighting was dim, making it cozy. It actually seemed like a cool place to hang out, definitely *not* a place I'd think to look for a black aura, but here I was.

I stepped up to the counter, looking up at the menu. It might as well have been written in a foreign language. It kind of was, actually. Latte, froth-a-grande, chai...I didn't know what any of that stuff was. I was not a coffee drinker. So I picked the safest looking thing on the menu, one with mocha in the title. Mocha was chocolate, right?

A middle-aged man took my order. He wasn't wearing a name tag, but I assumed he wasn't Joey. I couldn't picture this balding guy with a droopy middle pulling in high school girls.

I ordered a blueberry muffin to accompany my coffee and chose a plaid couch that ran along the wall so I had a view of the whole shop. My stomach growled in anticipation of the blueberry muffin. I'd skipped breakfast in the mad dash to make it to the bus stop so I wouldn't be late. Oh, the irony of it all.

I was halfway through the muffin when a guy came out of the back room with a box full of napkins. I hastily brushed the crumbs off my shirt and grabbed a magazine from the coffee table in front of me. I flipped through it, coffee in one hand, trying to appear nonchalant. He put the box down on a table and started refilling the napkin dispensers. It didn't take him long to notice me.

He looked over my way, his gaze traveling up from my legs, pausing at my chest, and eventually landing on my face.

This had to be Joey. The way he looked at me when he thought I wouldn't notice made me feel dirty. Like I needed to bathe myself in rubbing alcohol kind of dirty.

I took a deep breath, slowly letting down my guards.

I wanted his aura to be black. I wanted it so bad. Selfishly, I wanted to be done with this round of seeking.

For the sake of Morgan and the other unnamed girls, I wanted to turn his name in. Even if he was a rapist though, I wouldn't turn his name in unless his aura was black. I was treading a slippery slope as it was, and I had to stay true to the guidelines I'd set for myself.

He stepped over to me unexpectedly, and I quickly slammed my guards back into place, not wanting to be distracted by the glow of his aura.

He gave a dazzling smile, one that reeked of cockiness, probably the one he regularly used to get into girls' panties. "Interesting reading?"

I looked down at the magazine in my lap. I hadn't even looked at it when I picked it up, but now I saw it was open to an article on raising domestic chickens. What magazine did I pick up, anyway? I hastily flipped it closed. *Country Living in the City*. Of all the issues of *People* and *Self*, I had to pick up this one.

I smiled back, trying for coy. "Definitely." I even went so far as to twirl a strand of hair around my finger.

I hadn't planned on seducing any rapists today, so my hair was a mess, I had no make-up on, and I was wearing my usual faded jeans and hoodie. I didn't have a lot to work with, but I was putting it out there the best I could.

Damn, I wished I'd worn a push-up bra.

He looked at the cover of the magazine. "I wouldn't have taken you for a country girl."

"Oh?" I asked, fluttering my eyelashes and feeling ridiculous. "Why's that?"

"You're much too sophisticated." He smiled, but it didn't reach his eyes. His eyes, though a nice blue color, were dull and dead. Their eerie emptiness caused my smile to slip off my face before I remembered I needed to keep up the act.

I giggled at his comment as I assumed most girls did when he put on the charm.

Objectively, he was good looking. Sandy colored hair, blue eyes, straight nose. He was tallish, but probably not as tall as Cole. He dressed well. He wore the coffee shop uniform of khaki pants and a black polo shirt, but his shoes were high end and he wore a flashy watch that looked expensive. I didn't realize baristas made such good money.

The bell on the front door jingled and a group of elderly people walked in. He winked at me and went to the counter to help with their orders.

Satisfied he would be occupied for a while this time, I let down my guards. His aura surrounded him like black smoke. The smile, charm, and wink were nothing but camouflage for his true nature. I was in the presence of an evil soul.

A mixture of relief and apprehension washed over me. My plan was coming together. I slipped out while Joey was too busy serving the patrons to notice I was leaving.

I'd gotten my name for Xavier.

CHAPTER 8

AFTER SKIPPING MY MORNING CLASSES, I did the only logical thing—forged my mom's signature on a sick note and went to school. It wasn't like I had anywhere else to go.

We had a sub in history, which meant a movie. My poor history teacher was the sickliest woman I'd ever seen. She was allergic to just about everything and lactose intolerant on top of that. So I'd watched a lot of movies so far in junior history.

Today the class was chattier than usual. That might have had something to do with the fact that our sub was snoring softly, her head resting on the teacher's desk.

Snippets of conversation drifted my way. I caught a few words—*Morgan, slut, Joey.*

So much for keeping that a secret.

Brooke sat across the room in stony silence and shot me a dirty accusatory look. I shook my head silently. *It wasn't me.*

But honestly, what did she expect? The gossip mill showed no mercy. The only way to keep a secret was keep it to yourself.

At lunch, I sat with Kaley, which was becoming my habit—one I needed to break. She was a nice girl, too nice to be spending time with the Grim Reaper's seeker.

I was fond of her, though. If I'd had a little sister, I'd

want her to be like Kaley. Super smart and super sweet. I hoped she managed to survive the gauntlet of high school with those traits intact.

"Did you hear anything about Morgan Newby?" I asked.

Kaley pursed her lips. "Yes." That's all she said. Kaley was a wallflower with the keen power of observation, but she wasn't one to gossip. She didn't realize the power she wielded by basically knowing everyone's business. I wasn't going to tell her, though. Power corrupted even the saintliest.

"Do you know anything about it?" I prompted.

The look on her face said she didn't want to participate in the gossip, even with me. She didn't have a nearly white aura for nothing.

"I just want to know the truth," I said gently. "I have some experience with this sort of thing." That wasn't exactly a lie—after all, I did spend the morning with Joey the rapist—but it amazed me how quickly it was out of my mouth. I didn't plan on lying to coax Kaley to talk. It just happened.

Good thing the integrity of my aura wasn't on trial. It had to be getting darker by the day. If I kept turning in black auras, I'd have to turn myself in eventually.

The thought made me uncomfortable.

"Okay." Kaley shifted in her seat, the expression on her face saying this was anything but okay. "Apparently Morgan started seeing this guy, Joey, a few weeks ago."

"What do you know about him?"

She shook her head and put her palms up. "I don't really know him. He graduated last year. Anyway, he's dated a few other girls in the school and the rumors are he forced them—" she blushed and cleared her throat. "Into *things*."

"He raped them?"

"*Shhh*," she hissed, looking around to see if anyone was paying attention. That was twice now I'd scandalized girls at this school by using the "r" word, but I wasn't going to sugar coat it.

"But is that what happened?" I whispered.

"According to the rumors." Kaley looked very uncomfortable. I hated putting her in this situation, but I needed to know, and I trusted her judgment.

"What do you think?"

She shrugged. "It's probably true. Most rumors stem from some truth, and statistically, it's unlikely that all of these rumors are false." Leave it to her to apply logic and statistics to evaluating the rumor mill.

"Why do girls date guys like that?" I wondered out loud. "They have to know his reputation."

"He was voted best looking in the senior class last year," Kaley said. "Maybe that has something to do with it."

The cliché "don't judge a book by its cover" popped into my head. I'd always hated that saying, but I could see how it applied in this situation.

I looked around the classroom at all my classmates and thought about their auras that I had observed this week. The president of the Helping Hands club had a selfish streak running through his aura as wide as a four lane road. The junior class president was literally green with envy and guilt. One of the smartest kids in our grade was swarming in ignorance.

I sighed. "Yeah, well, looks can be deceiving."

MORGAN DIDN'T COME TO SCHOOL the next few days. I stalked the coffee shop, but Joey was still working as normal, his aura as black as it had been the first time I had seen him. Every day I was disappointed he was still there. I had hoped Morgan would have scrounged up the courage to go to the police.

I thought I was prepared to give his name to Xavier,

but as each day passed and Xavier didn't show up, the nerves and doubt set in. Even though Joey's aura was as black as coal, something about it didn't feel right.

Of course, nothing felt right about giving the name of someone with a white aura to Xavier, so there was that, too.

Or maybe it just didn't feel right to play God, interfering with people's fates.

I stopped Brooke at her locker. "How's Morgan?"

"How do you think?" she snapped, flipping her hair over her shoulder.

I held my hands up. "Sorry. I was just asking."

Brooke pulled a book out of her locker and sighed. "She came to school yesterday but left before the end of first bell. She couldn't handle it."

"Did she get any help with anything?"

She slammed the locket closed. "Of course not. She's the preacher's daughter. She can't let him find out she had sex." Brooke rubbed her temples. "Why am I talking to you about this?"

I didn't know why she was talking to me, either. I had genuine concern for Morgan, but she didn't know that. I wondered what she would think of my nefarious plans for Joey. He was a menace to society. But soon, he wouldn't be a threat to teenage girls anymore. The world would be a safer place.

So why did my stomach feel like it was in a blender?

I mean, what if I was wrong? Death was pretty permanent. There were no take-backs.

And who had the right to decide someone needed to die? Was it God? A jury of peers? I didn't know anymore. I just knew it didn't feel like a right or a privilege to sentence a person to death. It was a burden I wouldn't wish on anyone.

The uneasiness was eating away at me. My stomach churned all day, probably giving me ulcers.

At the shop that afternoon, saying I was distracted

was putting it mildly.

Cole tossed an oil-stained rag in my face. "Pay attention."

"I am." I used two fingers to lift the rag from where it lay on my shoulder. It reeked, but I didn't mind the smell as much as I used to. Perhaps grease monkey scent was an acquired taste.

"No, you're not."

I wasn't, but I wasn't going to tell Cole that. I was supposed to be learning about how to properly replace a catalytic converter. Cole had been explaining the process step by step for the last hour as he worked. I couldn't tell you the first thing about a catalytic converter other than it was metal and shiny. And it probably converted something.

I hopped off my stool and copped a squat next to the car Cole was working on, hoping if I were closer to the action I might actually pay attention. Slim chance of that, though. If I learned nothing else from this project, I learned that I did *not* want to be an auto mechanic.

I was content to let Cole do the heavy lifting on this internship, and he preferred me to stay out of the way for the most part. It wasn't just an internship for him like it was for most of our classmates. It was his job, and it wouldn't end when the project was over.

"Damn it," Cole cursed from under the car.

I tilted my head to look. "What?"

He sighed. "Just toss me a rag."

I did better than toss him one. I reached under and held it near his hand so he wouldn't have to fumble around looking for it.

How was that for good service? See? I was contributing.

When he took it out of my hand though, our fingers touched, sending currents up my arm and to the rest of my body. I jerked my arm away so quickly I hit my hand on the fender.

"Ow!"

"What did you do now?" His tone was slightly exasperated.

"I'm fine, thanks for asking," I said, rubbing the red mark on my hand. I'd never had such a reaction to a guy before, and it pissed me off. I needed to put a lid on it. I was untouchable.

Untouchable.

The butterflies in my stomach died and turned into dead weight. I couldn't ever get close to anyone, couldn't let anyone get close to me. It was dangerous, and beyond that, who would want someone like me, someone who essentially signed execution orders for good people?

I scooted backward to put some distance between me and Cole.

"The uh, first journal assignment is due this week," I said, trying for a safe topic.

"Shit," Cole said, sighing again. "I forgot about that. I'll have to work on it tonight."

"Do you need any help with it?" I groaned inwardly. I really needed to think before I opened my mouth. I had just given myself a lecture about not getting close to anyone, and then I volunteered to spend more time with Cole, the main person I needed to stay away from. My feelings toward him were already problematic.

Cole waited a few seconds before replying. "Why would I need help?"

"I don't know. I was just being nice?" My voice raised, making that last part a question.

"Just because I'm nineteen and still in high school doesn't mean I'm an idiot." His tone denoted he was clearly offended. *So* not my intention.

"I never said you were an idiot," I said, but since he brought it up, I was curious. "Why are you still in high school at nineteen anyway? Doesn't that put you like two years behind?"

I was treading on dangerous ground here considering

he was already sensitive about the subject. Whatever his reaction though, I won. If he answered, then my curiosity would be sated. If he got angry, then that would put some needed distance between us.

Okay, let me rephrase that. It would give me some distance. The problem was all on my side. There was no indication that he was attracted to me in the least. Most times, Cole tolerated me. On good days, he was friendly. *Friendly.* Like I was a friend's kid sister or something.

"I took some time off," he said gruffly.

I knew from the tone of his voice that the discussion was closed. The conversational door had just been slammed in my face.

Fine, he could keep his secrets. I had enough trouble dealing with another not-so-secret secret.

I couldn't get the Morgan situation out of my head. Joey Huslander was the slime of the Earth, the feces of human existence. So why did I still feel wrong about turning in his name? Granted, I felt less wrong than I had with the previous two, but still. This solution to my dilemma wasn't as worry free as I had thought it'd be.

I was hoping to spare my conscience from a beating. It was still sore from the last one.

How did I know if I was doing the right thing? I mean, the right thing would be not to choose *anyone* to die, but I didn't exactly have a choice in the matter, not if I wanted to go on living, and as crappy as my life could be, it was the only one I had. I'd like to hold onto it. Maybe I could create an online poll or something. *Check yes or no. Do rapists deserve to be killed?*

Death was the ultimate penalty. *Death penalty.* I closed my eyes and slapped myself on the forehead, shaking my head. I was the idiot, not Cole. There was an easy way I could get opinions on whether submitting Joey's name was the right thing.

Well, sort of. I couldn't mention the part about the world or the heavens or wherever having one less angel.

"What are your thoughts on the death penalty?" I asked.

I could hear him stop what he was doing for a second as he processed the abrupt shift in conversation. "Where's this coming from?"

"I have to write a paper on a controversial topic for English," I lied. Gosh, I was getting good at that. The lies just kept coming today.

He took a minute to answer. "The crime should fit the punishment," he said finally.

A vague answer. Classic Cole.

"But who gets to decide what punishments are fit for certain crimes?" I gnawed on my fingernail, then spit it out when I tasted oil.

Yuck. I pulled a tiny bottle of hand sanitizer out of my bag and squeezed a glob on my hands. I wished I had a tongue sanitizer. *Sheesh.* I needed to stop biting my nails before I ended up with bloody stumps for fingers, but my life was not exactly stress free these days.

"How about *an eye for an eye*?" Cole suggested.

"There are some crimes that don't have a matching eye, though. Like child abuse." I took a deep breath. "Or rape."

Cole rolled out from under the car. "Those fuckers should be killed." There was no hesitation. A dark look clouded his eyes.

I blinked, taken aback by his fierce expression and the conviction in his statement.

"Killing is also a sin, though," I pointed out. I worded this next part carefully. "So what about the person responsible for killing the child abusers and rapists? They'll have the deaths of those people on their conscience."

"They shouldn't," he said vehemently. "They're doing the world a service by killing them. I don't consider killing people like that a sin."

Tension left my shoulders and the urge to chow down

on my cuticle abated a bit. That was exactly the answer I wanted to hear, but I was still troubled. I would still be responsible for someone's death. Deserving or not, that still didn't sit right with me. Joey Huslander had parents, friends, people who cared about him and would grieve his death, even if he was a boil on the ass of humanity. So even if he deserved to perish, there would still be collateral damage. I'd seen it before.

As much as I tried to rationalize everything, my conscience didn't feel clear for what I was planning to do. Of course, it would never be clear. My birthright assured that.

"HOW'S YOUR PROJECT GOING?" MY mom asked as we cleared the table after a spaghetti dinner. She'd actually been home for dinner, which was rare.

I shrugged. "It's going."

"Do you think you want to be an auto mechanic?"

I gave her a look, handing her the leftover garlic bread. "Uh, no."

She chuckled. "I was surprised when you chose that for your project. I didn't think you had an interest in anything mechanical."

"We didn't have many choices." I turned on the kitchen sink. Our dishwasher was broken, so we had to hand wash everything.

My mom sighed at my comment and leaned against the counter. She knew my comment was referring to our situation and why we didn't have any relationships with people. Most kids were interning with a friend of the family.

We had no friends.

Except now I had Cole. And Kaley. I frowned, scrubbing my plate with more force than was necessary. I *liked* having friends. There was no way it could last though. Besides the fact that it was totally wrong for me to befriend people with white or nearly white auras, I would be moving sooner or later. Probably sooner.

"Do you want to see a movie tonight?" my mom asked.

"It's a school night."

"So what?"

That answer surprised me, but I was glad she was finally getting on board with my way of thinking. As long as I passed my classes, then what difference did it make? I wasn't going on to bigger and better things, so there was no reason to stress about my GPA.

We probably shouldn't spend the money though, and I was about to say so, but the expression on my mom's face stopped me. It was a mix of hopefulness and apprehension.

Our relationship had always been easy until recently. I didn't like constant tension between us, but there was no way things would ever be the same again.

My inheritance had changed everything.

Still, she was trying, so it might behoove me to meet her halfway.

"Sure," I said, wiping my wet hands on my jeans. As I was putting my shoes on, I started to get in the mood. I couldn't remember the last time I'd gone to the movies. A year, maybe two? Now that I was seventeen and able to get into rated R movies by myself, I wondered if she'd go for the new romantic thriller that was out. Her tastes generally ran more PG, but she could no longer use my age as an excuse to get out of seeing certain movies.

"Can we stop and get some candy?" I asked as we put on our jackets. The concessions at the movie theaters were always so expensive, so when I was a kid, my mom would load her purse up with snacks and candy from the grocery store.

My mom laughed. "Sounds like a plan. It's been a while since we've done that. It's a good thing my purse is huge."

"Just try not to drop your entire box of mini jawbreakers on the floor again," I teased. "I still can't believe how many people stepped on them and almost bit the dust."

She laughed again. "I know. You'd think after the first one people would get the idea not to step on them. I felt bad about it, though."

"Not bad enough to claim the jawbreakers!" It felt good to have an honest laugh with her.

She grinned and pulled open the front door.

The grins fell off our faces. Mine was replaced with a scowl. My mom's face aged ten years in those ten seconds.

Xavier stood in the hall just outside our door. He was using his finger to scroll through his cell phone. That struck me as odd. Even though Xavier looked to be in his thirties, I always thought of him as old, from another time. A cell phone in his hand seemed anachronistic somehow.

He slipped the phone inside his suit coat. "Ladies, it's a pleasure, as always, to see you both."

The pleasure was all his. I certainly wasn't happy to see him.

"You're early," my mom said, her hand balled into a fist at her throat.

I would have liked to bash my fist into Xavier's throat. Or into his beady eyes.

He took a step forward, and my mom moved back automatically, making room for him to come in.

Anger flared up within me. Why was she so passive with Xavier? Before I'd known about the whole seeker thing, I'd considered my mother a strong independent woman. She'd always taken care of me, made sure I had everything I needed. But now she was just rolling over and letting Xavier do anything he wanted. And now was the time I needed her most. Now was the time I needed her to take care of me, to shield me from Xavier and everything he represented.

Now she let me down, as she had this entire year.

I turned my head away, not wanting to witness any more of my mother's weakness where Xavier was concerned. He'd shattered my image of her, just as he'd shattered so many other things in my life.

I heard the protest of the springs on our ancient couch as he made himself comfortable. *Damn him.* Why should he be comfortable in our home when his presence made us the exact opposite? He just waltzed into our apartment, making himself at home, contaminating the one place we should consider a safe haven. I avoided our living room. Recently I noticed my mom did, too. Even long after he was gone, it reeked of cinnamon and cigar smoke. I couldn't lie on our couch without thinking of him sitting there, leering at us.

I straightened my spine and faced him. He might make my mother weak, but I wasn't my mother. He would not make me weak. I would not look away or cower, no matter how uncomfortable he made me, no matter how much I hated him.

"You're early," my mom repeated.

He struck a match on the heel of his shoe and lit a cigar. He took a few puffs before speaking. "I don't need an excuse to visit my favorite seekers, do I?"

My expression clearly denoted the contrary.

He chuckled. "I suppose you've caught me. As much as I would like it to be, this is not a social call."

I resisted the urge to snort, but just barely. Xavier's idea of a social activity was probably drowning puppies and making toddlers cry.

Hatred had to be oozing out of my pores. I couldn't contain it.

"Mary, you've got an assignment." He was all business now.

She nodded. "How long?"

"A month."

She nodded again. No doubt her mind was already churning, trying to remember the regulars at the restaurant, if they'd seemed particularly kind. Just another day on the job, right? How could she be so calm?

My stomach sickened to think about these poor people essentially sentencing themselves to death by having the misfortune of being a good person and being seated in my mom's section. It just wasn't right.

How had my mom been doing this for twenty years? How many souls had she turned over to Xavier?

How could she live with herself?

His gaze shifted to me. "What's your status?"

Show time.

"I have a name," I said quietly, my palms slick. My heart pounded, and I made an effort to breathe normally. Hopefully he would just take my nervousness for reluctance to submit the name. There was no reason for him to suspect otherwise.

"Oh?" he responded, looking only mildly interested.

I balled my hands into fists. I couldn't believe he could act so casually about this. He didn't even care that these people were losing their lives. As far as I knew, he wasn't involved in the reaping—he only supplied the names to the Reapers. They were just names to him, not human beings with families and people who loved them.

But what did Xavier know about being human? He looked human, but there was no soul behind his black eyes.

It was the moment of truth. I took a deep breath. "Joey Huslander." My voice shook.

He frowned. "Speak up, girl."

My confidence faltered for a moment, then I steeled myself against my wailing conscience. I was doing the right thing. Well, maybe not the right thing, but definitely the lesser of two evils.

I cleared my throat and looked Xavier in his unfeeling eyes. "Joey Huslander," I said clearly. "He's the one you want."

CHAPTER 9

I TUCKED MY HEAD DOWN and pulled my hoodie up. The fall days were pleasant, but once the sun went down, the cold crept in.

It wasn't my choice to be making the miles-long trek after dark, but I'd lost my phone. I'd searched everywhere in our tiny apartment and come to the conclusion I must have forgotten it at the shop. My immediate thought was *I'll call Cole and ask him if he's seen it.* Then common sense set in. I couldn't call him, *because I didn't have my phone.* Duh.

My mom had instituted a new policy of calling me on her break when she was working nights. If I failed to answer, she'd probably race back to our apartment, disregarding the possibility of getting fired for leaving her job a second time. Xavier's frequent visits had unnerved her.

They had unnerved me, too, especially since my mom was uneasy. I didn't know him as well as she did, and if she was apprehensive, then it couldn't be good. He had been coming around a lot more lately. What did that mean? It had to mean *something.* Xavier didn't do anything without a reason.

There was no point in worrying about that now, though. Xavier wasn't exactly free with information. Until he wanted us to know something, we'd be in the dark. I wasn't about to waste my energy worrying about things I didn't even know about. I had plenty of known things to worry about.

The shop was locked when I got there. I jiggled the doorknob and peeked in the windows before cursing and kicking the side of the building.

Not smart. I was lucky I didn't break a toe.

I banged on the door in futility. No one was in there, but it made me feel better to hit something.

I crept around the side of the building, running my hand along the bricks to guide me. Bill really needed to install outdoor lights, the kind that automatically came on when someone came near. It was pitch black.

The gate was locked, but I found the key under the rock next to the building where I'd seen Cole retrieve it once. Once in the back lot, I jiggled the doorknob on the back door. Locked. *Damn.* If only I'd seen Cole with a hide-a-key for this door. Then I'd be getting somewhere.

I checked all of the windows and hit gold on the last one. I dragged an empty crate over and stood on it, using my palms to push the window up. I had to hold it with one hand to keep it up, but the space was big enough that I could probably squeeze through it.

It was a challenge to hoist myself up while simultaneously holding the window open. It was even more challenging shimmying through the opening. I overestimated the size of it.

After getting stuck, not once, but twice, I landed on the concrete floor in a heap. So in addition to the nasty scrape I got on my stomach from the window sill, my hip would be sporting a purple bruise.

I stood up gingerly, seriously rethinking this whole idea. If I were smart, I would have walked to my mom's restaurant to let her know I didn't have my phone. Or started knocking on the neighbors' doors to borrow theirs. As they say, hindsight is twenty-twenty. It simply hadn't occurred to me to do either of those things or that the shop would be locked.

My phone was on the floor under my usual stool. It must have fallen out of my backpack. I gratefully picked it up and checked it for missed calls, happy to see that my mom hadn't called yet. At least this whole escapade wasn't in vain.

I closed the window and flipped the lock on it. Bill was lucky it was only me who decided to break in. I didn't know how much tools cost, but I imagined they weren't cheap. He probably had thousands of dollars worth of equipment lying around.

When I opened the back door to leave, I heard a click behind me.

"Don't move."

The voice was low and menacing. I froze. Maybe I wasn't the only one who broke into the shop.

Shit. How did I not realize I wasn't alone?

This was bad. Very bad. Fear took root in my heart, spreading through my veins with every heartbeat.

"Turn around."

I held my shaking hands up before slowly turning to find a gun pointed at me from about three feet away.

My eyes widened, fixated on the gun. I couldn't look away. I opened my mouth to speak, but only a squeak came out.

Was this what it was like for the poor pure souls my mom and I found? Sometimes they succumbed to illnesses or heart attacks compliments of the Grim Reaper, but other times the deaths were violent.

My adrenaline pumped, urging me to do something, *anything* to save myself, but my fear paralyzed me, and I stayed glued to the spot.

The gun lowered. Breathing became a little easier, and I sucked in huge gulps of air, my hands on my chest.

"What the fuck?" my would-be attacker said. Now that the gun was out of the picture, I looked at his face for the first time.

"What the hell, Cole?" I was simultaneously relieved and irritated to see him with the gun in his hand.

He did something to the gun—put the safety on? I didn't know anything about guns. All I knew was I didn't like being on the business end of one. He tucked it into the waistband of his jeans at the small of his back.

He was shirtless and shoeless, wearing only jeans that rode low on his hips, showing he was a boxers kind of guy. The sight of his bare chest made my hands shake for an entirely different reason. It was as tanned and toned as his forearms promised. He had to work out or something. That couldn't be natural.

"What are you doing here?" he asked, putting his hands on his hips.

"I forgot my phone. What are you doing with a gun?"

"How did you get in?"

I looked at him in annoyance. I *hated* when he ignored my questions and instead asked his own.

I pointed to the window. "I climbed in the window."

He crossed to the window and checked the lock.

I huffed. "It was unlocked. Don't worry, though. I locked it."

"Why didn't you just call me?" he asked.

I held up my phone and shook it. "I didn't have my phone, remember?"

"Are you telling me that that phone is the only phone within a one mile radius? You could have used another phone."

"Your number is programmed in it. Now I suppose you'll tell me I should have memorized your number."

"If you had, we wouldn't be in this situation."

I threw my hands up. "You are unbelievable. Also, can we revisit the fact that you just pointed a gun at me? *A gun!* Is that thing loaded?"

The look on his face told me it was.

"You pointed a *loaded gun* at me." I was oh-sothankful it had been Cole with the gun, but I was flabbergasted by the whole situation. *Flabbergasted.* And I didn't use that word lightly.

"An unloaded gun is pointless."

"You shouldn't go around with loaded guns! Why do you have that thing anyway?"

"I thought you were a robber." He rubbed a hand over his face. "You shouldn't break into people's businesses."

Probably not, but it wasn't like I was going to make a habit of it. This was a one-time deal. Lesson learned.

"Does Bill know you're walking around here with a gun?" I asked. "What are you doing here, anyway?"

"I live here."

I laughed. "No, seriously, what are you doing here?"

"I live here," he repeated. "There's an apartment upstairs."

"With your mom?"

"No. I haven't seen my mom in years."

"Wait, you live with Bill?" I was thoroughly confused.

He shook his head. "I live alone."

"Alone?"

"Yes, alone." His tone revealed annoyance. "I'm nineteen."

"But you're still in high school."

"No shit."

I scowled. "You don't have to be an ass. My reactions are perfectly reasonable. You're the one running around half naked with loaded guns." *Mental head slap.* I'd just drawn attention to the fact I'd noticed he was half naked.

But honestly? How could I not notice? Cole's hotness was never in question. His sanity and ability to rationalize like a normal human being? Always.

He ran both hands through his hair. "You. Are. So. Exasperating."

"Sorry to *bother* you." If sarcasm were water, we would have drowned. "I'll just go."

"You're not walking home alone."

How did we get to this again? Total deja vu.

"How do you think I got here?"

"It's dark outside."

"*No shit.*" I smirked, pleased at being able to throw his words back in his face.

"Come upstairs for a minute, then I'll drive you home."

I started to protest just because I didn't want to give in to his demands. But truth be told, I didn't want to walk home in the cold. In the dark. Alone.

So what was it going to be? Pride or practicality?

I looked over my shoulder through the window to the darkness outside. Trees swayed in the wind, creating eerie sounds and shadows.

Practicality it was.

He walked toward Bill's office and a door I hadn't noticed before. Behind it were stairs that apparently led to an apartment. The building didn't look tall enough from the outside to even have a second floor, much less an entire apartment.

I followed him cautiously up the stairs. It suddenly dawned on me that I'd never been to a guy's place. My mom had always been pretty strict, and then once I turned sixteen, getting close enough to a guy for him to invite me to his place was out of the question.

The stairs led up to another door that opened into a common room that served as a living room, dining room, and kitchen. It was more like a kitchenette than a kitchen, though, because it had one of those half stoves and tiny ovens that were sometimes in hotels, and the fridge was just half size, like the ones the teachers at school kept behind their desks. There was a small table with two chairs pushed against a wall and a futon. A small TV was mounted on the opposite wall. It was a good thing I wasn't as tall as Cole, or my claustrophobia would start to set in. The walls slanted so he could only stand up straight in the center of the room.

Cole disappeared through a doorway I assumed lead to a bedroom. I was tempted to peek in, but it felt weird. That was his bedroom. Where he slept. Where he got dressed. Where he got *un—*

I needed to stop right there. My thoughts were wandering into uncharted territory, places they had no business being. This was *Cole*, the guy who irritated me beyond reason. The same guy who tricked me into matching scrap nuts and bolts for over an hour.

My thoughts were on notice. Cole was eye candy, but that was it. Getting close to someone wasn't an option, especially someone with an aura like his.

Speaking of that, I wondered if his recent antics had colored his aura. Surely it couldn't still be white. The guy pulled a gun on me. Certainly that was *not* angel eligible behavior.

I crept closer to the doorway. This was the perfect time to check his aura.

His back was toward me, and the gun was no longer tucked into his waistband. I assumed he'd stashed it somewhere safe. At least, I hoped so. It gave me the heebie jeebies to think there was a loaded gun just lying around.

Please let his aura be colored.

I let my guards down slowly and held my breath.

Damn it!

I just didn't get it. He went creeping around with a loaded gun, cursed like a sailor, and acted like a major asshole a good part of the time. How could his aura possibly be white?

And why did he of all people have to be in possession of a white aura?

He pulled a t-shirt over his head, and I ducked back into the living area before he saw me. I took a seat on his futon, and then my phone rang.

"Hi, Mom." I could hear the hustle and bustle of the restaurant in the background. "It sounds busy there." Busy was good. Busy meant more tips.

"It is. We have two big parties, one for a birthday and the other for an anniversary, I think. Did you get your homework done?"

Cole slipped back into the room wearing a Bill's Auto Shop t-shirt. He had no shortage of those.

"Yup," I said. "Well, actually, I'm at Cole's place." I figured I'd better tell her, so she wouldn't flip out later if she found out I'd gone out. "We're working on our project."

Cole raised his eyebrows at that last sentence, shaking his head. I stuck my tongue out at him and then turned away.

"Ava, you need to tell me when you're leaving the apartment." She sounded more tired than angry. "We talked about this."

"I know. I forgot."

She sighed loudly. "Call me when you get home then, okay? I just want to know where you are."

I promised to let her know of my whereabouts and hung up the phone.

"Working on our project, huh?" Cole said, his eyes twinkling.

"Shut up."

"Have you actually done anything for the project?"

"Yes," I huffed, insulted at the insinuation I was a slacker. "I *still* can't believe you just pulled a gun on me. Why do you even have it?"

"In case you hadn't noticed, this isn't the safest neighborhood."

"Why do you live alone?" This probably crossed the line into too personal, but I figured what was a personal question between friends who pointed loaded guns at one another? I was not going to get past that anytime soon. It totally blew my mind. Figuratively, not literally, thank goodness. I really dodged a bullet there.

Okay, I needed to stop with the puns. That one was horrible, but it was hard to think with a blown mind.

He flopped down on the futon next to me. "The last time I saw my mom she was passed out with a needle sticking out of her arm. I'm better off alone." His tone was flat, detached, like he was reciting information out of a National Geographic magazine.

"I'm sorry."

"Don't be sorry for me. I'm not." He stood. "You ready to go?"

I did feel sorry for him though. My dad was a scumbag who'd bailed on me and my mom, but I'd always had my mom. I couldn't imagine what it would be like to have two scumbag parents.

Cole's orneriness made a little more sense now. Given his past, I was surprised he'd turned out as well as he did. He'd escaped the cycle.

"Yeah, I'm ready." I stood. Something in my face must have shown my feelings because he stopped.

"Don't look at me like that."

"I'm sorry." I looked away, not trusting myself to be able to wipe said look off my face.

"There's nothing to be sorry about," he said angrily. "I don't need your pity."

"I don't pity you." I frowned. That wasn't it at all.

"Yes, you do." He laughed bitterly. "This is why I don't tell anyone about my past. That *look* on your face. I can't stand when people look at me like that."

"I don't pity you," I repeated, "but I feel for your situation."

His face showed a mixture of emotion. He looked simultaneously vulnerable and angry. I looked past the man who stood before me and instead saw the young boy who had been unfortunate enough to be born to two delinquent parents, one who didn't care enough to stick around, and the other who cared more about getting high than her own son. I pitied the boy, but I didn't pity the man.

"It's time to go." He moved past me to grab his keys

off the table.

I sighed and took a few steps toward the front door. He turned abruptly and knocked into me. He steadied me so I wouldn't stumble, putting us chest to chest.

I looked up at him, my breath catching. He didn't smell like motor oil or grease this time. He smelled clean, fresh. He smelled *good*.

He stiffened, but didn't let go of my arm. His eyes were dark, and they scanned my face, seemingly searching, but for what I didn't know.

"Fuck," he said, before covering my mouth with his.

I had very few experiences with kissing, and if I'd had more time to prepare, I would have been nervous. Instead, I let instinct take over. I wrapped my arms around his neck and stood up on my tiptoes. He wrapped his arms around me, pulling me closer.

His tongue slipped between my lips and there was a moan—his? Mine? I didn't know, didn't care.

I ran my fingers through his hair. His hand snaked under my shirt, and his palm flattened on my back, bringing us even closer. My skin warmed at the feeling of his skin on mine.

More. I wanted more. I wanted to get closer. I arched my back.

Abruptly, he pulled away and stepped back, putting distance between us. "Fuck," he said again.

I looked at him, putting my fingers on my lips to find them swollen.

"I'm bad for you," he said.

I laughed out loud. "You have no idea."

"This isn't a joke."

"I wasn't joking," I retorted.

"We can't do this," he said.

I nodded, not trusting myself to speak out loud. My mind and body were both reeling. My mind was telling me the same thing he was. That this was a mistake. That this was bad for both of us. I didn't even want to think about

Xavier's reaction if he knew I was getting involved with a white aura. Because that's what they were to him—auras, not people.

My body was saying *screw it.* My body wanted to bridge the distance between us and feel his mouth and hands on me again.

And my heart—

I didn't want to think about that. That was dangerous ground.

I told myself it didn't matter what my heart wanted. As soon as my mom completed her assignment, we would be moving on anyway. Even if Cole and I did get involved, it would be nothing more than a fling. That was all it could be.

So it was probably better to just leave it alone. There were no scenarios where it could end well.

He sighed and ran his hand through his hair, following the path my hands had just taken moments before. "Let's go."

I followed him down to his car. We didn't speak the whole ride home, but he did wait until I was safely in the apartment before driving away.

CHAPTER 10

A LOUD CRASHING NOISE CAME from the front of our apartment. My mom and I looked at each other over our Cheerios, each of us with a *what the hell* expression on our faces. Then we both jumped up and ran to the front door.

Xavier had kicked the door in. His hair was disheveled, and his suit was wrinkled. This was the first time I'd seen Xavier not looking pristine. Normally he preened like a peacock in our presence. Now as he stood in our foyer, he reminded me of the Hulk, teeth bared and full of rage.

This could not bode well for us.

His eyes had a maniacal glint to them. Pointing at me, he growled, "You."

My mother automatically pushed me behind her, the mama bear in her surfacing as her cub was threatened, but Xavier batted her away like she was a pesky mosquito.

He picked me up by my throat and held me against the wall. My fingers wrapped around his hand, trying to pry it off. My legs dangled against the wall.

"Put her down!" My mom clawed at his back.

He spared her a glance. "Settle down, Mary, or I won't even give her a chance to explain." He turned back to me and shifted his hand ever so slightly so that he was holding me up by my jaw rather than my throat. I gasped, air returning to my lungs.

"Tell me about Joey Huslander." His eyes bore into mine, searching.

My brain couldn't process the situation quickly enough to come up with a plausible answer. The only thing I could think about was my next breath.

He removed his hand, and I fell to the ground in a heap, banging my left knee hard. My mom rushed over and wrapped her arms around me. I clung to her.

"That's what I thought," he sneered. He smoothed his hair and straightened his jacket, also realigning the red pocket square that had come askew.

This was good. This was the Xavier I knew, sleek and sophisticated. He'd always been menacing, but never dangerous. This new side of Xavier scared me.

I'd never experienced violence before, having led a pretty sheltered life thanks to my mom. I longed for those days of blissful ignorance.

Xavier walked into the living room and sat in his usual place on the couch, pulling a cigar from inside his suit coat.

My mom examined my neck. "That's going to bruise," she said quietly. "Go get some ice. I'll stall Xavier."

I did as I was told, no questions asked.

When I walked into the living room holding a baggie of ice to my throat, my mom was sitting across from Xavier. It looked so *normal*. There was no indication Xavier had just broken bad on me moments earlier.

"Tell me about Joey Huslander."

"He works—" I coughed at the effort it took to get the words out. "—in a coffee shop." It was the first thing that popped into my mind after *oh, shit—he knows*. I clamped my mouth shut.

Xavier chuckled. "You're trying my patience, my dear."

"Why don't *you* tell me about him?" I asked. He obviously already knew something or he wouldn't be questioning me like this. I wasn't being obstinate and pushing my luck with Xavier for the sake of being stubborn. It would waste less time if he told me what he already knew.

Yeah, right. Even after he choked me until I nearly blacked out, I still couldn't bring myself to willingly cooperate with him.

This time Xavier threw his head back and laughed. "Ava, how you amuse me." He put out his cigar on the heel of his shoe. "But I'm not in the mood to be amused. This is your last chance."

I swallowed and immediately winced at the pain in my throat. I looked to my mother. It's not like she could tell me what to do. As far as I knew, she'd always been a model seeker. She'd certainly always been subservient to Xavier in my presence.

I suddenly got lightheaded and swayed, grabbing hold of a chair for balance. My temperature felt like it was rising. It felt like when I had the flu when I was eight and had to be hospitalized for my fever. Except much, much worse.

"Ava?" My mom's voice was alarmed. It sounded far away, like I was in a tunnel or something.

"You feel that, Ava? It's your blood. It's slowly beginning to boil."

My mom jumped up and came over to me. She pressed the rapidly melting ice to my forehead. "What are you doing to her?"

"Oh, don't worry. It won't kill her."

I begged to differ. It felt like my insides were being roasted over a fire, like Xavier was going to make a s'more with my organs. I clenched my teeth and moaned.

"Xavier." Her voice was calm over a layer of frantic. "There are no Reapers here to save her."

"She doesn't need saving."

My vision blacked out, and I sank to my knees. Screams spilled from my mouth as the fire roared through my veins, erupting through my skin.

"Ava, hang on." My mom smoothed my hair back from my face. "Xavier, stop it! Look what it's doing to her."

"I told you. She'll be fine."

"The lesions on her arms are *not* fine. She's bleeding!"

Sure enough, I had little volcanoes erupting on my arms, spewing blood instead of lava. I closed my eyes and rode the waves of pain as streams of blood rolled down my skin.

"Ava, stay with me, baby," my mom said. She huddled down on the floor next to me and wrapped her arms around me.

From my fetal position on the floor, I opened my eyes for a few seconds to see Xavier leaning forward, looking at me curiously. "How very interesting. I wonder what would happen if—"

"*No*," my mom said firmly. "This needs to stop. What do you want?"

"She robbed me of a white aura."

Auras don't belong to you! I wanted to shout.

"I have a name," my mom said. "I'll give it to you. Just stop this now."

"Ah, but you see, that simply won't do. I need a teenager. And she's the only one who can give me that."

A wave of heat rolled through me, and I screamed again. I bit down to silence myself, tasting blood in my mouth.

"Just give her two more weeks. She'll get you another name."

Xavier sighed. "Fine."

The pain stopped immediately, and I gasped, sucking in air with tears running down my face. The tears were hot, like they'd just come out of a squealing tea kettle.

This shit just got real. The pain was real. The blood flowing out of the sores all over my arms and legs was real.

I couldn't believe this was my life.

"Oh, thank goodness," my mother clutched me to her,

and I moaned as her clothing rubbed my bleeding skin.

"This name will not take the place of your assignment, Mary. That still must be completed on schedule."

"Yes, of course," she murmured, stroking my hair.

"Well?" Xavier said. "Are you going to make good on your bargain?"

"Julie McKenner," my mom said quietly.

Xavier stood, then knelt down next to me. "You can't get one over on me. You can't cheat the system. You can't win, Ava. Don't even try."

I knew me. No matter what he said, I wouldn't stop. I couldn't live the rest of my life answering to him. I had to at least try to change my destiny.

It seemed I might literally die trying.

He stood and walked toward the front door. I mustered what little strength I had to flip him the middle finger before everything went dark.

MY LATEST EXPERIENCE WITH XAVIER proved what I'd suspected all along.

He wasn't human.

I didn't wake up until the next day. My mom had cleaned and bandaged the sores on my arms and somehow gotten me into bed. She didn't manage to get me dressed, though, so I was just wearing underwear. Bandages covered various parts of my body. It appeared my arms took the brunt of it. I didn't check beneath the bandages, afraid of what I'd find there.

I didn't attempt to get dressed and instead slipped on a robe and hobbled out to the kitchen. Having my blood boiled made me hungry.

My mom was sitting at the kitchen table. Just sitting. Not reading, not eating, not doing a crossword puzzle, nothing. It was a little disconcerting to see her sitting there staring off into space with a disconnected expression on her face. She just looked plain out of it.

"Hi," I said through cracked lips, my voice hoarse. Her head snapped over to me, her eyes coming into focus.

"Ava, I didn't hear you get up." She rose and pulled out a chair for me. "You should stay in bed."

"I'm okay," I said, but I gratefully sank down into the chair. I was far from okay, but I wasn't going to let my mom know how bad I really felt.

I felt like I had a lobster-red sunburn on the inside of my skin.

The effort to make it to the kitchen resulted in a bead of sweat along my forehead. I felt moisture beneath some of the bandages, signaling that the lesions had probably started to bleed again, or at least ooze.

Yuck. I hoped they didn't scar.

"Are you hungry?" she asked.

"Starving."

As calm as I was acting about all of this, I was anything but calm. My insides were churning, and only part of that was due to the whole internal sunburn thing.

Xavier had power. Freaky, pain-inducing power. And I doubted that was all he had in his bag of tricks. I was sure his antics yesterday were meant to discourage me from defying him, but every twinge of pain I felt made me feel even more vengeful.

I couldn't live like this. I *wouldn't* live like this. I wasn't going to bow down to Xavier for the rest of my life like my mom had.

I'd just have to be smarter next time. Underestimating Xavier had been a huge mistake—one I wouldn't make again.

My mom pulled out stuff to make me a chicken salad sandwich, one of my favorites. As she was cutting celery with her back toward me, her hands shook.

"Mom, are you okay?"

She dropped the knife and held onto the edges of the counter, her shoulders shaking silently.

I stood unsteadily. "Mom, it's okay. I—"

She turned, wiping her eyes. "No, you sit. But it's not okay. Xavier could have killed you."

"Have you ever seen him do anything like that?"

She shook her head. "I knew he was powerful, but I had no idea. I should have protected you. I should have—"

"There's nothing you could have done," I said firmly, and I meant it. I didn't want her to be punished for something I did. It was time I stopped expecting her to stand up to Xavier for me. If I was big enough to make my own mistakes, then I was big enough to handle the consequences.

She sighed and turned back to the celery, resuming her chopping. "This sucks."

Truer words were never spoken.

I laughed, then stopped abruptly at the pain in my throat. I gulped down some water.

"I should tell you something," I said quietly.

"You knew Joey Huslander didn't have a white aura." Her tone wasn't accusatory, but I still felt like I was being scolded.

"Yes." I filled her in.

"This isn't a game, Ava."

I straightened my spine. "No, it's not. People die because of us."

She flinched slightly. "There is no other way."

"It was worth it to try," I said forcefully.

She dropped some bread slices in the toaster. "No, it wasn't. Look at yourself."

I didn't want to. I didn't want to know how bad I looked.

"What did you think would happen?"

I picked at the edge of the placemat that was coming unraveled. "I don't know, but I can't live like this."

"You don't have a choice." She placed a sandwich in front of me. "Chips?"

I nodded, and she shook a few of them out of the bag

and onto my plate.

After putting everything away, she stood in front of me, her arms crossed. "I'm scheduled to work today, but I can call in."

I shook my head. "Go to work. I'll be fine."

"I don't know..."

I took a huge bite of my sandwich, making a show of chewing enthusiastically and swallowing. "I'm fine. I'm just going to lie around and watch TV."

She looked me over in the way moms do. "Okay, but you call me if you need me, and I'll come straight home. I don't know how long recovery will take. Normally seekers heal pretty fast, but this—" She gestured to all of my bandages with a helpless look on her face. "This is different."

Different didn't even begin to cover it.

I normally avoided the living room because it reminded me of Xavier, but it was time I reclaimed our space, a little act of rebellion. Once she'd left, I shuffled in to lie down. Every movement hurt. Basically anything involving my skin hurt.

I didn't bother turning on the TV and instead stared at the popcorn ceiling. I had two weeks to find a new name for Xavier. Actually, now it was one week and six days.

I'd only found one white aura so far, but I was still perplexed by that one. Cole should *not* have a white aura. The reason for it eluded me, and I'd spent more time than I'd like to admit thinking about it. He simply was not angel material. And there was the whole throbbing thing. Something about his aura was just off. It wasn't fated anyway though, so I couldn't turn Cole in unless I wanted to run the risk of being boiled from the inside out again.

It had absolutely nothing to do with my feelings for him. Feelings that I was too scared to explore. I'd rather face Xavier again. Those feelings stayed locked away, safely in the land of forbidden thoughts.

Was it just the other night, less than forty-eight hours

ago, that I was kissing him in his apartment? It felt like another life.

I wished it were another life. I wished *I* had another life instead of being cursed with the life of a seeker.

The story went that one of my ancestors was an angel. So, yes, I guess that meant I was part angel, only a tiny part though as it had been diluted over many generations. That was why my mom and I rarely got sick, and when we did, we recovered quickly.

My angel ancestor—I didn't even know his name— apparently fell in love with a woman, which was forbidden. He left heaven to be with her and fathered a child. After a few years on Earth though, he decided he wanted to return to heaven. In exchange for his re-admission, all of his descendants became seekers.

It was a pretty crappy story. The love story part started out okay, but then he ended up leaving her anyway. So she really got the short end of the stick. Not only did she lose her man, but her descendants were cursed for all of eternity.

I yawned. Even though I'd slept over twenty-four hours, I was still tired. Seekers might heal fast, but it took a lot out of us.

I was just drifting off to sleep when there was a pounding at the door.

I stilled, clutching at the couch cushions. I sniffed the air, but I didn't detect any cinnamon. That meant it probably wasn't Xavier, but there were no guarantees where he was concerned. He'd never attempted to mask his scent before, and I didn't see any reason he'd start now. He wasn't the type to sneak up on people—he made his presence known. Still, he was unpredictable.

The knocking at the front door continued, so I hefted myself off the couch and secured the belt on my robe so I didn't give the UPS man or whoever it was a show. I looked through the peephole to see Cole standing there, his hands on his hips, an annoyed expression on his face.

I silently backed away from the door.

"I can hear you, Ava," Cole called.

I pursed my lips. "How do you know it's not my mom?"

"Obviously it's not since you just answered me."

How much of an idiot was I? I slapped myself on the forehead, then winced. Xavier must have fried some of my brain cells.

Cole pounded on the door again. "Open up."

I sighed. I knew Cole, and he wouldn't go away until I answered the door. Stubbornness was one thing we had in common.

I unlocked the door, leaving the security chain on, and cracked the door a few inches.

"What do you want?"

"Why weren't you at school?"

"I'm sick."

"You should've let me know you weren't going to be at the shop."

"Why?" I huffed. "It's not like you let me do anything worthwhile."

He grinned. "Do you really want to do anything worthwhile?"

He had a point. I had no desire to be up to my elbows in grease.

"What do you want?" I asked again. Then I got annoyed. "You know, I tell you I'm sick, and you don't even ask what's wrong with me or how I'm feeling."

He sighed. "Are you going to let me in or are we going to continue this conversation through this three inch gap?"

I considered. I didn't want Cole to see me like this, but on the bright side, once he did, I didn't have to worry about a potential relationship with him. My current state of being would scare away anyone in his right mind.

Though it was questionable whether Cole was in his right mind.

"Ava? What the hell?"

"I'm thinking."

It was not like any girl wanted a guy to be repulsed by her under any circumstances though. But for both of our sakes, I was going to take one for the team.

I shut the door to undo the chain. Then I opened the door and sauntered—okay, more like hobbled—back to the couch.

"Nice outfit," Cole said from behind me.

My cheeks reddened. "Thank you," I called over my shoulder in what I hoped was a flippant tone. Then I hid myself from the neck down under a blanket.

"You should call maintenance to fix this door. It looks like someone bashed it in or something." He inspected it. "Has it always been like this?"

"Um, I haven't noticed," I lied.

He observed me from a safe distance across the room. "Maybe you really are sick." Did he think I was lying before? Then he added, "You look like shit."

I looked up at him using my best bitch stare. "What do you want, Cole?"

"Sorry. I meant you look like you feel bad." He tossed a folder on the coffee table. "Here's the work you missed. Kaley asked me to bring it to you. Can I get you something? Water or something to eat?"

On one hand I was touched by his concern, but on the other hand, it was proof I really must look like hell.

"No, thanks. I'm good. Do you need anything else?"

He sat and rested his elbows on his knees. "What's wrong with you?" He quickly corrected himself, "I mean, what's got you sick?"

"It's, um—" I hadn't thought of an excuse because I hadn't planned on seeing anyone until I was recovered. "I had an allergic reaction to something."

I was pleased with myself for coming up with that explanation on the fly. An allergic reaction could certainly cause lesions on my skin, right?

He frowned. "Do you know what from?"

I shook my head.

"That's weird. Did you eat anything unusual?"

"Um..." I acted like I was trying to remember when really I was cursing the irony of the situation. At first he was a little too unconcerned, and now he was *too* concerned. I didn't have answers to all of his questions.

"I really don't know," I said lamely, hoping he'd let it drop.

Luckily he had something else on his mind. "Listen, about the other night—"

I put my hand up to silence him. "We really don't need to talk about it."

It happened, it was wonderful, and it was over. We'd both agreed it couldn't happen again. As long as we didn't make a big deal out of it, then I believed we could work together for the remainder of the project without any more...*incidents.*

Even though it was utterly depressing.

He shifted uncomfortably. "Are you sure?"

I nodded, and he looked relieved. His relief was like a needle in my heart.

Don't think like that, I told myself. *It's better this way. It's what you wanted.*

He grinned. "I think Bill misses you."

"What?" I snorted. "No way." I was more likely to win the lottery, and I wasn't even old enough to buy a ticket.

"He asked about you and everything."

I laughed. "Tell me what he said, word for word?"

"He said—" Cole cleared his throat in preparation for impersonating Bill's gravelly voice. "*Where's the red-headed chick?*"

I laughed again, shaking my head. "I don't think he remembers my name."

"Sure he does. He gives nicknames to people he likes."

I looked at him skeptically. "Red-headed chick is my nickname? Okay, then, what's your nickname?"

"I don't have one." Cole smiled, one of his rare genuine smiles, the kind that hit me right in the heart. Only this time, it caused the hole in my heart to grow from needle size to pencil size. "He doesn't like me as much as he likes you."

I stared at him wistfully for a moment, wishing things could be different between us.

Then just as quickly, I snapped out of it. *He was relieved, Ava, relieved that he wouldn't be making out with you again.* Even if I weren't a seeker, things probably wouldn't be any different between me and Cole.

I rolled my eyes. "Cole, you are so full of shit."

He flashed a wicked, unabashed grin. *Strike three.* The hole in my heart transformed into a black hole, sucking the rest of my heart into it.

The last forty-eight hours had been emotionally exhausting, going from cloud-level highs to abyss-deep holes. I needed to hibernate for a season to recover. With my new deadline from Xavier though, that wasn't an option.

Physical exhaustion took over and my mouth opened in an obnoxiously long yawn.

Cole took the hint and stood. "I'll let you get some rest. See you tomorrow?"

I nodded and started to stand, careful to keep the blanket wrapped around me.

"Don't get up. I'll see myself out."

I sank back down onto the couch, grateful not to have to try not to trip on the blanket by walking with it. Uncovering myself was *not* an option.

Cole opened the front door, then turned. "Ava, try not to look like shit the next time you have guests, huh? It's bad manners." He grinned and shut the door behind him.

I just shook my head. Jerk.

CHAPTER 11

TODAY WAS THE DAY, THE day Cole was taking me to a car auction. I was irrationally excited. It's not like I was getting a car, but it was the most exciting thing I'd done in a while.

It made me a little sad to realize that, but I was too excited to stay sad for long.

Bill had decided to expand his business by flipping cars. It was like those house flipping shows on TV, except he was going to do it with cars—buy beat-up cars, fix them up, and sell them for profit. Being the antisocial being he was, Bill had sent Cole to bid on a few cars at auction. It showed the level of trust that existed between Bill and Cole.

When I saw Cole pull up, I grabbed my jacket and ran out the door, calling good-bye to my mother as I slammed the door. Cole was on the bottom step when I got there. I grabbed his jacket and kept moving toward the car, pulling him with me.

"I was going to come up," he said.

"I know."

He stopped in his tracks, stopping me. No matter how hard I pulled him, I could not get him to budge.

"Isn't your mom curious about who you're spending all your time with?"

"Yes."

He looked pointedly up at my apartment window where my mom was indeed peeking out from behind the curtains. She ducked when she realized she'd been caught.

Cole looked back to me. "Okay. I don't mind meeting your mom though."

"I'll keep that in mind."

He allowed himself to be pulled to the car. "It seems like I'm your dirty little secret." His tone was light and joking, but I could tell his feelings were a little hurt. We weren't a couple or anything, so there was no reason to introduce him to my mom. Considering his bad relationship with his own mother, I was guessing he had lingering mommy issues.

"It's not like that. It's complicated."

"Right," Cole said, disbelief in his voice, but he let it go.

I got into the Rustinator and buckled up, sighing. I didn't want Cole thinking I was hiding him from my mom, but I wasn't taking any chances that she'd see his aura either. Even though the chances of that were slim to none considering we could only see auras in our own age group, it still wasn't something I wanted to risk. It was safer this way.

Half an hour later I stood in a sea of cars, some shined to a gleam while others looked like the Rustinator's long lost siblings.

I pointed to a shiny mint green one. It was an older model, but it looked clean and well kept.

"How about that one?"

Cole glanced at it for half a second, then shook his head, dismissing it.

"Why not?" I asked, miffed that he didn't even consider my suggestion.

"It's a fair price," he said.

"*Exactly*," I said. Duh? Wasn't that why we were here?

He looked at me and chuckled, shaking his head slightly. "We need to find ones that are way below fair price so we can make a profit after we fix them up."

"Oh," I said, a little deflated.

"This is more like what we want." Cole was standing next to a junker. It was missing a side panel and the other panels were all different colors. The bumper had a huge dent in it. The rearview mirror was broken.

"That looks like hell, almost as bad as—"

"*Don't* say it," Cole cut me off. His attachment to that car of his was mystifying.

He popped the hood and poked around. I stood beside him and looked down, pretending to know what I was looking at and smiling at people walking by.

It was...an engine, I guess. Even after weeks of hanging out at the shop, I still didn't know much about engines. I could—in theory—change the oil and a tire, but engines still looked like a bunch of metal and tubes and grease.

"How does it look?"

He pointed to some rubber tubes. "These are rotted."

"Oh, that's too bad."

He shook his head. "No, that's good. A lot of people won't look past that, so it might keep the auction low. Hoses like this always need to be replaced eventually. The cost is minimal. If you look past them though, the engine looks to be pretty sound. I need to crawl under it to know for sure."

"Oh." I stood back to give him space, feeling pretty useless.

"You can take a look inside and let me know what you think," he said.

I smiled and climbed in the car. Maybe he was just taking pity on me, maybe he was giving me another nuts and bolts job, or maybe he really did want to know what I thought. I didn't care. I wanted to feel useful.

The inside was clean for the most part. There was a

mysterious stain on the back seat that I didn't want to think about, but there were no rips or tears. It reeked of cigarette smoke though.

I also noticed the radio was missing and there were holes in the doors where the speakers should be. Even I knew enough about cars to know those were easily replaced.

Given the condition of the outside of the car, I was surprised how well kept the interior was.

I poked my head out the window to see Cole's feet sticking out from under the car. He started scooting out, and as he did, his shirt scrunched up, revealing his stomach.

His toned, tanned stomach.

The top of his boxers peeked out from underneath his jeans.

I quickly pulled my head back into the car, trying to unthink the thoughts in my head, as if that were even possible. I banged my forehead against the steering wheel.

Don't go there.

Cole stood up and brushed his hands off on his jeans. He nodded. "Looks pretty good, actually."

"Are you going to bid?"

"How's the inside look?"

He opened the passenger side door, looking around as I gave him my report.

Even though he agreed this car was worth bidding on, he still wanted to inspect as many cars as he could before the auction began, so I slogged around behind him. After what seemed like forever, but was more like an hour, Cole picked up a little paddle, and we found seats.

He noticed me eying the paddle and the corners of his mouth quirked up. "Do you want to hold it?"

"Yes!" It was silly, but I wanted to be the one to hold up the paddle. I'd seen an old movie once where a glamorous woman raised her paddle nonchalantly to bid on a diamond necklace as if she hadn't a care in the world and had millions of dollars to spend. I'd always thought it'd be cool to be like that.

This auction was nothing like the one in the movie though. Instead of being surrounded by glamorous people in evening gowns and tuxes, it was beer bellies and trucker hats in a hastily constructed tent. No elegant auction hall. It wasn't leisurely, either. If you blinked, you'd miss it.

The car we wanted was one of the first ones up. Cole let me bid, but in about ten seconds he was holding my arm down and shaking his head.

"Too high," he said.

I was disappointed. Out of the three cars Cole had selected, all of them went for thousands over what he was willing to pay for them.

As we walked to his car, I kicked at the gravel. "Well, that sucked," I commented.

He shrugged. "No big deal. There will be other auctions."

"Will Bill be mad?"

"He'd be mad if I overspent on a car."

I pouted. "I wanted to buy a car today."

"Patience, grasshopper."

Patience was not one of my virtues. I was sure I had a thick streak of impatience running through my aura. It could be worse though.

It could always be worse.

Cole drove me home, stopping at the curb in front of my apartment building.

"See you later," I said, shutting the door.

Cole leaned over and rolled down the window. "Hey, Ava."

"Hey, what?"

He rolled his eyes. "I was wondering if you'd mind, uh—" he stopped and swallowed before continuing, "—looking over this paper I had to write for English. You know, help me edit and revise and all that junk."

"Sure. Just email it to me."

This was a huge step in Cole's world. He trusted me enough to ask for my help. I was sure he saw asking for help as a sign of weakness, and Cole didn't do weakness. Nothing about Cole was weak.

I smiled as he drove away.

Yup. Things could be a lot worse.

MY MOM CRADLED A GLASS of dark wine. A mostly empty bottle sat on the table in front of her. It was ten a.m.

"Hey, Mom," I said tentatively, looking over my shoulder at her as I pulled a bowl out of the cabinet.

She nodded to me and brought the glass up to her lips. I poured myself a bowl of cereal. As I reached into the refrigerator for the milk, I noticed the newspaper sitting in front of her.

I sat down across from her and pulled the paper toward me. The headline read, "Mother of Three Killed in Car Accident." The article was only one paragraph long, so the details were sparse—it didn't even mention the victim's name. The headline summed up the entire article.

I took of bite of Apple Jacks and eyed my mother. I'd never seen her like this. She wasn't a drinker. She especially wasn't a morning drinker. Other than the rare cocktail if we went to a nice restaurant, I'd never seen her drink.

This must be her. This must be the name my mom submitted so Xavier would stop torturing me. This woman unknowingly gave her life because of my mistake.

My mom had been seeking for twenty years, but this was the first time a death had broken through her carefully constructed defenses. She'd always managed to stay detached. Until now.

Her eyes were glassy and unfocused, and her skin was splotchy. She absentmindedly ran her fingers along the headline, almost as if she were petting it.

Mother of Three Killed in Car Accident.

That wasn't the whole story. The headline should read *Mother of Three Killed Because Teenage Girl Thought She Knew it All.*

I pushed my cereal away.

I wondered if my mom would consider sharing her wine.

"I'm sorry," I said quietly.

She silently raised her glass in a toast, then took a big swallow. I cradled my head in my hands, and we sat in silence while she finished her wine. When she drained the last in her glass, she put it in the sink and grabbed the bottle. She walked down the hall toward her room with one hand on the wall to steady herself.

She still hadn't said one word to me.

She didn't have to.

I knew this was my fault. And there was absolutely nothing I could do to fix it.

CHAPTER 12

THE PARTY WAS IN FULL swing by the time I got there. Parties weren't my thing, and normally I didn't even pay attention to the social scene of whatever high school I happened to be attending. You had to be blind not to know about this party though. Fliers were plastered all over the school, and no matter how quickly the teachers and custodians took them down, more appeared like multiplying bunny rabbits. I'd personally thrown away six different fliers that had been shoved into my locker.

The party was in the better part of town, in a largish house with a white picket fence. It was exactly the house you'd expect a family in a sitcom to live in. I wasn't even sure whose house it was. I just paid my three dollars and headed straight for the keg, red plastic cup in hand.

This wasn't me. I wasn't a party girl, but I couldn't deal with my thoughts any more today. I was willing to try anything to get out of my own head for a few hours.

I'd sat in the library for hours, obsessively researching the mother of three who'd died as a result of my mother turning in her name. Julie McKenner, formerly of Charlotte, North Carolina. One of her three children was a boy with special needs she'd adopted, and she'd quit her job to stay home with him. She taught Sunday school every other Sunday at her church and volunteered at the local women's shelter.

Way to go, Mom. She sure knew how to find them. Julie McKenner was class A angel material.

And it was my fault her three children would never see her again. If I hadn't tried to trick Xavier, Julie might have lived. My mom might have found someone else's name to turn in for her assignment next month.

But that was the problem. There was always going to be another name. It never ended.

I chugged the beer, nearly gagging. This wasn't the first time I'd had beer, but it was the first time I'd had a purpose for drinking it.

The music thumped, some song I didn't recognize. I'd become disconnected from that sort of thing lately. Somehow having the latest hit on my iPod while I was checking out auras didn't warrant my attention.

Brooke was across the room chatting with a guy I didn't recognize. He looked older, like maybe he was in college. When she caught my eye, I nodded. She lifted her chin in acknowledgment. She had no idea what role I played in Joey's injuries, but she hadn't missed the connection between my interrogating her about him and his getting held up at gunpoint and ending up in the hospital soon after.

If only I had those kinds of connections. There was a certain black suit wearing prick I'd like to take a hit out on.

Could Xavier die? I didn't know the answer to that, but I certainly wouldn't mind taking part in an experiment to find out.

I refilled my cup and tried to mingle a little. No one approached me, though. I guessed I had a little *fuck off* vibe going on. I didn't care. I wasn't here to socialize.

What was the point in even attempting to fit in? I grabbed an empty cup someone had left lying around, not feeling guilty at all that that person would have to pay to get another cup. This was the least of my sins. *Finders, keepers.* I filled my two cups and cut through the living room to the sliding glass door that led to the backyard. I sat on the edge of a large planter that had a dead plant in it and carefully nestled my spare cup in the loose dirt.

I closed my eyes for a moment, willing my eyes to absorb the tears forming there. What right did I have to cry? The kids who just lost their mother had a right to cry. Not me. Not the person responsible.

I drained my cup and looked up at the stars. I knew from science class not all stars were white, but from my vantage they all looked that way. There was probably a metaphor there that related to white auras, but I couldn't see it right now.

The beer was taking effect.

The sliding glass door opened and two guys and a girl appeared.

"Hey," the first guy said. "Do you care if we smoke out here?"

I waved my hand in the universal *go ahead* sign. When they lit up though, I realized they weren't talking about smoking cigarettes. The second guy offered me the joint they were passing around, but I shook my head, content to sip my beer.

The girl giggled, catching my attention. I glanced back over and almost did a double take. I blinked, then rubbed my eyes.

Their auras were in plain sight even though my guards were up. At least, I thought they were up. I hadn't lowered them.

God, the last thing I needed was my guards failing. I couldn't deal with this right now. I'd come to the party to forget about all this aura crap for a few hours.

I kept my face turned away until I heard the glass door opening and closing, and their chatter disappeared. Then I breathed a sigh of relief.

I stood and swayed a little. The beer made my head feel fuzzy, and even though I was pretty sure I was standing straight, it felt like my body was moving in little circles, as if moving in time to music that no one else could hear.

I turned my head at the sound of the glass door sliding open. A light as white and bright as the stars above appeared. This light didn't blind me as the others had because it was familiar. I was used to seeing it.

"What are you doing here?" I asked.

He'd taken it up a notch and had on a green polo shirt instead of his usual t-shirt. No jacket. I was bundled up in my heaviest coat and scarf. Underneath? You guessed it. Jeans and hoodie.

Cole looked me up and down. "I could ask you the same thing."

"What does it look like I'm doing? I'm enjoying a party."

He looked around, taking note of the lack of people. "This looks like a lot of fun."

"It is," I said, a little too loudly. "You didn't answer me. You *never* answer me. What are you doing here?"

He leaned against the door frame and crossed his arms. "The same thing as you."

"Bullshit." I jumped forward, sticking a finger in his chest. It was solid, and I resisted the urge to explore it with more than just that one finger. Instead, my fingers walked up his chest to his nose and gave it a little pluck. "You're not the high school party type."

He cocked one eyebrow. "And you are." It was not a question, but his words were loaded with skepticism.

"Definitely." Or at least I totally could be. I could do this. I could live this life. I tilted my almost empty cup above my mouth, catching the last few drops. "And if you'll excuse me, I need to get back to it." I pushed past him. I didn't need to explain myself to him, and I certainly didn't need him looking down his nose at me.

I stumbled into the living room, almost taking a nose dive into the green shag carpet. My two red cups were still clutched in my hands. When I looked up, I was assaulted with bright auras of every hue. I threw my arm up to cover my eyes, my cups clattering to the ground.

Passion red, creative yellow, and sweet pink mixed with the more wicked ignorant orange, and jealous green. The energies overwhelmed me, making me even dizzier and more light-headed.

Someone bumped into me, and I fell to my knees. I stayed there, whimpering, needing to get out, but paralyzed by the onslaught of energies.

Strong hands gripped me under my arms and hauled me to my feet.

"Are you okay?" Cole asked.

"The colors...they're too bright. I can't..."

"Colors?"

I clutched at his arm. "I need to get out here. The colors, oh God, they're so bright. They're blinding me."

He wrapped his arm around me. "I've got you."

I leaned into him, taking shaking steps with my eyes squeezed shut. It wasn't until I felt the cool night air that I dared to open them.

I wished I hadn't. The scenery around me swirled, and I keeled over, losing the contents of my stomach in the bushes.

I hadn't thrown up since I was seven years old. Why did I have to break my streak in front of Cole of all people?

When I was sure I'd gotten everything up, I straightened and wiped my mouth with the back of my hand. I looked over at Cole who was standing a few feet away. I expected a smirk and was surprised to find a look of sympathy instead.

"It burns, doesn't it?" he asked.

I nodded, wishing for a glass of water and a Tic Tac.

"Come on," he said. He wrapped his arm around my waist to guide me, and I was grateful for the support.

Now that the alcohol had left my system, my guards were starting to work again, and Cole's aura faded into the background. I was also coming to my senses.

I'd gone to the party not to socialize with my dazzling peers, but because I'd known there would be a keg there, and I'd hoped the alcohol would dull what I was feeling. I'd just wanted to forget, even if it would only be temporary.

The joke was on me, though.

Apparently alcohol intensified my aura seeing abilities to the point where I couldn't block them out. Who knew? I certainly didn't. I now understood why my mom was drinking alone rather than at a bar.

We walked the few blocks in silence to where the Rustinator was parked. When we got to it, he opened the passenger door for me.

I was so humiliated. It would be better if he were in asshole mode right now. Then I could focus my energy on being pissed at him. Instead, I was overcome with a mixture of self-pity and self-loathing. I hated myself for what my recent actions caused, but I felt sorry for myself for being forced into a role I desperately didn't want. I was a seeker, and it seemed there was nothing I could do about it.

The silence made the thoughts in my head loud and unbearable, exactly what I'd been trying to avoid.

"You don't strike me as the high school party type," I said, rehashing our conversation from earlier.

He buckled his seatbelt and started the car. "I'm not."

He turned in the direction of my apartment, but I reached over and put a hand on his arm. He glanced at me, a question in his eyes.

"I don't want to go home right now."

He did a U-turn, speeding off in the direction of the shop. Well, old man style speeding, anyway. I think we actually went a mile over the speed limit.

I laid my head against the back of the seat and closed my eyes. The motion of the car was making me queasy. I willed my stomach to settle, not wanting to yak in his car. It would be both embarrassing and unforgivable to desecrate the Rustinator.

When we got to the shop and his apartment—still getting used to that one—Cole pulled a glass out of his cupboard and filled it with tap water. He pressed it into my hand.

"Drink. You'll thank me later."

I took the water and gulped it down, sinking down onto the futon. Cole sat next to me, leaning back and stretching his legs.

"What the hell were you doing, anyway?"

Ah, there was the Cole I knew and loved.

I shrugged. "Partying."

He shook his head. "Someone needs to teach you how to party."

I put my face in my hands. "I know," I mumbled miserably.

I wanted to tell him I wasn't just some loser teenage girl who couldn't hold her alcohol. I had a valid reason for wanting to dull my senses. And for the first time, I wanted to share my secret. I wanted to tell Cole about the burden I carried.

But I couldn't.

First of all, Xavier would find out, and he would go ballistic I'm sure. I'd never been told any rules about secrecy, but I had to believe they existed.

Second, would Cole even believe me if I did tell him? He might write me off as crazy. But in the slim chance he actually believed me, what then? What would he think of me?

A clanging noise in the kitchen area interrupted my thoughts.

"What are you doing?" I asked.

Cole spun a bag of bread, twisting it open. "Grilled cheese," he said. "I assume you like grilled cheese?"

"Who doesn't like grilled cheese?"

He grinned. "Exactly."

I watched as he made our sandwiches. His approach

was much like his approach to working on cars—methodical and capable.

Minutes later he placed a paper plate holding a perfectly golden grilled cheese sandwich on my lap. He sat down next to me with three sandwiches piled on his own plate.

I took a bite and nearly moaned out loud as cheesy goodness filled my mouth.

"Good, right?" Cole had been waiting for my reaction and was smiling.

I nodded, wiping a stray bit of gooey cheese off my mouth. "This is better than the average grilled cheese."

He nodded. "I know. There's a trick to it."

I waited. "Are you going to tell me?"

He leaned in conspiratorially. "You have to grill both sides of the bread."

I checked the bread closer, and sure enough, both sides were grilled. "Huh," I said. "I never would have thought of that."

We sat and chewed in companionable silence for a few minutes.

"Why are you being so nice to me?"

"Would you rather I were an asshole?" he asked dryly.

"No, I mean, sometimes you are though."

He raised his eyebrows and my cheeks reddened.

"You have to admit," I said in a hurry, "that you can be an asshole."

"Yeah," he said begrudgingly. "It just comes so naturally."

"So why are you?"

"An asshole?"

"No, being nice to me." I swallowed the last of my sandwich and seriously considered licking the cheese and crumbs off the plate. It was that good.

He shrugged. "You're having a rough night. I've had a few of those. It would have been nice if someone had been nice to me." He grinned. "Someone older and wiser, that is."

I shoved him playfully. "You're only two years older than me."

He grabbed my wrist and twisted it, holding my arm hostage.

"Hey!" I protested.

"Don't push someone if you're not prepared for retaliation."

I tried to wrench my arm free, but he held it firm. I was getting a taste of what it would have been like to have a brother as I imagined siblings probably tortured each other like this.

But Cole was most definitely not my brother. And he definitely had me overpowered. I might as well play to my strengths. Feminism be damned.

I bit my lip and looked up at him. "You're hurting me."

He loosened his grip immediately. I shot my foot up to hook under his knee. The idea was to knock him off the futon—mature, I knew, but he started it. I was just going along.

Instead I found myself tumbling off the futon and landing on my butt on the floor while Cole maintained his position on the futon.

He leaned over to peer at me, his eyes twinkling in amusement, though he somehow managed to keep a straight face. "Are you okay?"

I could tell he was trying not to laugh. I admired his restraint, really I did. If our positions were reversed, I probably would not have been able to stop the eruption of giggles.

I lay back and threw an arm over my face. "Fine," I mumbled. Tonight just really sucked. But nothing that sucked about tonight could be blamed on anyone but me.

He laughed, a loud belly laugh that actually brought tears to his eyes and made him gasp for breath.

Okay, I take that back. Some of the blame was his. His hyena laughter was unnecessary and definitely made me feel like an even bigger ass than I already did.

When his laughter subsided, he stood and held a hand out to help me up. I grabbed it and pulled myself up, but my feet got twisted and I ended up stumbling into him. He wrapped an arm around my waist to steady me.

Our chests and the lengths of our bodies were touching. He stiffened but didn't step away. I could feel his every inhale and exhale.

His fingers stroked my back a little, causing tingles to run up my spine.

Why weren't we separating? We'd agreed to be no more than friends, but at this moment, that didn't seem to be on the forefront of either of our minds. Being this close to him felt good. It felt *right*.

And when so many things were wrong in my life, it was a delicious distraction for something to feel so right.

Pressing my face into his chest, I cursed myself for puking earlier. I so wanted to kiss him, but with post-puke breath? Wasn't gonna happen.

"You should probably take me home," I said, my voice laced with disappointment.

He still didn't move, not releasing me. "Yeah."

Putting his hand under my chin he kissed me softly on the lips, then abruptly released me.

"Let's go," he said gruffly, grabbing his keys and walking out the door, not looking behind him.

What was that?

I put my fingertips to my lips. The sweeter side of Cole was going to be my undoing.

I ran my hands through my hair and let out a frustrated sigh, then trudged down the steps after him.

CHAPTER 13

I STARED BLANKLY OUT THE window in my English class.

Right at Xavier.

I did a double take, sitting up straight and blinking rapidly.

Unfortunately, my eyes weren't deceiving me. There he was lounging in the courtyard outside the school, smoking a cigar. I looked around the classroom to see if anyone else had noticed him, but the other kids were all looking toward the front of the room.

Any minute now, security would come by and escort Xavier off school property. They were known for regularly patrolling that area and busting the kids who snuck outside, thinking they were going to have a quick smoke.

I would just ignore him. That was the smart thing to do. Security would take care of it. But what if Xavier pulled one of his tricks?

No, that wouldn't happen. Xavier wasn't stupid.

Was he?

I looked at the front of the room and tried to focus on Mrs. Gregory's lecture on the symbolism in *Death of a Salesman*.

This wasn't my problem. Catching trespassers wasn't my problem, even if I did happen to know the trespasser.

My gaze drifted over to the window again and my eyes

met Xavier's. *Shit!* He smiled and crooked his finger at me. *Come here.*

Shit, shit, double shit. I couldn't pretend to ignore him anymore. I sighed and stretched my hand in the air.

"Yes, Miss Parks? Is there something you wanted to say about the symbolism of diamonds in *Death of a Salesman?*"

"Um, no, ma'am. Can I—May I go to the restroom?" My classmates snickered at Mrs. Gregory's scowl.

"You're interrupting my lecture to ask me that?" she said sternly.

"I'm sorry. It's, uh, a bit of an emergency."

She narrowed her eyes at me, and when I didn't back down she huffed. "Fine. Take the pass."

I shot out of my seat and grabbed the pass hanging on the chalkboard on the way out the door. I jogged down the hallway as fast as I could without getting myself in trouble.

I burst through the courtyard doors. "What are you doing here?"

Xavier blew out a breath of smoke, dropped his cigar on the ground, and stepped on it with his foot, grounding it into the pavement.

"Hello, Ava."

"What are you doing here?"

"Is that any way to treat your dear Uncle Xavier?"

"Cut the bullshit. We both know I've never liked you. There's no reason to pretend otherwise. What do you want?"

Xavier gave an approving smile. He appreciated my candor.

"I'm just checking on your progress. Any white auras yet?"

"If I'd found one, you'd already have the name. My mom's going to be pissed you came here."

He waved his hand, dismissing my warning. "What Mary doesn't know won't hurt her. Understand?"

While his gesture was blasé, his tone was not. It was

threatening.

I stuck my chin out and nodded.

"You don't have to be picky. Turn in the first white aura you find and you can go back to your life."

Yeah, until the next time he demanded a name.

I glanced over my shoulder at the building. If anyone saw me out here, Mrs. Gregory would surely write me a referral and send me to the principal's office. I wished Xavier would get to his point.

"Okay, well, if that's all you want, I need to get back to class."

He closed the distance between us and put his hand on my arm. I jerked it away. "Don't touch me."

"I want to make sure you understand, Ava. *Any* white aura will do." Xavier enunciated each word, saying this sentence slowly, to make sure what he was saying sunk it.

I frowned at him. We were only supposed to turn in fated auras. I opened my mouth to remind him of that but clamped it shut. I wished I had pressed my mom more about the difference between fated and non-fated white auras. I had a feeling I was missing something here, but I had no idea what it was.

"I need to go back to class." I turned on my heel and stalked away.

"Remember, Ava," Xavier's voice drifted across the courtyard with an eerie reverberating quality. "*Any* white aura will do."

I kept walking, Xavier's words echoing in my mind.

A WEEK PASSED. THEN ANOTHER day. Another. I was no closer to finding a fated white aura. What could I tell you? My high school was a cesspool of mediocrity. Kaley was the closest I'd found. Every morning when I saw her, my stomach clenched. Would today be the day her aura turned white and I'd have to submit her name for reaping?

She was the first pseudo-friend I'd had in a year. Pseudo because I couldn't even claim her as a real friend.

Real friends didn't hold the pen to potentially sign the other's death sentence.

I kicked a rock as hard as I could, and it ricocheted off a trash can. I was taking my sweet time getting to the shop today. Cole would probably bitch at me for being late. Bill wouldn't even notice. Sometimes I wondered who the real boss was.

I was tempted to play hooky from the shop and go home for a nap instead. That would really set Cole off, though, since he'd seen me at school and knew I wasn't sick. I was so exhausted that his wrath might be worth the risk. I wasn't sleeping much these days, and when I did sleep, I had nightmares about chasing white auras, only every time I actually caught one, the aura changed colors.

I'm sure it meant something, but I wasn't sure I wanted to know.

It took copious amounts of caffeine for me to stay awake today during school. I desperately wanted to sneak a snooze during history when we watched yet another movie, but I couldn't. Apparently sometimes I projected my aura when I slept.

I'd never witnessed it myself because it happened when I was, you know, sleeping, but it shocked the hell out of my mom the first time it happened when I was seven. The best she could figure, it happened when I was in a meditative state, like sleep. And it was rare. So rare, in fact, my mom had never heard of it happening before. I was a freak among the freaks.

Awesome.

Needless to say, I never got to go to any sleepover birthday parties as a kid.

Cole wasn't in the shop when I walked in. It was void of cars, and Bill was in his office with his feet propped up on his desk, TV blaring.

I hovered in the doorway. "Um, Bill—"

His feet fell from the desk, and he sat up straight. "Sorry," he said, fumbling with the remote to turn down the volume.

"No, it's okay." I ran my fingers along the doorframe. "I'm sorry to bother you. Is Cole here? Or is there something you need me to do?" I added that last part as an afterthought. Even though Bill was my boss for this internship and signed off on all my hours, he'd never actually given me any direction. All my orders came from Cole.

"Rain's coming," Bill said as if that explained everything. As if on cue, raindrops splattered on the window.

"Uh-huh." My face must have looked as confused as I felt.

"Rain scares the customers away. Cole's upstairs."

"Thanks."

Bill grunted in response and hit the volume button on the remote.

That conversation was downright impressive for him. It was the most words we'd ever exchanged.

I climbed the stairs slowly and noisily. I could see the door was open at the top, and I didn't want to surprise him. That last time I'd done that, he'd almost shot me.

Okay, so maybe that was exaggerating a little bit. Cole had been in control the entire time. In the short time I'd known him, I'd never seen him *not* in control.

Cole looked up from where he was lounging on the futon with an open textbook in his lap.

"Hi." I tucked my hair behind my ears.

He closed the textbook. "Hey."

"What are you working on?"

"Studying for a government test." He waited a beat. "You can come in, you know."

I crossed over to sit on the other end of the couch. "You don't have to stop."

He opened the book and sighed. "I'll be so glad to

graduate."

I pulled an e-reader out of my backpack. That was one good thing that had happened this week. My mom won it in a raffle at work and surprised me with it. The library loaned out digital books, so I could read whatever I wanted, wherever I wanted without anyone knowing what I was reading.

Like now. I was in the middle of a historical romance novel. I would never, *ever*, read that in front of Cole. His teasing would be merciless.

I took off my shoes and curled up on the end of the couch. The rain hitting the roof created a soothing white noise that had a calming effect on my nerves. For the first time in the last nine days, I was able to relax. I *so* needed this, and I was totally still listing these hours on my internship log sheet. I was on the premises, and it wasn't my fault the shop was empty during my scheduled hours.

I had just finished reading the second page when a yellow Skittle skidded across my screen and flew off, landing under the coffee table.

I looked over at Cole, but his nose was in his book.

Whatever. I went back to reading.

No sooner had I read another paragraph than a green one bounced off my leg. Seconds later, a red one hit my shoulder.

"You know," I said, my tone bland, "your aim is terrible."

He grinned and tossed a few Skittles in his mouth. "No, it's not."

I laughed. "Anyone can make it into their own mouth from two inches away. What were you aiming at before?"

"Skittles are shaped weird," he protested. "The shape affects their trajectory."

I coughed, and it mysteriously sounded like *bullshit*.

"Open your mouth," he said, his tone challenging. "I promise I'll make it."

I made a show of putting my e-reader down and

stretching out my jaw.

He frowned at me. "What are you doing?"

"Stretching out my mouth. You're going to need as big a target as possible."

He pursed his lips. "All right, wiseass. Open up."

I opened my mouth and closed my eyes a split second before a Skittle bounced off my eyelid.

"Are you trying to blind me?"

His response was a Skittle that bounced off my front tooth. That one kind of hurt, but I plucked it off my stomach and popped it in my mouth, chewing it with a wide grin.

He handed me the bag. "Okay, hotshot. You try it."

I shook a few of them into my hand. I arched my wrist to throw the first one but lowered it. "No fair. Open your mouth all the way."

He obeyed, and I sent it hurtling through the air. Just before it would have sailed into his mouth, he snapped it shut.

"Cheater!"

He grinned. "Okay, okay. I'll keep it open this time. Promise."

I looked at him, my gaze clearly conveying the doubt I held. Fool me once and all that.

But he was true to his word, and I sunk the next five out of six candies I lobbed over his way.

"Do you admit defeat?"

"Who's defeated? I'm the one getting to eat all the Skittles. It was all part of the master plan."

I snorted. "Keep telling yourself that, ace." I picked up my e-reader. "Now study."

"Come on, best two out of three."

"No," I said, using my best teacher voice. "You've got to study. You *do* want to graduate this year, right?"

"You're just scared." Cole popped a Skittle in his mouth and chewed with a smug look on his face.

I put down my e-reader. "Scared?"

"'Cause you know I'll win. It's okay. You can admit it."

I opened my mouth to fire off a snappy retort but clamped it shut. He was goading me, and one of us had to be mature.

I shook my head and turned my attention back to my book. "*Study*, Cole."

He was obviously easily distracted today, and I didn't want to contribute any more than I already had. It was weird. Normally he was really focused on whatever task was at hand, whether he liked it or not.

The rain must have been affecting his brain.

And I really wanted to get back to my book. It was just getting to the good part, anyway, *if you know what I mean.*

I'd read about six words when Cole snatched the e-reader out of my hands. He held it above his head.

"Give it back," I said.

"Not until you agree to a rematch."

"*Cole.*"

"*Ava.*"

I narrowed my eyes at him. Was he *mocking* me? And this was after he stole my book? Oh, it was on.

I launched myself at him, but he anticipated my move and held the e-reader farther behind his head, holding me back with his other arm.

Damn, he was strong.

"What are you reading anyway?" he asked, twisting his neck so he could see the screen.

I stilled momentarily, the blood draining from my face.

Oh, no. This was bad.

I redoubled my efforts to reach it, but he held it too far away.

"*She licked her lips in anticipation as his hands roamed...*" he stopped reading and turned to look at me.

The blood returned to my face in a hurry.

"Really?" he said through barely stifled laughter.

"That's what you're reading?"

I used the opportunity to lunge further toward the e-reader. I didn't get it, but I was successful in knocking it out of his hands.

The next thing I knew, I was on my back and Cole had hold of my right foot and was pulling my sock off. *What the hell?*

I was taken too off guard to react in a timely manner. By the time I got my wits about me, Cole was tickling my bare foot.

"Stop!" My voice was part shriek, part squeal.

Cole grinned down at me and held tightly to my ankle with one hand, attempting with the other to gain possession of my other foot.

I kicked his knee as hard I as could before he could catch hold of my foot. I kept whacking him and finally hooked my foot around the back of his knee and pulled hard.

He fell on me, and I made a sound that was a cross between a pig's snort and a puppy's high-pitched yelp. Not my most graceful of moments.

Cole was heavy. I only had a second to register this before he propped himself up on his knees and started attacking my sides.

I laughed, and not a dainty, girly laugh, but a tears-streaming-down-my-face, can't-catch-my-breath, snort-inducing laugh.

"Stoooo—" was all I managed to get out in protest.

I put my hands on his shoulders and pushed, only to confirm how wimpy I really was. He didn't even budge. He took the opportunity to grab my wrists and pin my arms above my head.

This was a guy with experience.

"I'm...going...to...pee...my...pants!"

That got his attention. He stopped abruptly, but didn't move, his one hand paused on my stomach and the other keeping my hands pinned above my head.

His face hovered a foot above mine and he looked into my eyes.

"Really?" he asked.

"Really what?" I said without thinking.

"Are you really going to pee your pants?" he asked drily.

My cheeks flushed. "Um, no, I'm good." Desperate times had called for desperate measures, but I was now regretting my words. The last thing I wanted was Cole to think of me as the girl who pees her pants.

"I tickled someone who did that once. My mom was pissed." His voice was detached. Even though he said the words, they weren't what he was thinking about.

"Uh-huh." That was about as coherent as I could get.

Cole was on top of me, pinning me down. What had seemed like innocent tickling moments earlier had warped into something else, something less innocent.

His eyes scanned my face. I tried to read them, but they were giving mixed messages. Desire was definitely there, but so was trepidation, uncertainty.

But with my arms and hands immobile, the ball was in his court.

Mostly.

The thought that I shouldn't be doing this flitted through my mind, being dismissed as quickly as it had come.

I scooted up a little, closing the distance between our faces.

I wanted to lean in, *so* wanted to, but the change in his expression stopped me. It was as if I was on the other side of his gun again. Only this time, he pulled the trigger.

He released my hands and moved to the other end of the couch, getting as far away from me as possible.

Denied.

I rushed into the bathroom and closed the door behind me, turning the faucet on full blast. I leaned on the counter and stared at my reflection. I half expected a cyclops or Medusa to be staring back me. Why else would his expression have turned to stone so quickly?

Had I misread the signals? Had I been so preoccupied with what I wanted I'd totally ignored what he wanted?

Or in this case, *didn't* want?

No, I'd seen the look in his eyes. Before he'd locked himself down, he'd felt something. But the last time we'd been in this situation, we'd each made it clear it was a bad idea.

And it was a bad idea. As much as I wanted to be a normal girl with a normal crush, I wasn't. I never would be.

It sucked. It just sucked.

Get it together, Ava. I couldn't stay in the bathroom forever. In the next minute or two, I'd have to go out and face him.

God, it was humiliating. I'd put myself out there only to be shot down. *Stupid, stupid, stupid.*

I turned the water off and raked my fingers through my hair. Then I squared my shoulders and opened the bathroom door.

Cole was still sitting on the couch, his elbows on his knees. He looked up when I walked out.

"I'm sorry," he said.

"There's nothing to be sorry for."

"I...we can't do this."

"We're not *doing* anything, Cole."

"Just now, on the futon—"

"Hey, you started it," I said, a half-smile on my face that didn't quite reach my eyes. "You tickled me, remember?"

"I know." He ran his hands through his hair. "That's what I mean. We can't be friends."

"Wait...I thought that's what we agreed to be—friends."

"It's getting too complicated."

He didn't know the half of it.

"I'm sorry," he said again.

"Stop saying that."

"If we're not in the shop," he continued as if I hadn't spoken, "then we shouldn't hang out."

Bang goes the gun.

"You're being ridiculous."

"No, I'm not. I'm not good for you."

"Don't you think I should be the judge of that?" It slipped out before I realized I was going to say it. I didn't mean to argue with him. It *was* a bad idea for us to be together, just not for the reasons he had come up with. Maybe I wasn't as ready as I thought I was to give up on him.

He was the bright spot in this fiasco I called my life.

"You're young—" he started.

"*Don't* even go there."

"You're two years younger than me. I've done some bad shit. You don't know anything about my past."

"Because you refuse to talk about it."

"This is best." His tone was resigned and final. There was no point in arguing with him. I might as well have been arguing with any of the tools in the myriad toolboxes down in the shop.

Come to think of it, I kind of was, because Cole was acting like a total tool.

He stood. "I'm going downstairs. You're welcome to stay up here and read. I'll let you know if the shop gets any business."

I retrieved my e-reader from the floor and shoved it into my bag. "No. This is *your* apartment. I'll leave." I stalked over to the door and yanked it open.

"Ava—"

I turned on my heel. "*What?*"

He hesitated. "Do you need a ride?"

That stopped me. There was the Cole I knew, the Cole who was thoughtful, the Cole who cared about me even when we were fighting. How could he possible think he was bad for me?

It *was* a bad idea for us to be together. But not because of him. It was because of my status as a seeker and his pesky white aura.

God, I wished things were different. I wished I could afford to show him how right he was for me, despite his claims that his shady past made him unsuitable. I wished I could just be with him.

I wished things weren't so complicated.

But they were.

I looked at him, allowing his aura to slip in. It shimmered a throbbing translucent white.

"I know who you are. I *see* you," I said sadly. "I just wish you could see yourself."

Then I turned and left.

CHAPTER 14

THE STAIRWELL SMELLED LIKE BURNED cinnamon, like someone had lit a Cinnabon on fire. I used to love Cinnabons as much as the next person, but in my world the smell of cinnamon was foreboding.

I still had twenty-four hours. Xavier was early. This was not good.

I dragged my feet, wishing I had anywhere to be but home. At least my mom's car was in the parking lot. I wouldn't have to deal with him alone.

Xavier had assumed his normal position on our couch, presiding over our living room while my mother sat across from him. How many times had I witnessed this exact same scene in the past month? His visits were more frequent than they'd ever been. I wondered, as I had many times before, if we were Xavier's only...clients? Charges? I didn't know how to describe our relationship with him.

I did know he called the shots.

I dropped my backpack inside the front door and hung my coat on the coat rack.

"Ava, darling, is that you?" Xavier's voice was coated with saccharine.

He knew damn well who it was.

"Hello, Xavier," I said, my voice equally sugary. I smiled an obviously fake smile, one that didn't reach my eyes. They were full of rancor.

He grinned, an honest grin. Good to know I amused him.

"Today's the day!" he said brightly. He sat up straighter, his eyes wide with excitement. It was sick. Just sick.

I shook my head. "I still have until tomorrow."

He sighed dramatically, sinking back into the couch. "Don't you know it's bad form to wait until the last minute? Procrastination will get you nowhere in life."

I frowned. "It's not the last minute. I still have twenty-four hours." What was the reason for this lesson on punctuality? I looked over at my mom, but she was sitting with her arms wrapped tightly around herself, her eyes boring a hole into the floor. I could expect no help from her.

He stood. "Because of the grace I showed you after your last little incident, I would have thought you'd want to prove yourself by delivering early."

Even if I had a name, I wouldn't give it to him. I wouldn't rob that poor person of any more days than I had to.

"I'm not ready."

He turned to my mother. "Mary, I thought we agreed you were going to teach your daughter some manners?"

"She hasn't missed her deadline, Xavier," my mom said smoothly, finally looking up and participating. "She'll come through."

Xavier rose and slowly circled the room. "I'm not so sure. You see, I've lost faith in her. She and I don't have the same relationship as you and I do, Mary." Xavier ran his fingertip along my mom's jaw. She stiffened but didn't shrink away. Points for her.

He turned to me. "Your dear mother has been a loyal seeker for quite some time now. Let's see, it's been...how old are you, Ava?"

"Seventeen."

"So that would make it almost eighteen years since Mary's last indiscretion."

This was news to me. I looked over at my mom, my eyes questioning, but she avoided my gaze.

Why was I always the last to learn about things like this? And why did I have to find out from *Xavier* of all people?

How many more secrets was my mom keeping from me?

And worse—how many of these did Xavier know?

"Do you have a point?" I snapped at Xavier.

He cocked his head, looking at me through slitted eyes. He bared his teeth just a little.

Across the room my mom gasped, her hands clutching at her throat.

I knelt next to her, panicked. "Mom?"

What was he doing to her?

She continued to gasp, which turned into choking. I held her hands so she couldn't claw at her throat anymore. She'd already dug several deep scratches. Her eyes bulged and were filled with raw fear.

Oh, God. She couldn't breathe. He was suffocating her.

"What are you doing?" I tried to remain calm, not wanting to show Xavier how scared I was, but I couldn't keep the panic out of my voice.

He merely smiled, and I wanted to punch his teeth in.

I had to *do* something. I couldn't just stand by and watch him hurt my mom. I searched around our living room for something to use as a weapon. The only thing that might work was the heavy glass lamp. Would I be able to heft the thing and swing it hard enough to do any damage to Xavier?

Then my mom started coughing and sucking in air.

Oh, thank God.

I squeezed her hand. "Are you okay?"

She nodded, tears streaming down her face.

I stood and stepped toward Xavier. "What is wrong with you? You just said she's a loyal seeker. If you have a problem with me, then take it out on me, not her."

He tapped his fingers together gleefully. "But you see, I am, my dear. You don't seem to care about yourself all that much, but there are others you care about."

My mom, Kaley, Cole...

I fisted my hands and bit my lip to keep from screaming out in frustration.

Xavier inclined his head, his point made. "Keep that in mind."

He left without another word.

I'D EXHAUSTED ALL OF MY options at school. There were no white auras.

Well, other than Cole's. But that wasn't an option.

I needed access to a lot of teenagers to search for auras. On the weekend or in the evening, that wouldn't be a problem. During the school day was another story. Unfortunately, there were no more weekends or evenings left. I had exactly eight hours.

I nervously watched as my mom called yet another private school. We'd come up with the plan to tour a Christian school under the guise that I might be enrolling. Christian schools were bound to be full of saintly people, right? Wasn't that the point? So far my mom had been coming up blank, though. Most schools wouldn't give a tour on such short notice.

"Ten? That's the only time today? Okay, we can be there by ten. Thanks." My mom hung up the phone.

"Well?" I said.

"Trinity Christian," she said. I looked at the address she had pulled up on the laptop.

"That's at least an hour's drive," I exclaimed. "We'll never make it."

Her expression was determined. "We have to."

Five minutes later we were zipping down the interstate and weaving in and out of traffic. I gripped the edge of the seat. I might give Cole a hard time about driving like an old man, but I much preferred that to my mom's current frantic driving. I kept my mouth shut though and watched the clock, praying we wouldn't get pulled over. If our luck held out, we would arrive just after ten.

The student tour guide was waiting for us just outside the front door. She was dressed in the quintessential Catholic schoolgirl outfit—maroon and gray plaid skirt, tucked in white button down shirt, knee socks, and heeled Mary Janes. Her arms were crossed and she was literally tapping her foot. When she caught sight of us, she flipped her long pale blonde hair over her shoulder.

"Mrs. Parks?"

"Actually, it's Ms.," my mom murmured.

She cocked her head. "Did I have the time wrong? I thought you were supposed to be here at 10:00, but it's 10:09."

My mom and I exchanged a glance. "We hit traffic," my mom said.

"Oh. Well, in that case, welcome to Trinity Christian Academy. I'm Brittany." Her voice was bright and an obviously fake smile was pasted on her face. I didn't bother checking her aura. I didn't need to see it to know she wasn't angel worthy.

She handed us two visitor name badges to clip on our shirts.

"Here's the front office. Over there is the auditorium, but we'll have to look in there at the end of the tour because they're rehearsing for the winter show. Our theatre troupe has won multiple awards at festivals all around the state." She looked at us expectantly, and we nodded, trying our best to look impressed. Once she turned around again, my mom looked at me and rolled her eyes. I stifled a giggle.

"What grade are you in?" she asked me, looking over her shoulder as she sashayed down the hall to our next stop on the tour.

"Eleventh."

"The same as me!" she squealed.

Oh, goody, I wanted to squeal back sarcastically. Instead I mustered up a smile.

"Where are most juniors at this time of day?" my mom asked.

"Excellent question!" Another smile flashing perfectly aligned bleached teeth. "You're just in time to observe the chemistry lab."

My mom kept her busy with questions while I checked out the auras of the students in the chemistry lab. Right before I lowered my guards, I got that sick, twisted feeling in the pit of my stomach.

I was hunting. Wasn't that basically what seeking was? I didn't have a rifle or anything like that, but for all intents and purposes, I was stalking prey.

I was a predator.

Bile rose in my throat. We came here for the purpose of choosing someone to die.

Some people might consider it a blessing to be chosen to be an angel. But I never found out if my selections made the cut. I never found out what actually happened to their souls.

And besides that, what kind of existence did an angel actually have? I didn't even know what I was condemning the person to if they made it through. For all I knew, being an angel was a crappy job. I just didn't know what to believe anymore.

And I had nowhere to turn for answers.

I forced my eyes open and peered around the lab. Students were crowded around tables in groups of two or three, just starting to light their Bunsen burners. I let my guards down and slowly their auras began to fill the room.

There was a lot of brown. It made sense there would be a lot of dogmatism at a Christian school. But what I didn't expect to find was no sign of a white aura. There were tinges of white, but no aura even came close to being pure white.

I looked over my shoulder in dismay at the kids laughing over their Bunsen burners as Brittany led us away.

We continued our tour, and Brittany started to ignore me after it was clear I wasn't going to engage in perky conversation, focusing instead on my mother.

It was more of the same everywhere I looked. No white auras. Part of me was relieved.

The other part of me, the larger part, was terrified. What was Xavier going to do when I had to ask him for another extension? I clung to the hope he wouldn't do too much damage. He needed me. If I was incapacitated for too long, then it would be that much longer until I could find him a white aura.

I trembled thinking of his earlier threat. I was prepared to do whatever it took, even beg, to keep him from hurting someone on account of me. I'd literally grovel at his feet if I had to. Appealing to his vanity was probably a better strategy than trying to attack him with a lamp.

The tour ended, and Brittany flounced away, leaving us with an enrollment packet. We tossed it in the trashcan on the way out the door.

When we were back in the car, this time traveling home at a much safer speed, my mom glanced over at me. "Well?"

I shook my head. "Nothing."

Her knuckles whitened on the steering wheel. She exhaled. "It's okay. I found one."

My head snapped in her direction. "What?"

"The chemistry teacher," she said grimly.

I didn't know my mom had been seeking, too.

I hadn't paid much attention to the teacher since I couldn't see her aura. I tried to remember her, but failed. She simply wasn't memorable. I was finding that was relatively common with white auras. Some of the best people around were the most easily overlooked.

I stared out the window. "It's a good thing for her that Xavier wants a teenager."

"We'll use the name to bargain."

The name. The poor teacher had changed status from person to name. Detachment at its best.

"No," I said firmly. "This is my mess. I don't want anyone else punished because of me."

She opened her mouth to protest, but I beat her to it.

"No," I said again. My conviction must have convinced her I was serious.

"Damn it, Ava." She pounded her fist on the steering wheel.

My eyebrows skyrocketed. My mom almost never cursed.

"This isn't a game," she said angrily.

"You keep saying that," I said harshly. "But you're the one reducing people to names. That chemistry teacher isn't just a *name*. She's a person."

"I am your mother," she said quietly. "I will do whatever it takes to keep you safe."

"This isn't something you can fix for me, Mom." I took a breath for this next part, bracing myself for her argument. "I don't want you there when Xavier comes."

"I don't think so. I'm not leaving you alone with him."

"Look, like it or not, being a seeker is my birthright. You keep telling me it's not a game, and I need to take it seriously. But you don't take *me* seriously. I bear the same responsibility as you with this."

Her chin quivered. "I never wanted this life for you."

It's a little late for that, I thought bitterly. I wouldn't wish this life on anyone.

"Well, this is the life I have," I retorted. "And I don't

want you taking heat because I didn't follow through with my responsibilities. And I don't want someone to die because of me if they don't have to."

"Xavier has a lot more power than I knew," she said quietly.

I ruminated on that comment for a moment. Had he always had the power and kept it hidden, or had his power increased over the years?

There was so much about this seeker business we didn't know. I had more questions than answers.

"I think we should try to find others like us," I said.

She frowned, turning on her signal and merging into the exit lane. "What do you mean?"

"Other seekers. We can't be the only ones."

"I don't see what good that would do."

I ran my hands over my face in frustration. "At least it would give us some more information. Don't you want to be free of this?"

"That isn't possible," she said immediately.

"How do you know that?"

She just shook her head. "This is what I'm talking about Ava. This isn't a game. This is your life. This will always be your life. The sooner you learn how to accept it, the sooner you can move on with it."

I stared out the window. I might as well have been talking to a brick wall. My mom was a smart woman. I didn't understand why she was so close-minded when it came to this. She was cowed under by Xavier, and part of me hated her for it.

She was so adamant about not leaving me alone with Xavier, but she'd only ever bowed to his demands anyway. What was she really going to do?

When we pulled into the parking lot, my mom dropped the f-bomb. My eyebrows shot up. The second curse of the day for my mom could not mean good news.

Xavier was there in the parking lot leaning against a light pole. The ever-present cigar was between his lips.

When he saw us, he took the cigar in his hand, and his lips curved into a sinister smile.

He walked over to our car, his hand casually in his pocket. Opening the back driver's side door, he slid into the back seat.

"Ladies, did you enjoy your little field trip? Mary, I'm surprised at you, allowing your daughter to be truant. You know that's illegal in Virginia."

My mom kept her hands on the steering wheel and looked straight ahead. I could see her pulse was racing from the vein in her neck.

Xavier sucked on his cigar and blew out the smoke, filling our tiny car. I wanted so badly to roll the window down, but for once I was taking a cue from my mom and staying completely still.

He wasn't supposed to be here yet. I still had at least another couple hours. I wanted my mom gone, out of this situation I created.

"Xavier," I said, trying to keep my voice even. "Do you mind if you and I talk upstairs in the apartment? My mom needs the car to get to work. She's already late."

"But we're all so cozy in here," Xavier said, leaning back. He put his cigar out on the backseat, leaving a burn mark the size of a quarter and causing the small space to fill with the smell of burnt fibers. "Tell me, Ava, did you find what you were seeking?"

I closed my eyes, dread setting in. "No," I whispered.

"Speak up, girl."

"No."

Immediately my mom began gasping and clawing at her neck.

"Mom!" I shrieked. I put my hands on her throat, kneading it in an attempt to massage some air through.

"It won't do any good," Xavier said in a bored tone.

"It's me you want! Leave her out of it. She has nothing to do with it."

She was gasping and clawing much more frantically

than she had yesterday. Whatever he was doing, he was doing it much, much worse. All the mean things I said to my mom ran through my mind. If she died now, I'd never get to make up for them. I'd never get to tell her I was sorry.

"Aw, Ava, you'll hurt her feelings. I've found the mother is a child's biggest influence."

"What do you want?" Massaging her neck wasn't doing anything, so I squeezed her hand and swept her hair out of her eyes. I pleaded to a God I thought had long since forgotten me.

I'd do anything, *anything*, not to lose my mom right now. I couldn't lose her.

"A name." Xavier voice was flat. How could he be so unfeeling? He'd known my mom for years. She used to treat him like family.

Now she was nothing but a tool to him, and a disposable one at that.

"I don't have one!"

My mom's face was getting pale, and she had stopped fighting as much. Not good.

"Mom," I whispered, putting my hand on her face. "Mom, hold on."

"It's been one minute now that she's been without air. Some can last up to three minutes before passing out, but I don't think your mom will be one of those."

As if on cue, her eyes rolled to the back of her head and she slumped over the steering wheel.

"Just over a minute." Xavier tucked a gold pocket watch back into his pocket. "Pity. I had hoped she'd last longer."

Tears streamed down my face. I didn't know what to do. I had to save her, but how? I didn't have what he wanted.

Xavier leaned forward and whispered in my ear, "You know what you have to do."

"I can't," I sobbed. "I can't give you what you want." I

clutched my mom's clammy limp hand.

"The risk for brain damage will greatly increase in about twenty seconds. Come on, Ava, any white aura will do."

I simultaneously felt like I was going to throw up and pass out at the same time. My hands shook.

"*Any* white aura, Ava." At my silence, he sighed. "Fine, that's five, four, three—"

"Cole Fowler!" It flew out of my mouth before I knew I was going to say it.

"That's a good girl. I knew you had it in you." Xavier exited the car and went—I didn't know where. I didn't care. He probably went back to that special corner of hell for beings like him.

I put my hand up to my mom's mouth to check if she was breathing. I exclaimed in relief when I felt a steady rhythm of air coming in and out of her body.

"Wake up, Mom," I whispered. Her eyes fluttered, a sure sign she was coming around.

I collapsed in my seat, sobs wracking my body.

I was relieved. I was horrified. Above all, I was scared. *Cole.*

Oh, God. What had I done?

CHAPTER 15

DREADED ANTICIPATION FORMED A KNOT in my stomach. I wore a groove in the shop's concrete floors from my pacing. I couldn't help it—I was a woman on the edge. Bill seemed to be getting irritated by it. He looked at me a few times like he wanted to tell me to sit still, but in the end his weird aversion to females won out and he locked himself in his office.

My heart raced as Cole slid under a truck and all I could see were his feet. I needed to see him. I needed to see he was okay.

I didn't know exactly how these things worked. What I did know was that death could come at any time. The Reapers could be outside the building right now, just waiting to pounce.

Cole didn't know it, but he was on the eve of death. It could be anything. The truck he was working on could fall on him, or he could choke on a jawbreaker. He was a bit young for a heart attack, but stranger things had happened.

The uncertainty of it was eating away at me. How could I protect him if I didn't know what I was protecting him from?

I stopped my pacing and hopped up on my stool. Trying to calm myself, I took deep breaths. Simply watching over him wasn't going to save him. If the truck fell on him, it wasn't like I could lift it off.

A plan—I needed a plan.

I chewed on my cuticle and bounced my knee up and down.

Nope, I couldn't do it. I couldn't sit still, not while the Reapers had Cole's name.

I resumed my pacing.

"Are you almost done under there?" I asked.

Cole slid out from under the truck, looking up at me. "What's your deal today, Ava? You're freaking Bill out, and to tell you the truth, you're freaking me out, too."

"Nothing," I choked out. "I don't have a deal."

Cole looked at me like I'd sprouted an appendage in the middle of my forehead, and then he slid back under the truck.

"I'm almost done," he said, his voice muffled. Then he coughed.

I dropped to all fours to peer under the truck. "Oh, God, Cole, are you okay?"

Silence.

"Cole!" I shrieked. *Oh God, oh God, oh God. Why wasn't he answering?* Fear fed on my insides.

"Okay, you've moved past freaky to psycho." The tension left my body at the sound of his voice and I collapsed a little. "What the hell is up with you?"

"Can you just come out from under the truck?" I asked as calmly as I could, which meant my voice was still several octaves above normal.

He slid out and sat up, resting his elbows on his knees. "I can't change oil without being under the truck." He spoke slowly, like he was explaining something to a small child.

I sat back. "It just makes me nervous."

He sighed. "You're lucky I like you."

He liked me? The churning in my stomach was momentarily replaced with butterflies.

"Otherwise I would have kicked you out of here an hour ago," he continued. "You've got to chill out. Is it, you know, that—?" He grimaced.

I crossed my arms, my nostrils flaring. "Don't even ask me if it's that time of the month. That is such a stereotype."

He grinned. "All stereotypes begin in truth."

I narrowed my eyes at him, and he slid back under the truck. If statements like that kept coming out of his mouth, the Reaper would have competition for taking Cole out.

I hopped back on the stool and put my head in my hands. What was I doing? Cole's smart ass comment had snapped me out of my frenzy. It pissed me off that he was right. I *was* acting like a psycho. Lord only knew the permanent damage I had caused poor Bill. The man was scared enough of estrogen as it was.

I would just have to undo this, I decided. I'd find a way to get in touch with Xavier and tell him I made a mistake. I'd tell him that Cole's aura wasn't white after all. I'd made a mistake.

I *had* made a mistake.

I never should have given Cole's name. But what choice did I have? My mom was suffocating.

I felt like I'd cut off one hand to save the other.

Maybe we could fake Cole's death. I got excited for a moment, then realized what a stupid idea that was for multiple reasons. For starters, the Reaper who was assigned to Cole would know if he'd killed someone. It's not like we could pull the wool over the Reaper's eyes in that regard. A faked death meant Cole's soul would remain in his body, so there would be no potential angel soul to evaluate.

Lastly—and most importantly—I would have to give Cole some reason we needed to fake his death. I could just imagine that conversation.

Guess what, Cole? The Grim Reaper's out to get you.

And yeah, I'm the one who sicced him on you. Now play dead.

There was a loud bang and I screamed.

"Cole!" I frantically rushed over to the truck, my heart racing, my eyes wild. I lay on my stomach, preparing to army crawl under it to get to him.

Oh God, oh God, oh God. Had he been shot? Was he bleeding out?

He grabbed my wrist, and I screamed again.

"Stop, just stop," he said firmly. He slowly rolled the creeper out from under the car so I could also scoot back out without him letting go of my wrist.

I sat on my butt, shaking.

He knelt next to me, his dark eyes trying to read mine. "What's going on, Ava?" His voice was gentle. My heart broke a little for how kind he was being to me when I had sentenced him to death less than twenty-four hours before.

"I...I—" I had to tell him something, but what? "What was that noise?" I asked instead.

He pointed to where Bill was standing near the front of a car. Bill's eyebrows were raised, and he looked a little bit frightened, truth be told. Poor Bill. My erratic behavior would probably traumatize him for life.

"Bill just put the hood down," Cole explained.

Of course. My cheeks reddened. After a month of hanging around the shop, I should know the difference between a car hood slamming and a gunshot. Then again, I'd never heard a gunshot in real life.

"Do you want me to take you home?" Cole asked. I tried to read his face, but it was carefully blank. Was he trying to get rid of me or was he concerned? I couldn't tell.

I shook my head. "I can't go home." What I meant was *I can't leave you.* Not until I fixed this. He'd have to get over his new *we can't hang out* policy.

Cole looked like he wanted to say more, but he let it go. "All right." He stood and held out his hand to help me up. "I've got to get a car that's blocked in the lot. Do you want to help move some cars around? I'll be done with this truck in a few minutes."

Nodding, I sat back on my stool and chugged half a bottle of water, then put the cool bottle up to my forehead. I was sweating from the sudden rush of adrenaline.

Cole finished with the truck and tossed me the keys. "Think you can manage parking that on the far side of the lot?" When I nodded, he said, "I'm going to start shifting around the cars."

He selected several sets of keys from the hooks by the side door while I adjusted the driver's seat and mirrors in the truck. I was only moving it to the parking lot, but my driver's ed teacher had all but etched driving safety in my brain, so I couldn't even fathom starting a car until everything was properly adjusted.

I checked the mirrors one last time and the image reflected in the side mirror made me stop. I backed the truck up a few feet, put it in park, then turned around so I could see better.

A guy I didn't recognize was in the lot talking to Cole. Nothing seemed out of the ordinary, just two guys shooting the breeze, but the hair on the back of my neck stood up. Something felt off, like there was an electric current in the air or something.

And dang, the guy looked familiar. Something about the way he held himself. Like he had a grudge against the world.

Then it dawned on me who the guy was. I didn't know him per se, but he was one of the guys I saw outside the Quik In when I was looking for black auras the first time. I never did find out why Cole was there that afternoon. Maybe he knew this guy.

But wait, wasn't he the one to warn me away from those guys? Didn't he say they were gang members or something?

I continued to watch. The guy said something and

Cole laughed.

Then suddenly Cole wasn't laughing anymore.

He was too busy staring at the gun pointed at him.

I didn't think. I just acted. I threw the truck in reverse and slammed my foot on the gas pedal. I pressed my palm flat on the horn.

Shots fired.

I heard and felt a thud as the back of the truck hit something. Hit *someone*.

I put it in park and jumped out, running around to the back of the truck. "Cole!"

He caught me in his arms. I sobbed, saying his name over and over and holding onto him to prove to myself he was whole. He ran his hand over my hair and said, "Shhh" in my ear.

"I thought you were going to die," I whispered. "I thought he was going to shoot you."

"He tried," Cole said grimly. "Stay here."

He went around the back of the truck. I crept closer until I could see what he was looking at. The guy lay on the ground. I thought I heard a low moaning, but I couldn't be sure.

I raised my hand to my mouth, horrified. I'd just hit another human being with a truck.

A human being who was about to kill Cole, no doubt influenced by the Grim Reaper.

See, the Grim Reaper didn't always do the dirty work himself. In fact, that was rare. Reapers usually worked through others.

Cole nudged the guy with his foot, but his body was limp.

"Is he alive?" I whispered.

Cole look at me, annoyed I hadn't stayed put like he'd told me. "Yeah."

He put his hands on his hips and surveyed the situation, saying just one word. "Fuck."

That about summed it up.

He kicked the guy's gun into an open gutter a few feet away where it clattered down and disappeared.

"Did he see you?" Cole asked.

"Wh...What?" My eyes were wide. I was having trouble processing the events of the last few minutes.

"Did he see you?" His tone was urgent. "Did this asshole see you?"

"I can't see how he missed me. I hit him with a truck."

"Yeah, but did he see your face?" Cole put his hands on my shoulders and looked in my eyes. "Think hard, Ava."

I did think hard but not about if the guy saw me or not. I thought about why Cole would want to know if the guy saw me. I noticed he made no mention of calling the police and in fact had already disposed of evidence.

I tilted my head. "What's going on, Cole?"

"Did...he...see...you?" He enunciated each word.

"Maybe. I don't know."

"Shit."

I definitely heard a moan this time. We both turned to look at the guy, whose eyelids were fluttering. Cole let go of my shoulders, strode over to him, and kicked him twice. The moans stopped.

I'd like to say I was surprised Cole had violence in him, but I wasn't. He'd had a rough childhood, and I was sure he'd seen his fair share of brutality. I *was* surprised to see how Cole was handling this situation, like he knew what to do.

What the hell was in his past that he knew how to deal with a gun wielding gang member who had just been mowed down by a pickup truck?

He walked back to me. "Ava, we've got to go. These guys don't usually travel alone. I don't know why this one was."

I had a good idea.

"Where do we have to go?" I asked.

Cole paced a few feet, running his hands through his

hair. "Away. You've got to trust me on this."

I didn't answer. I was too busy thinking about this crazy turn of events.

This could work though. Cole was a sitting duck if he stayed around here. The Reaper would catch up to him eventually, but this would buy me some time to figure out a plan.

"Ava..." Cole said, pleading in his voice and torment in his eyes.

There was so much I wanted to say to him, so much I probably should say to him, but I couldn't.

Instead I looked up at him and said what he wanted to hear. "I trust you."

CHAPTER 16

COLE GRABBED MY HAND, AND we ran inside. He flung open a cabinet door and reached his arm up and in, into some kind of hidey hole. His hand came back out with a wad of cash.

He ran up the stairs two at a time, and I followed him, not sure what else to do. Outside with the passed out gang member everything seemed to move in slow motion. Now we were in fast forward.

I watched as Cole opened a duffel bag and threw some clothes in it. He grabbed his laptop and his coat and we ran down the stairs. We were in and out of the apartment in literally one minute.

I had barely buckled my seat belt when we peeled out of the parking lot. The tires actually squealed.

"Are we going to my apartment?" I asked, breathless. With one hand I gripped the seat, and with the other I held onto the seat belt. I didn't trust the integrity of anything in the Rustinator, and Cole had dropped the old man driving routine and was driving like someone was after him.

Which technically someone was, if you counted the Grim Reaper as someone. Maybe even two someone's if the gang members had figured out what happened to their friend.

Cole switched lanes, cutting off a minivan and

running a red light. "When we get there you have two minutes to get whatever you need. We can't—"

Cole stopped talking abruptly as he looked in the rearview mirror. "Shit."

I twisted to see what he was looking at. "What is it?"

"See that black SUV back there?"

"Yeah."

"I think they're following us."

I frowned. "How can you tell?"

Cole gripped the steering wheel with a grim expression on his face. Then without warning and barely slowing down he took a sharp right turn into a neighborhood. Behind us was the squeal of tires as the SUV made the same turn.

"That's how."

We sped past rows of houses with tiny front yards. Children played in one of them, jumping in piles of leaves. An elderly couple walked a scruffy looking dog down the sidewalk. A boy practiced flips on the curb with his skateboard.

"Cole, we have to get out of this neighborhood," I said. "There are people out there, kids. This isn't safe."

"We're almost there." He squinted and leaned forward, staring intently at something. Then he took a sharp left, almost hitting another car going straight. We zoomed away leaving angry honks in our wake.

I have to admit I was impressed at how well the Rustinator was taking these turns. My grips on the seat and seat belt relaxed a little.

He took another left, then another, and finally a fourth, putting us right back where we were. Why had he taken us around the block? Then he gunned it, and I watched the speedometer continue to climb.

Up ahead, a block after where we'd made that first left, there was a red light.

"Red light, Cole! Red light!" I shrieked.

"It'll turn."

I tensed, bracing for impact. At the last second the light turned green and we sailed through the intersection. As soon as we were through, I turned in my seat to see the SUV come to a sudden stop to avoid being t-boned by a barrage of traffic.

I turned to Cole. "How did you know the light was going to turn?"

He glanced over at me. "I timed it."

I shook my head, still in shock my organs weren't splattered all over Fordham Boulevard. "How?"

"This is a shortcut I take sometimes to get to school. I can tell exactly to the second when that light is going to change. It's a short light."

I leaned my head back against the seats and breathed deeply, waiting for my heart to stop racing. It helped that Cole had resumed his usual old man style of driving.

"I take it we're not going to my apartment now."

Cole shook his head. "Sorry. We can stop at Walmart or somewhere and pick up whatever you need."

I bit my lip. "I have exactly three dollars."

"Don't worry. I have cash."

We hopped on the interstate and exited ten miles later at a Target. Once in the store, he handed me a stack of twenties, and we split up, thank goodness. I didn't want to pick out new underwear with Cole hovering.

I didn't know exactly what I would need, but I assumed at least one change of clothes. We hadn't discussed exactly what our plan was. All I knew was a gang was after us, and Cole thought it was because of him.

It technically was, just not in the way he thought.

It was less complicated to let him think that. That was my story, and I was sticking to it. It had nothing to do with being a coward and not wanting to tell him the real reason his life was in danger.

I picked out two sets of clothes, a pair of pajamas, and some basic toiletries before turning my cart in the direction of the food section. Somehow I didn't think we'd be dining at Applebee's anytime soon.

I found Cole waiting for me at the front of the store when I checked out. I tried to offer him what was left of the money he gave me, but he shook his head, telling me to keep it.

Once in the parking lot, he veered to the right.

I stopped, looking over at the left side of the parking lot where the Rustinator was parked. "Aren't we parked over there?"

"We're not taking my car. It sticks out too much."

It stuck out like a dying dandelion in a bouquet of roses, yet it took a high speed chase through a residential neighborhood for him to admit his car was unsightly. And he called *me* stubborn.

I didn't know what he had in mind, so I followed behind him, curious. He went down an aisle next to a large white van and stopped.

He glanced around nonchalantly, then pulled out a long metal pole I hadn't noticed he'd been holding next to his leg. I couldn't see exactly what he did because his back was to me, but he was sitting in the driver's seat of a late model Honda Accord in about twelve seconds.

My jaw dropped. He leaned over and opened the passenger side door. "Get in."

Speechless, I did what he said, tossing my bags into the back seat.

He pulled out a screwdriver—where was he getting these tools? The screwdriver had a tag on it, and I realized he must have done some shopping of his own in Target. He lined the screwdriver up on the steering column and hit it with a hammer—tag still attached—to bust it open. He used the hammer again on the ignition, tossing the metal piece over his shoulder when it broke free. Then he jammed the screwdriver in where the ignition used to be and twisted. The engine sputtered and then turned over.

He was perfectly calm when he pulled out of the parking space. Still calm as we waited on a red light to let us out of the shopping center. He hadn't even broken a sweat as we got back onto the interstate.

I couldn't say the same for myself.

He fiddled with the temperature controls. "Are you cold?"

"What was that?" I asked. My back was pressed against the door and I gaped at him.

"What?"

"You just stole a car."

He shrugged a little bit. "Borrowed."

"Do you plan to return it?" I asked pointedly.

"No, but it's not like I'm going to hock it for parts or something. They'll get it back eventually."

"Still..." I crossed my arms.

He glanced over at me, a half-grin on his face. "You have no room to talk. You hit someone with a truck today."

I put my face in my hands. Why did he have to remind me? That was not something I would put on my college applications. If I were to fill out college applications anyway.

"Too soon?"

I nodded. "Yeah. Too soon. *Way* too soon."

He nodded and focused on the road. Any lightness in the mood dissipated and gave way to tension.

Were we fugitives? Even though that guy had pulled a gun on Cole, what I did was a hit and run. Wasn't it? Or was it self-defense? Except I hadn't been defending myself—I was defending Cole. I didn't feel bad about what I did—okay, well, just a little bit, especially when I thought about the sickening thump sound made by truck's impact with the guy's body. I would do it again, though.

There was no point in thinking backward. I had to look forward. My prerogative was keeping Cole safe, and dwelling on the past wouldn't help. It happened. I couldn't change it. Now I had to deal with what was in front of me.

"What's the plan?" I asked.

"We'll drive for another couple hours, then stop for

the night."

"Then what?"

He tapped on the steering wheel with his thumb, the only indication he might not be as cool and collected as he appeared. "I don't know yet."

That made two of us.

I reached into the back for my bag of food. "Cheese Nips?"

He wrinkled his nose. "I only eat Cheez-Its."

I rolled my eyes. "Really? You're being a cheese cracker snob? Now? *Really?*"

"What else you got?"

"Granola bars and some bottled water."

"Are they s'mores granola bars?"

"Chocolate chip. And wipe that look off your face," I said in response to his grimace. "You should have bought your own food."

"That's something we can agree on." He took the granola bar I offered and ripped it open with his teeth.

It was hot.

Down, girl. That *had* to be the adrenaline talking.

Who was I kidding? It wasn't adrenaline. It was Cole. He had an effect on me, even more so now that I'd witnessed his bad boy skills. They somehow made him more attractive to me, even though I spent my days looking for pure auras.

That reminded me—it was his pesky white aura that got us into this mess in the first place. After his recent hoodlum activities, that problem might have resolved itself.

Cole was focused on the road, so I took the opportunity to lower my guards and look at his aura.

I bit back a rush of expletives.

His aura was whiter than it had ever been before. How could that be?

This wasn't the first time I'd wished for another person who could see teenage auras, but I needed someone else now more than ever. There had to be a malfunction with my aura sensing skills or something. Maybe when Xavier boiled my blood, it affected my abilities. None of this made any sense.

And there was no one I could talk to about it. Well, not no one.

I pulled out my phone. "I'm texting my mom."

A flicker of unease crossed Cole's face. "What are you going to tell her?"

"That I won't be home for dinner. I'll have to call her later and tell her something else though." I'd probably tell her the truth, but Cole couldn't be in earshot for that. I wasn't looking forward to that conversation. Even though I was going to be honest with her, she was still going to be pissed.

Dealing with her anger would have to come later. I had more immediate problems. Like the one sitting next to me.

And he had some explaining to do.

Well, so did I, but he didn't know that.

"Cole, do you have something you want to tell me?" I asked. "Or perhaps several things?"

He sighed and looked out the window. "I'm a mechanic. It's not a stretch that I'd know how to break into cars."

"True, but I don't think that guy wanted to shoot you because you're a mechanic."

"Yeah." He rubbed the back of his neck, obviously uncomfortable with my line of questioning.

"And I don't think those guys in the SUV were chasing us because you're a mechanic."

He sighed again. He seemed at war with himself, trying to figure out how much he wanted to disclose. Cole wasn't big into sharing about himself, and I was usually okay with that, because hey, who was I to judge? This time, though, that wasn't going to fly.

I needed to know everything I could about Cole so I

could figure out how to save him. If I had to play the *you put my life in danger because of your sketchy past so you owe me* card, so be it.

"I got mixed up in some stupid shit after I left home," Cole said. "Stealing cars, stripping them, stuff like that."

"Were you in a gang?"

"No," Cole said quickly. "I wasn't that stupid. But I did business with some. It...didn't end well."

I waited for Cole to elaborate, but he didn't. He must have met his sharing quota for the day. I left it alone.

What he told me confirmed what I'd been thinking for weeks now. For all intents and purposes, he should not have a white aura. Either my aura sensors were out of whack, or it had to mean something.

And I intended to figure it out.

CHAPTER 17

IT WAS LATE BY THE time we went through a drive-through to pick up some dinner. We ate in the car in the dark parking lot. Neither of us wanted to maintain the facade of normalcy we'd need to sit and eat in the restaurant. Plus I didn't want Cole exposed to any more people than were necessary. I didn't know where the next death attempt was coming from, but I knew it was coming.

It was only a matter of time.

After that, Cole found a crowded movie theater parking lot. He wanted to exchange cars, thinking the one we were in was probably already reported stolen. So while he went to take care of that, I sat on the curb to wait and make the dreaded phone call.

I briefly considered sending a cowardly text that said *Staying overnight at a friend's house. It's important. Sorry for the late notice.* It was sort-of true. Of course, that violated her no sleepover rule. I wasn't worried about projecting my aura, though. I was filled with too much stress for that.

I would have preferred going that route for now because I was emotionally drained. But I couldn't because of one factor that was literally the bane of my existence.

Xavier.

He had boiled my blood when he'd learned I'd given

him a name with a black aura. He had suffocated my mom when I wouldn't produce a white aura name. What would he do when he learned I'd intervened in the Grim Reaper's work?

I was fairly confident my mom was safe at the moment. She was working a long shift at the restaurant, and Xavier had never visited her at work. He preferred to spread his poison in the private setting of our home, where it could seep in and contaminate the one place we should feel safe.

Then again, he'd never visited me at school before, either, so all bets were off.

But the only reason Xavier hurt my mom was because of me. He and my mom seemed to have a cordial working relationship, and I didn't think he would have hurt her if he weren't trying to strong arm me into giving him a name. That was a big *if* though, so I couldn't put off calling her any longer.

She answered on the fourth ring. Although it wasn't allowed, she'd started keeping her phone on her at work just in case.

"Hi, Mom," I said.

"Are you okay?" she asked immediately.

I fiddled with a piece of grass growing up from a crack in the curb. "Yes."

"You don't sound okay." The background noise had died off. She had probably walked outside.

I sighed. "It's Cole."

"Oh, honey, I'm so sorry."

"He didn't die."

"He didn't...why didn't he die?" There was suspicion in her voice.

"I saved him."

There was silence from her end. I took the phone away from my ear and looked at it to make sure the call hadn't disconnected.

"Tell me what you did, Ava." Her voice was calm, the

kind of forced calm she had donned when I was in trouble as a little kid, and she'd known I was guilty but wanted me to confess to my crimes.

I explained everything in a rush, and she let me, not interrupting.

"Have you ever heard of someone having a white aura who just shouldn't have one?" I asked. "Or an aura that throbs?"

"No." She sounded troubled. "That has to mean something."

"Maybe it means my aura reading skills are on the fritz."

"I don't think so," she said thoughtfully. "I think it means something else."

I breathed a sigh of relief. I needed that confirmation.

Now I needed to warn her. Hearing her voice on the other end of the line was both comforting and distressing. Despite all the grief I'd given my mom recently, I couldn't imagine my life without her. She'd kept Xavier and all that seeking entailed away from me for as long as she could. At first, I'd felt betrayed at the secrecy, but I now realized she'd done that to allow me the best childhood possible given the circumstances. Now I'd repaid her by putting her life in danger.

"You need to hide," I told her. "I'm sorry, Mom, I'm so sorry, but Xavier—"

"Don't worry about me," she interrupted. "I can take care of myself."

I was shocked with how well she was handling this. Before she'd done nothing but reprimand me for not falling in line with what Xavier wanted me to do. Now I'd gone against him and the Reapers in probably the worst way possible, and she supported me.

Moms were weird.

"I'm sorry."

"I'm not," she said slowly as if she were coming to terms with it. "You're standing up for what you believe in.

I don't like doing...what we do, but I've never fought it, at least not hard enough to make a difference. And then I had you, I couldn't risk it. I couldn't risk you."

"Thanks, Mom," I said quietly. Her words brought tears to my eyes, and her support bolstered my confidence. I didn't know what I was doing. I just knew I wanted to—needed to—save Cole. Failure was not an option. And once I saved him, I would figure out how to retire from being the Grim Reaper's seeker.

I hung up with my mom after she promised to go into hiding. She made me promise not to call her. If Xavier did catch up with her, she couldn't share what information she didn't know. That part made me uneasy, but it made sense. I didn't know a lot about surveillance technology, but I'd seen enough cop shows to know it was easy enough to tap phone lines and track someone using their cell phone. Instead, I would email my mom once a day with a single sentence: *I'm okay.* Though emails could also be traced, it wasn't as easy as tracing a phone. Or so we hoped.

Cole pulled up in another Honda and I got into yet another stranger's car. A CD was playing—some kind of new age music that sounded like a bunch of wind chimes combined with the sound of ripping cardboard. Not a fan. I pressed the stop button on the CD player.

"Why did you stop it?" Cole joked. "That was my jam."

I couldn't find it in myself to come up with a snarky retort.

Cole noticed my silence and glanced over at me. "Everything's going to be okay, Ava. I promise. I'm so sorry you had to be involved in this, but I'm going to take care of it."

I nodded and busied myself scrolling through the radio stations. I should be the one reassuring him, but I wouldn't even know what to say. Cole seemed so much more capable than me in this situation. I didn't have a plan or any useful skills. I had nothing.

"What'd your mom say?" Cole asked.

We'd come up with a story I could tell her about Bill taking us out of town for a last minute car auction. It was a crap story, but it was the best we had been able to come up with. I'd always planned on telling my mom the truth, but I couldn't let Cole know that, because well, *he* didn't know the truth.

"She was a little mad, but she calmed down once I convinced her it would help my project grade."

"Good."

"What about Bill?" I asked. "What did you tell him about why you suddenly took off?"

"The truth." At my shocked expression, he added, "He already knows about my past."

"Did he call the police about that guy?"

"Nah. He was gone by the time Bill got there."

"What about the damage to the truck?"

Cole shrugged. "He'll probably just fix it."

I was starting to get the impression Bill was more than just the woman-fearing man he seemed to be. What kind of a guy didn't bat an eye when his teenage employee almost got gunned down in his parking lot and then took off after hiding the evidence?

Either a saint or a sinner. Which I didn't know.

We drove for another hour before Cole decided we'd gone far enough and checked us into a hotel.

Into one room.

Awkward.

That part of us going on the run together hadn't dawned on me. The room had two beds, but there was only about a foot between them, so we might as well have been sleeping in the same bed. I could reach my arm out and touch him if I wanted to.

If I wanted to...I didn't know why I tried to kid myself.

Cole slept in pajama pants. Just that. Pajama pants. We watched some TV before calling it a night, some kind of show. Maybe some *Duck Dynasty* re-runs? Or it could have been *Donald Duck*. I was pretty sure ducks were involved somehow.

You try to maintain proper brain function with a shirtless Cole just a foot away.

Stupid me had picked up the cheapest pajamas I could find at Target, which were hot pink *Hello Kitty* pajamas. I should have thought that one through better, but I didn't want to spend all of Cole's money. I hadn't considered I'd be wearing them in front of him. *Stupid, stupid, stupid.*

It didn't seem like I had the same effect on Cole that he had on me. While I lay awake worrying about snoring and drooling on my pillow, his breathing was low and even, and dare I say he even snored slightly.

That should have made falling asleep easier, but I was plagued with other thoughts, thoughts of the last time I saw Cole with his shirt off.

Did he even remember that night we kissed in his apartment? Of course he remembered it—after all, he wasn't senile—but did he ever think about it? He acted like it hadn't even happened, but I thought about it more than I would ever admit.

It was a restless night, so I awoke tired. In addition to lusting for Cole (there, I admitted it), I was stressed about my mom and worried about what Xavier would do when he found out I intervened in the Grim Reaper's work.

I blinked, holding my hand over my eyes as the morning sun shone through the cheap hotel curtains. The clock read 7:37. Too early to get up. We had no schedule. I flopped over and snuggled under the covers, closing my eyes.

Then they popped open again, and I bolted upright. Cole's bed was empty. I didn't hear water running in the bathroom either.

Oh, shit. Some kind of protector I was. *You have to keep track of the guy you want to keep alive, Ava*, I scolded myself, grabbing my clothes from where I had thrown them on the chair last night. I would have to find him. But how? I couldn't call him on my cell because Xavier might track my number. I didn't have a car, nor the skills to steal one, and even if I did, how would I find him? I had no clue where he would go. I didn't even know exactly where we were. Somewhere off interstate 64, north of Richmond.

I darted into the bathroom to take care of business and noticed a note tucked in the corner of the mirror.

Went for breakfast.

There was no time, so who knew how long he'd been gone? I slumped down and sat on the edge of the bathtub. I needed to be more like Cole—calm, cool, and collected. At the first sign of trouble, I started running around like a chicken with its head cut off. Rational decision making was needed, not emotional reactions.

I was tired, physically and emotionally. I'd been on edge, ready to implode ever since I gave Xavier Cole's name.

A long hot shower was in order. Hopefully it would clear my brain. It had been overloaded for the last twenty-four hours and could stand to take a break.

As I stood under the hot stream of water letting the steam soak into my pores, my brain didn't clear, instead filling with thoughts of how I could save Cole.

I needed to find out what happened to Joey Huslander. I hadn't realized until now I didn't know exactly what happened to him, other than hearing about him being held up at the coffee shop and ending up in the hospital. After Xavier had gone berserk on me and my mom's selection died, I'd been a little too preoccupied to worry about him. I couldn't believe I hadn't thought about this until now.

I sat on the bed in a towel with my hair dripping water down my back waiting for Cole's computer to start up. Luckily it wasn't password protected.

I quickly did a search and learned Joey had been

working late one night by himself when a robber came in and held him up at gunpoint. He'd handed over the money immediately, but the robber shot him anyway. It was touch and go in ICU for a few days, but he pulled through and was expected to make a full recovery. He was already posting pictures of his gunshot wound and making comments about how chicks dug scars. What a douche bag.

Why hadn't he died? Maybe the Reaper realized his aura wasn't pure and halted the reaping. That was what it sounded like to me. I'd never known a reaping to go awry before.

Well, not including Cole, of course.

I had to figure out a way to sully Cole's aura. Then if the Reapers did come for him, he wouldn't die. He might end up injured, but it was the best I could come up with.

The lock on the door clicked, and I jumped, clutching the towel tighter around me.

Cole walked in carrying a Dunkin' Donuts box. The smell of sugary goodness filled the room. My stomach growled in response.

He took one look at me and the corners of his mouth tilted up in a sly grin.

"You're back," I squeaked, hiking the towel up around my neck. That only served to expose more of my thigh. I cleared my throat and hunched over, trying to cover as much skin as I could with the tiny hotel towel.

"I am. Good timing." His gaze roamed all over my body before he cleared his throat and turned his head. The way the mirror over the dresser was positioned, he could still see me, but I didn't think he knew I realized that.

I raised my eyebrows. Maybe I was too quick in thinking I had no effect on Cole.

Taking a deep breath, I stood, letting the towel drop slightly to reveal more of my back, and walked toward the bathroom, swaying my hips a little more than normal. I couldn't see Cole's reaction, but I heard him go still and clear his throat.

Lust was one of the seven deadly sins, right?

My saucy behavior was for his own good. It was strictly to sully his soul.

Yeah, right.

I shut the bathroom door and leaned against it with a silly grin on my face, thinking of about a thousand ways I would like to help Cole sully his aura.

If only it could be that easy.

CHAPTER 18

WHEN I CAME OUT OF the bathroom in my new Target clothes, Cole was lounging on the bed feasting on donuts and coffee, idly scrolling through his phone.

I sat on the edge of the bed and continued to towel off my damp hair. "Did you come up with a plan yet?"

"Working on it." He pushed the box of donuts toward me. "I didn't know what you'd like, so I got a variety."

I selected a chocolate covered glazed one with sprinkles, wrinkling my nose at the sight of a cinnamon one.

"Thanks," I said.

He pulled a small carton of milk out of the bag. "I've never seen you with coffee, so I figured milk was a safe bet. Everyone likes donuts and milk, right?"

"Thanks," I said again. I didn't usually drink coffee, but I could've used a strong dose of caffeine this morning. Still, it was thoughtful of Cole to try to figure out what I'd like. My stomach fluttered at the thought that he remembered my preferences. And he was right—donuts and milk were fantastic.

"There's a mall with a movie theater a couple miles away from here," Cole said. "We could go see a movie to kill some time."

I picked at some loose threads in the comforter.

Under different circumstances, I would have loved for Cole to ask me to a movie.

No, I take that back. My feelings toward Cole were complicated. *We* were complicated. But his life being threatened made me realize some things, namely that I cared about him beyond him making my body tingle. I cared about him a lot.

Now I was trying to come up with a covert way to convince Cole we should stay on the move. He had been making phone calls trying to get the situation with the gang members resolved, and he could do that from anywhere now that there was a healthy distance between us and them. So from his point of view, there was no reason to keep driving.

But I knew the longer we stayed still, the easier it would be for the Grim Reaper to find us. Although, I'd read somewhere car accidents were one of the leading causes of death for young men, so perhaps spending a lot of time in a car wasn't a good idea, either.

I put my donut down on a napkin, my appetite gone. I was between a rock and hard place, one of those damned if you do, damned if you don't situations.

"Fuck." Cole's curse had me looking up sharply.

I raised my eyebrows in a silent question, looking over to where he was staring at his phone.

He crumpled up his coffee cup and threw it into the trash can. "No movie for us today. I've got to go to D.C." He grabbed his duffel bag and started throwing clothes into it. Then he stopped with a frustrated sigh and ran his hands through his hair. "Ava, I swear, I'm sorry about this. The last thing I wanted to do was drag you into this shit."

"It's okay," I said. "Let me pack my stuff."

I smiled to myself as I walked to the bathroom to stuff my things into the plastic Target bag. My immediate problem had resolved itself. We were going on the move again. I could only hope my luck would hold out.

Out in the parking lot, I looked around for the dark

green Honda we'd been using. Parked in its place was a silver Toyota.

Cole opened the driver's door. "Are you coming?"

I gaped at him. "You're a klepto! This is the third one you've stolen!"

He leaned on the open door and slipped his sunglasses on. "For starters, we're not stealing them. We're just borrowing them."

"Keep telling yourself that," I muttered.

"And it's safer this way. The longer we stay in one car, the more likely we'll get caught."

I slumped in the passenger seat of the car, noticing the booster seat in the back.

We were terrible people.

I perked up a little at that thought. I checked Cole's aura, then slumped down further in the seat, crossing my arms. It was whiter than ever.

It wasn't until we were several miles down the interstate that I asked him why we had to go to D.C.

He gripped the steering wheel, his mouth in a thin line. "My brother."

My head whipped around. "*Your what?* You have a brother? Since when?"

"Since I was five, I guess. He's fourteen."

"You told me you didn't have any siblings."

"No, I didn't."

I could've sworn I asked him about having siblings. Now that I was thinking about it though, I couldn't remember the exact answer to the question. He'd probably avoided it in classic Cole style.

"So what's the deal with your brother, then?"

Cole sighed. "He's gotten himself mixed up in some gang shit. Stupid stuff."

"Huh," I said, not stating the obvious, but I was definitely thinking it. Like big brother, like little brother. "And he texted you?"

"No, an old friend did."

He left it at that, and I stared stonily out the window. It would be nice if Cole would confide in me. Then again, it wasn't like I had any room to judge.

I decided right then that I wasn't going to look at his brother's aura. What if the freaky *shouldn't be pure but was whiter than snow* aura thing was genetic? I didn't want to risk knowing the identity of another white aura I wasn't willing to submit for reaping.

Other than the stop and go traffic around Fredericksburg, we made good time. We got a hotel room in Alexandria, which Cole told me was about five miles from the capital.

"Is this where you grew up?" I asked.

"More or less," Cole replied. "We moved a lot. You hungry?" When I nodded, Cole continued. "You're in for a treat then. If we hurry, we have just enough time to catch lunch."

We piled back into the car—same one. Cole hadn't swiped another one, though I was sure it was just a matter of time. He took me to a little Italian mom and pop restaurant called Joe's Place that had red and white checked table cloths and played traditional Italian music. Their lunch buffet had everything Italian you could ever want—pizza, spaghetti, chicken Parmesan, baked ziti, alfredo, and salad.

And Cole ate all of it. I could see why he liked this place. He easily ate four times as much as I did. It would have cost a fortune in a regular restaurant.

"When are you going to see your brother?" I asked while I watched him devour his fourth plate of food.

"Not sure yet. Probably tomorrow."

We had some time to kill, so we took the metro into the city. I'd never ridden the subway before, and the metro was quite the experience. I'm pretty sure a prostitute and her pimp sat across from us, and let me tell you, the prostitute was not a Julia Roberts from *Pretty Woman* look alike. On the other side of us was an older couple obviously doing the whole tourist thing. The man had a huge camera hanging around his neck, and the woman clung to the hot pink fanny pack strapped around her waist, looking suspiciously at anyone who came near her.

I wanted to go to a museum, but it made me nervous to even think about being in huge crowds. Anyone could be our enemy at this point. I felt like I was in *The Matrix* where anyone could turn into an agent at any given time. It was similar in that the Reapers could use anyone to get to Cole.

Instead, we sat at the reflecting pool, despite the cold. Cole was quiet. It was obvious he had a lot on his mind, so I used the time to do some reflecting of my own.

I stared at the Lincoln Memorial. It was strange seeing it in real life after seeing it in every history textbook I'd ever had. Lincoln had gone down as one of the best presidents in our country, but he had the blood of a lot of Americans on his hands. I paid enough attention in history to know that the American Civil War had the most American casualties of any war our country had ever been in. My American history teacher was a nut for statistics, so I'd had to memorize a lot of random facts and surprisingly still remembered most. There was an average of over four hundred deaths per day during those four years.

No one mentioned that when they talked about Lincoln. At the end of the day, his actions made our country a better place, and his intentions were always noble, so I guessed that was what mattered in the grand scheme of things. But still, over four hundred deaths a day? Not something that could be overlooked.

I had to wonder what color his aura was.

Did the ends always justify the means?

Eventually it got too cold to just sit there, so we decided to walk around some of the outdoor memorials, starting with the FDR memorial. It was interesting, like taking a walking tour through his years as president. I found it amazing that one man was able to touch so many different lives. His legacy was leaving the world a better place than he found it.

I couldn't say the same thing for me.

I didn't get the whole angel thing. I just didn't get it. I'd never seen any evidence of angels on Earth, and the world needed angels. There was some seriously messed up stuff going on these days. I witnessed lots of it just this afternoon with my dubious metro companions and the numerous homeless people strewn about the streets of D.C. And it seemed there were reports of mass shootings every time you turned on the news. Where were the angels? Why weren't they helping people? Why then did good people who might make a positive difference in the world have to die to become angels?

I'd been asking these same questions a while now, and I'd yet to come any closer to answering them. Maybe if I had the answers I'd be more okay with my role as a seeker.

On our walk back to the metro, I saw different groups of homeless people clustered around steam vents. It made me sad. And guilty.

I'd heard somewhere that something as simple as smiling at other people could brighten their day. There was no time like the present.

We were coming up to a homeless man who was huddled on a bench. His clothes were dirty and a layer of filth coated the skin that could be seen under his overgrown beard and unkempt hair. My first instinct was to cringe and look away. Instead, I forced myself to make eye contact with him and smile. I couldn't do anything else for him right now, but I could do that much.

"Got any change, miss?" He was missing several teeth.

I shook my head, my smile wavering a bit.

"Keep walking," Cole murmured in my ear.

"What about you?" the man asked Cole. "You got any spare change?"

Cole kept walking, not acknowledging him.

"I'm talking to you!" the man shouted. He lunged at Cole, and I saw a flash of metal.

"He's got a knife!" I shrieked.

Cole reacted just a second too late. The man slashed the knife down Cole's arm and over his hand. His jacket protected his arm and wasn't even damaged by the dull knife, but Cole's hand did not fare as well. A line of blood stretched across it.

The man raised his arm to try to slash Cole again. This time it looked like he was aiming for Cole's throat. Cole ducked out of the way and used his foot to sweep the guy off his feet. The man lay in a heap, moaning.

"I just wanted some change," he mumbled between groans.

The whole incident took seconds. Unlike with the gang member when I'd jumped into action, this time I'd been paralyzed. I was the worst bodyguard ever. I should have thrown myself in front of Cole. And then what? What would I have done? Would I have knocked the guy to the ground like Cole did? Nope, I didn't have that skill. I could have *smiled* at him or come up with some other equally effective facial expression. Cole had handled the situation much better than I could have because he was capable.

I, on the other hand, seemed to be confirming how *not* capable I was at every opportunity.

I reached for Cole's hand. "You're bleeding."

He glanced down as if he hadn't noticed it before. "It's fine," he said as several drops of blood splattered onto the pavement. "Let's go back to the hotel."

"What about him?" I pointed to the homeless man. He had begun to crawl back to his bench and seemed to have already forgotten about us.

Cole's expression was a mixture of pity and disgust. "I'm not trying to make that guy's life any worse than it already is. Let's just go."

We set off to the nearest metro station, and I grabbed

some napkins from a street vendor's cart.

"Give me your hand." I pressed the napkins to his wound, and the blood immediately seeped through. "This looks bad Cole."

He pulled his hand away from me and lifted the napkins, inspecting it. "It'll be fine."

I kept my mouth shut throughout our ride on the metro back to our hotel while I watched napkin after napkin become saturated with blood.

Cole was an idiot. He had been attacked by the guy and cut pretty badly, and he was being blasé about it. No way was I going to let Cole survive an attempted stabbing and then succumb to infection.

Uh-unh. Not going to fly on my watch.

On our walk from the metro station to our hotel, I slipped into a pharmacy and picked up some antibiotic ointment and an assortment of bandages.

Cole was leaning against the outside of the brick building waiting for me. He was about to pull the napkin up to check out the wound when I closed my hand around it.

"Ow," he whined. "Why did you do that?"

"If you lift the napkin, it'll probably start bleeding again. Let's go."

Cole sulked the few remaining blocks to the hotel.

I made Cole let me wash the wound in the sink. Well, no one could really *make* Cole do anything. I should say he *let* me wash it.

I thoroughly dried his hand, careful not to get any fibers from the towel in the open wound. I squeezed a glob of antibiotic ointment on it and slapped on a big Band-Aid.

"You're pretty good at this," he observed. "I could've used someone like you when I was a kid."

I raised my eyebrows as I packed up the medical supplies. "Why?"

"I was always doing dumb shit. Skateboarding off the roof. Typical kid stuff, I guess."

I laughed and crossed my arms, leaning against the sink. "That is *not* typical kid stuff. I think *you're* the one with the death wish."

He shrugged. "Probably." His eyes clouded over, and I knew he was thinking back to his past. I realized why he could've used someone like me when he was a kid—because his mother was a crappy mom.

I cleared my throat. I moved to squeeze past him to exit the bathroom, but he stopped me. "Thanks," he said.

In the tightness of the bathroom, we were only inches apart. His face hovered above mine.

"Anytime," I breathed. I looked up into his eyes and I noticed flecks of gold for the first time, like there were bits of caramel mixed with the chocolate.

He looked at me for a few moments with a conflicted expression, then he abruptly left the bathroom. I heard him grab his jacket off the bed.

"I'll go get us some dinner," he called, shutting the door behind him.

I let out a breath, allowing a few seconds to collect myself. I shuddered looking at the bloody napkins in the trashcan. Now that I was alone, it really hit me. That was Cole's blood. Cole's blood had been shed.

I gripped the edge of the sink and stared in the mirror. Seeing Cole's blood hardened my resolve. I would do whatever it took to keep Cole's blood off my hands.

No matter what the consequences.

CHAPTER 19

WE WERE MEETING COLE'S BROTHER, Kyle, at a McDonald's. When I questioned whether the breakfast would make Kyle late to school, Cole just gave me a blank stare.

Okay, so school wasn't a priority. I guessed there were bigger concerns.

I knew Kyle the minute we walked into the restaurant even though there wasn't much resemblance between Cole and his brother. It wasn't hard to pick him out—he was the only patron under sixty. Kyle had dirty blond hair and a paler skin tone. When I slid into the booth across from him though, I stared into the same dark eyes and impossibly long lashes, and I knew beyond a shadow of a doubt they were brothers.

"Who's she?" Kyle asked, giving me the once over.

Cole slid in beside me. "Don't be an ass."

Kyle gave me the universal chin jerk, which meant a bevy of things depending on the occasion. "'Sup."

"I'm Ava," I replied in response.

"Are you his girlfriend or something?"

My chin dropped a little. This kid was direct.

"Did you eat yet?" Cole asked in his classic avoid-the-question style. This time I was grateful. The answer to Kyle's question was a clear *no*, but it was still awkward.

"Nah."

Cole stood and pulled some bills out of his pocket. "Ava, do you mind getting food for all of us?"

I took the cash he offered. "Sure, what do you want?"

Kyle opened his mouth to answer, but Cole cut him off. "Surprise us."

"Get me a Coke," Kyle called as I walked off.

If Kyle was anything like his brother, then he could pack away some food, so I ordered half a dozen breakfast sandwiches and several orders of hash browns in addition to the requested soda. As I waited for my order, I watched them talk. Cole played the role of the serious big brother, Kyle the petulant little brother.

Cole still hadn't told me exactly what prompted this visit. I hadn't asked, both because Cole was so tight-lipped about everything and because, more importantly, in this case he had the right to be. Whatever was happening with Kyle wasn't Cole's secret to spill. I would have offered to wait at the hotel, but I hadn't wanted to leave Cole alone, and he seemed to expect that I would come along anyway.

When I finally brought the tray full of food to the table, Cole's expression was one of anger and Kyle's one of annoyance. Kyle took the Coke I put in front of him and sucked at the straw.

"I hope everyone likes eggs," I said a little too brightly, trying to break the tension. Kyle ignored me. Cole gave a tight smile.

I sighed. This was going to be one uncomfortable breakfast.

"So Kyle," I said, "what grade are you in?"

He snorted. "School's for pussies."

Cole leaned over and smacked the side of his head. "Watch your mouth."

"Stop acting like you're my dad, Cole."

This time it was Cole's turn to snort. "That jackass never gave two shits about you, and now he's in prison. I'm nothing like him. If I were, I wouldn't be here."

"Now who needs to watch his fucking mouth?" Kyle retorted. "You act like you're so much better than me."

"I am," Cole said, his expression serious, "*now*." He let out a frustrated breath. "I don't want you making the same stupid mistakes I did."

Kyle slumped down in his seat, a scowl on his face. "Mistake is just a matter of opinion."

"You think those guys are your family, your brothers, but they're not. They'll roll on you so fast it'll make your head spin."

I picked at my food, wishing I could disappear. The curious part of me was happy to get the dirt, but the decent part of me wanted to leave the two brothers to hash this out in private. This wasn't a conversation suitable for bystanders.

"Just 'cause they rolled on you doesn't mean—"

"That's exactly what it means," Cole interrupted. "If they do it once, they'll do it again."

"It isn't like that."

"It's *always* like that."

"Are we done here?" Kyle said. "I've got shit to do."

Cole laughed bitterly. "No, you don't. You need to go back to school or you'll be nineteen like me and still stuck in high school."

"Damn it, Cole, I'm not like you. I'm not gonna be like you. I'm gonna make my own way." Kyle stood and pocketed two remaining sandwiches. "I'm outta here."

Cole grabbed his arm as he walked past, nearly decapitating me in the process. "Just give me until June. I'm gonna make this right for you, I promise."

"All words and no action, bro." Kyle stalked away, pushing angrily through the exit door.

Cole sat in silence, obviously brooding.

"So that's your brother," I said, breaking the silence.

"Yeah," Cole grumbled. "And despite what he says, he's exactly like me. I was a know-it-all little shit just like him when I was fifteen."

"And now you're so old and wise."

Cole looked at me and smiled, though the smile was sad. "They're trying to suck him in. I knew enough not to join, but Kyle...he's different that way. I didn't care if I belonged. I liked being a loner. Kyle needs to belong."

"Is he...is he part of a gang?"

Cole flexed his fist, angrily. "Not yet, but it's just a matter of time. I'd hoped he would stay away until I could get my diploma and auto certifications. Then I could get him away from all this."

"Does he still live with your mom?"

He shrugged. "Technically, I guess. I think he crashes on friends' couches more often than not. Fucking mother of the year."

He worked the muscle in his jaw and looked away, anger simmering just below the surface.

Cole was hurting. Beneath the anger, I knew he was hurting, and I didn't know how to help him. I awkwardly put my arm around him and patted him on the shoulder.

His lips curved up in a small smile, and we both sat there in commiserated silence.

The moment ended when the phone in his pocket buzzed, and he pulled it out to check the message. He raised his gaze to the sky. "Will this shit ever end?"

"What is it?"

"I've been out of the game for a year now, but they're claiming I took one of their cars. Stripped it. That's why that guy came to see me. Someone set me up."

"So what do we do?"

"Bill's trying to figure out who is stripping the cars."

"*Bill?*"

"Yeah, Bill." Cole seemed annoyed I was surprised Bill was apparently acting as a detective. "He's a good guy. I keep telling you that."

"So what now?" We dumped our trash and walked out to the parking lot to drive back to the hotel.

"I'll give Bill another day to see what he can come up

with. Then I'm going home to straighten this shit out myself."

My eyes widened.

"Don't worry," Cole said. "We won't go to the shop. But I've got to get closer so I can start asking around. I'll keep you safe."

I wasn't worried about myself. Even though the Reapers seemed to have caught up with us here in D.C., Cole would be an easier target closer to home. Or so I assumed. I cursed myself for not forcing Xavier to give me more information about how the Reapers worked.

Yeah, like I could force Xavier to do anything. I sighed. I felt so helpless. It was laughable that I named myself Cole's protector. If there was any real danger, what chance did I have? I got lucky that first time and happened to be behind the wheel of a big truck. I certainly couldn't have *big ass truck* be my weapon of choice. I needed a gun or knife or something. Unfortunately, unless it was a water gun or I was going to slice up an apple or something, both of those weapons would be useless for me since I didn't know how to use them. It never occurred to me I'd need to be trained in combat.

Much of my life over the past year had never occurred to me. Most people wouldn't believe me if I told them. Heck, I wouldn't have believed me either before my sixteenth birthday. I still couldn't believe my mom had been seeking souls my whole life right under my nose, and I never knew about it.

Traffic was heavy on the beltway, especially near our exit. The heat in our most recent car was temperamental, and it wasn't working at the moment. I shivered, wishing I had thought to buy some gloves when I bought those clothes at Target. At that point, I had no clue we'd be venturing further north where it was about ten degrees colder. And if we didn't go home soon, I'd either have to find a Laundromat or buy more clothes.

I lurched forward suddenly, feeling the pull of the

seatbelt against my chest.

Cole looked over at me. "You okay?"

I nodded. "Did someone hit us?"

"Yeah."

"Should we stop?"

He gave me a bland look. "This is a borrowed car, remember?"

Oh, yeah. I hoped there wasn't too much damage to the rear bumper. It was bad enough we *borrowed* the car.

My body slammed into my seatbelt as we were hit from behind again, the nylon cutting into my neck. *Ouch.*

"What the fuck?" Cole said.

I twisted to see who kept hitting us. The driver was a middle aged lady in a minivan with one of those flowers that danced back and forth in sunlight perched on the dash. I squinted, trying to get a better look. That was when I noticed the glazed look in her eyes, like she was possessed or something.

My eyes widened.

She wasn't in control of herself.

The Reapers had found us.

I turned back around, panicked. Another powerless situation. Cole was behind the wheel. Short of launching myself out the window onto the minivan's windshield, there was nothing I could do but watch.

We were hit from behind again, and this time Cole lost control of the steering for a brief moment, sending us careening toward the guard rail on my side. He straightened us out, but there was nowhere to go. We were blocked in by traffic.

Several other drivers gaped at the scene unfolding, but none of them tried to help. Realistically, there wasn't much they could do without making the situation worse.

There was a loud crunching noise behind us as the van hit the vehicle beside it to pull up beside us. The woman steered the van into the driver's side of our car and the impact was brutal. I screamed as my body slammed into the passenger door. Cole's neck jerked, but he kept a grip on the steering wheel and tried to keep us off the guard rail.

He eased up on the accelerator and as soon as the woman realized we had slowed down, she matched her pace to ours, continually ramming the minivan into us.

She didn't turn her head toward us a single time. She was on auto-pilot. There, but not really there. The Reapers had to be involved somehow. There was no other reasonable explanation.

"Hang on," Cole said. "An exit is coming up."

A saw a flash of red and blue lights flare up as we sped past a break in the median. Soon sirens were in our wake.

"Come on, come on," Cole said, using his peripheral vision to keep an eye on the van while simultaneously watching for the exit. He glanced up every few seconds to look in the rearview mirror to monitor the cop pursuing us.

The van crashed into us again as we came to the beginning of the exit ramp.

"You're missing it, Cole," I shrieked over the squealing tires.

"Hang on," he said through gritted teeth.

At the last second, he veered off onto the exit ramp. The van continued straight. I craned my neck and held my breath until I saw the red and blue lights follow the van. Involving police would only complicate things.

Cole pulled to a stop just off the exit ramp in a commuter lot next to the metro.

"Are you okay?" he asked, eerily calm.

I nodded, shaking all over. "Cole, your forehead. You're bleeding." There was a gash from the corner of his left eyebrow that ran halfway up his forehead.

"It's fine. We've got to go." He leaned against the driver's door, but it was jammed shut. "Ava, open your door."

I looked over at him. I'd heard him, but I couldn't

bring myself to raise my hand to the door handle. "You're bleeding," I said again.

He took my face in his hands and looked into my eyes. "Ava, you've got to snap out of it. That cop probably called this in. Cops might be here any minute."

I nodded but didn't move. All I wanted to do was stare into his deep brown eyes. He was bleeding, but alive. They didn't get him. We'd escaped. We were safe.

He broke eye contact and climbed into the back seat, letting himself out of the back passenger side door. Once out he yanked on my door handle several times until he managed to get it open. He pulled me out by my hands and wrapped his arms around me, pressing his lips to my forehead.

I could've melted from the warmth of his lips on my cold skin.

The fog that surrounded me lifted, and I wrapped my arms around him, squeezing tightly. "Oh, God, Cole, did that just happen?" The events of the last few minutes ran through my mind in a montage. I was not cut out for this shit.

He stroked my hair and kissed my forehead one more time. "Yes. Now we've got to go."

I nodded and he held my hand, leading me to the metro station. I stopped, clutching his arm. "Wait, my bag."

He jogged back to the car and rooted around the floorboard until he found it. Faintly in the distance were sirens.

We took off at a run toward the metro, ran our tickets through the turnstiles, and hopped on a train just pulling away without knowing where it was going. That little detail didn't matter. Anywhere was better than here.

We collapsed on a pair of seats in a heap. I put my fingertips up to the wound on Cole's forehead. He must have banged it on his window. The clot had already formed, and it was starting to scab over.

Tears came out of nowhere and silently streamed down my face, my shoulders shaking. He wrapped his arm around me and tucked me into his body. It was comforting, but I had no right to his comfort. Twice now he had been injured because of me. It was only a matter of time before the Reapers completed their task, and I was no closer to stopping it.

We rode the train to the end of the line, only then getting off and taking a look at the metro map to figure out which line we needed to take to get to our hotel. Half an hour later, Cole checked us out of the hotel, and we walked a few blocks over to a restaurant parking lot where he boosted another car.

While we looked for another hotel, Cole was quiet, brooding. He had a lot going on right now, so it was understandable. Plus, a deranged woman did just try to kill him with a minivan.

I slid a sideways glance at him and sighed. I needed to tell him.

Cole lay flat on his back with his hands behind his head on the bed in our new room, which was an upgrade from the last one. Usually, he'd be channel surfing or scrolling through his phone or something. I could handle his smart ass comments, but this quiet worried me. The last forty-eight hours was weighing on him.

No more secrets.

But how did one go about starting a conversation to confess to being the Grim Reaper's lackey? *Gee, Cole, I forgot to tell you about my other part-time job. Those murder attempts these last few days? My bad.* Because that's what this was—murder. I didn't care if his death might serve a greater purpose if he became an angel. It was murder, just as the deaths of the names I submitted before were murder.

I was a conduit for murder.

I closed my eyes. *Best not to think about that now. Focus.*

"Did you, um, notice anything strange about the woman driving that van?" I asked tentatively, tracing the pattern of the comforter with my finger.

He snorted. "Other than the fact that she was trying to kill us?"

She wasn't actually trying to kill me. If I had died, I would have been a casualty, my death a by-product of the Reaper's work. This was not the time to point that out, though.

"Actually, yes."

He turned to his side and propped his head up on his hand. "Did you notice something?"

I looked at his eyes and saw doubt there. He'd noticed something. I hoped that would make my confession easier, that he would believe me more readily.

"Yes," I said slowly. "But I want to hear what you have to say first."

He flopped back onto his back. "This is crazy. These last two days, I mean. This is twice now since we've been up here, and three times if you count the gang member back home, but I can't help thinking the universe has it out for me, you know?"

I did know. Only it wasn't the universe. Just a Grim Reaper.

"It doesn't seem like a coincidence, does it?" I said quietly.

"I only got a look at that woman's face for a few seconds, but she seemed possessed."

"I saw that, too."

"And that homeless guy? Same look."

"Maybe they *were* possessed."

He laughed bitterly. "It's just my karma. I've done some shitty things in my life. I guess it's catching up to me all at once. I'm just sorry you got caught up in all this shit. I swear, Ava, I'll keep you safe. You won't pay for my mistakes."

I closed my eyes as my heart broke. He was so

adamant about protecting me he didn't even realize I was the one he needed protection from.

"It's not a coincidence."

"It's freaky luck, that's what it is."

I took a deep breath. "I'm going to tell you something, and I need you to hear me out, okay? 'Cause it's a little freaky."

He sat up and grinned. I was glad to see he was getting back to his normal self, but sad it would be short lived once he heard what I had to say.

"I have a job." I paused, trying to figure out the best way to explain it. Perhaps I should have prepared for this conversation a little more, but I didn't know how I would have done that.

"A job?" he prompted.

"Do you believe in angels?"

He frowned at the seemingly abrupt shift in the conversation. "Not really, no."

I blew out a breath. This was going to be harder than I thought.

"Pretend you do. You know how when some people die, people will say God must have needed another angel?"

He nodded. "It's horse shit, but yeah, I've heard the saying."

"The saying is sorta true. Sometimes God does need another angel and people are selected to die specifically because they have the potential to be angels."

He raised his eyebrows. "I didn't know you were crazy religious."

"I'm not," I said impatiently. This wasn't going well. I might as well just spit it out. "My mom and I are both seekers. We find people who can become angels. Then we give their names to the Grim Reaper. Well, not directly. We have a middle man."

Cole looked at me like he clearly thought I'd hit my head a little too hard earlier in the car. "Okay," he said finally.

I stood up and paced, everything coming out in a flood. "So I can see auras. They're like colors, you know? The whiter and the lighter the colors, the better the person. And the darker the colors, the more evil the person." I paused. "Your aura is white."

I didn't mention the fact his aura throbbed like no other I'd ever seen. I also didn't get into the whole fated and unfated part. That would just complicate things, and it was hard enough to explain it to him already.

Cole took a second to put it together. "So you're saying I'm a good person? Because my 'aura' is white?"

I nodded. "More than just good. You're in line to become the next angel. Well, potentially, if you pass whatever tests await once your soul has been reaped."

"Okay," Cole said.

I waited for him to say more, but he just stared at me. I didn't know what I expected him to say. I had hoped he would believe me, but I knew better than that. Cole was one of the most down to earth people I'd ever known, and by that I meant the least likely to believe in ghosts, extra-terrestrials, or psychics.

And seekers for the Grim Reaper.

I needed to prove it to him. How did I do that? I slumped against the wall, feeling defeated, until I noticed the silver of Cole's gun in his bag.

Xavier's words echoed in my mind. *Do you have any idea how much pain can be inflicted on someone who can't die?*

"I'll show you," I said to Cole and grabbed the gun before I lost my nerve.

Cole jumped up and put his hands up. "What are you doing with that?"

He stepped toward me as if to take the gun from me. I turned it on him to stop him, gripping it in sweaty hands. "I have to show you something."

I trusted that the gun was loaded since Cole had once said unloaded guns were worthless. I fiddled with it for a second, and it clicked. *Safety off.*

"Put the gun down, Ava," Cole said, carefully taking tiny steps toward me. His eyes were wide. I almost laughed. I finally managed to shock the unshakable Cole. *Just wait until he sees what I do next.*

"Do you trust me, Cole?" I asked.

He nodded. "You know I do. Just give me the gun, Ava."

In one swift motion, I turned the gun on myself, pointing it at my temple. Though I had just claimed not to be religious, I sent up a quick prayer I was right about this.

Then I squeezed my eyes shut and pulled the trigger.

There was a dull click, then nothing.

I was still standing. I was still breathing.

I opened my eyes just in time to see Cole flying across the room toward me. He wrapped his arms around me in a tackle, simultaneously wrestling the gun from my grasp and restraining me on the floor.

He popped the cartridge out of the gun and shoved it deep in his pocket. He tossed the gun on the bed.

"What the fuck, Ava?" His face was inches from mine. Terror was in his eyes, like I'd never seen before. It was not there when the gang member had the gun pointed at him, when the homeless man was slashing at him, or when the soccer mom was trying to run us off the road in her minivan.

I cocked my head. "You said you trusted me," I whispered.

He took a few deep breaths, then crushed his mouth to mine. I moved to wrap my arms around him, but he still had me restrained on the ground, his body covering mine.

So I kissed him back, fiercely, holding nothing back.

It was urgent, our mouths tearing at one another's. He shifted his weight so his body wouldn't crush me and dipped his hand under my shirt, running it up my side. I dug my fingers into his back.

He pulled away first, breathing deeply. The terror in

his eyes had faded, but it wasn't completely gone. I regretted putting it there, but Cole had never been one to be convinced by words. He was more of an *actions speak louder than words* guy. If he was going to believe me about the whole seeker thing, he needed to see it.

Abruptly he stood and brought me up with him. He pulled me to his chest. "Never do that again."

"I don't plan to," I said. "I just had to show you."

He stepped away from me. "Show me what? That you're crazy? I know you were in shock after the thing with the minivan, but I thought you had snapped out of it."

I laughed bitterly. "Unfortunately, this isn't something I can just snap out of."

He scrubbed his hands over his face. "I'm taking you home."

I shook my head. "We can't go home. You're too vulnerable to the Reapers there."

He stilled. "Reapers? Like *Grim* Reapers? What does any of that shit you said before have to do with you turning a gun on yourself?"

In my haste to give him tangible proof, I hadn't clearly explained. Oops. Minor flaw in my plan.

"Seekers can't die. Well, not until the Reapers are done with us anyway. It's like divine intervention or something. Like that day I stepped into traffic, the first day we met."

He sat on the edge of the bed, resting his elbows on his knees. I knelt in front of him. "I know it's a lot to take in, but what I'm telling you is true. I wish to God it weren't, but it is. The gang member, the homeless guy, the minivan? All of that was orchestrated by Reapers. You're on their list."

I conveniently omitted how he got on their list. That was a conversation for another time. Or never.

I preferred never.

Cole looked at me in disbelief, shaking his head.

"Has that gun ever messed up like that before?" I

asked.

"No, it's never misfired," he admitted begrudgingly.

"Look, I know it sounds crazy, but these near death experiences aren't going to stop until we figure something out. It's just going to get worse. The Reapers won't stop until they've succeeded." I took a shaky breath. "Until you're dead."

CHAPTER 20

WE STAYED IN THE HOTEL room the rest of the afternoon, not even leaving for food, ordering in Chinese and pizza. Though Cole had the TV on, he kept one watchful eye on me at all times. After I came out of the bathroom one time, the bulge in his pocket from the clip was gone and the gun was nowhere in sight. I had no idea what he did with them, but I was sure he put them somewhere I couldn't find them.

That was fine with me. I had no desire to put a gun up to my head again. I had made my point. I just hoped Cole had easy access to the gun in case we needed it. I wasn't kidding about the Reapers not stopping until they'd succeeded.

I didn't think Cole believed me, but I'd convinced him not to take me home, and he seemed content to let me think he believed me. Whatever. As long as he did what I told him, he could take me to the loony bin later. After he was safe.

Project Corrupt Cole's Aura started tomorrow. I still wasn't sure how this was going to work, but I had the rest of the night to figure it out.

I pulled Cole's laptop onto my lap to check my email. I'd emailed my mom this morning before we'd met his brother at McDonald's. That seemed like so long ago.

I frowned when my inbox was empty, not even a single email telling me how I could lose twenty pounds in three days. My mom always kept her phone with her. She should have responded by now. Of course, she wasn't always the most tech savvy, but I couldn't shake that nagging feeling. I debated calling her but decided I couldn't risk it. I'd just have to trust her word she could take care of herself.

I closed the lid of the laptop and shoved it off my lap onto the bed beside me.

My first thought for corruption was the seven deadly sins, but when I thought of what those were, I didn't know how that would work. I almost giggled at the thought of Cole committing gluttony. I could just see him with a bulging belly, food all over his face, and crumbs on his shirt. That one wouldn't work anyway. Cole was a glutton on a regular basis, but he apparently had the metabolism of a jack rabbit.

Sloth wouldn't work either. For one thing, I couldn't see Cole just lying around being lazy. Even now I could tell he was getting twitchy from being cramped up in the hotel room all day. Besides, that one would take too long.

Lust...now that was one I could work with. I looked at Cole out of the corner of my eye. He was lounging on his bed with one arm behind his head, TV remote in the other hand. What would be involved in committing the sin of lust?

My belly tightened and my eyes glazed over at the thought.

Focus, Ava.

It was hard to focus with the memory of his mouth on mine so fresh in my mind. We hadn't talked about it, and I didn't want to be one of those needy girls who always wanted to *talk* about everything. Besides, we had bigger problems right now than discussing the meaning of a kiss.

Even if that kiss was the *knock your socks off* type.

To be truthful, it probably fell more into the *I'm glad*

you didn't just blow your brains out variety.

Either way, I'd take it.

But first things first. I had to figure out a way to get the Grim Reapers off his back. After that there would be plenty of time to discuss our relationship.

Our relationship.

Did what we have qualify as a relationship?

I tried to picture us holding hands at the lunch table at school and kissing each other good-bye at our lockers. Nope, couldn't picture it. That would never be us. For one thing, that just wasn't who Cole was. Me neither, really. Maybe once upon a time, but that time had passed.

I was forgetting the most important factor here. Cole's life was in danger because of me, because I let myself get attached. I owed it to him to step away once he was free of the Reapers. He didn't deserve me. And I didn't mean that in a way that was flattering to me.

Cole was better off without me. I'd let myself forget these last few days, but it was time I remembered.

Once Cole was safe, I'd walk away.

COLE OFFERED TO TAKE ME to the national zoo the next morning. I think he couldn't handle another day cooped up in the hotel, and he'd arranged to meet up with his brother again later in the afternoon, so we weren't ready to leave the area yet. He probably figured the zoo was safe. How much trouble could we get into in a zoo? It wasn't likely we'd get mauled by a tiger. Although, I wouldn't put it past the Reapers to try something like that.

As we climbed the hill from the metro stop to the zoo's entrance, I walked with a bounce in my step and a goofy grin on my face. Despite our circumstances, or maybe because of them, I was giddy with excitement. I hadn't been to the zoo in years, and I'd never been to the national zoo. They had giant pandas. I mean, *come on*. What's not to get excited about?

Apparently not everyone felt the same as me. At the entrance to the zoo, we passed a surly preschooler with his nanny. His arms were crossed and he stamped his foot, loudly exclaiming that the zoo was stupid. His poor nanny looked frazzled. I stuck my tongue out at the kid behind the nanny's back. His look of indignation made me giggle.

Cole grinned. "What's so funny?"

I shook my head, not wanting to explain I was taunting a little kid. I was so happy to see a genuine grin on Cole's face. A good night's sleep did us both good, and the tension in the air had definitely fizzled a little.

He hadn't mentioned the whole Grim Reaper thing, probably hoping I'd forgotten about the whole thing.

As if. Being a seeker was always simmering in my mind, even if it was on the back burner. With Cole's life on the line, it was boiling over.

The need to turn his aura hounded me. I was no closer to figuring out how to do it since none of Cole's previous questionable acts had any effect on it whatsoever. Cole needed to commit some serious sins if his aura was going to change.

But if his aura turned, would he still be the same Cole I'd fallen for?

I had developed a theory that intentions mattered as far as auras were concerned. Cole's intentions were usually good, so it was like his intentions canceled out his nefarious actions. Now I needed him to do something bad, but the problem was the sins wouldn't matter unless Cole's intentions were bad, too. So how did I convince him to change his intentions?

That was the thing. If the intentions weren't his, it wouldn't work. If he committed sins to please me, then wasn't that still a noble intention? This was a real doozy. I wasn't sure about any of it. I mean, if he committed murder just because I told him to, then would his intention really matter? Cold-blooded murder was always evil, right?

I just didn't know anymore. There were so many gray areas, exceptions to rules, and loopholes that my head spun.

We strolled around the Asia Trail, stopping where a crowd of people had gathered around the clouded leopard exhibit. I went up on my tippy toes and could just barely make out the cat along the back fence line. I turned to point it out to Cole.

He was standing back a few feet. I smiled at him and motioned for him to come closer. As he took a step toward me, a toddler who was perched on her father's shoulders began to slip, but the father was too busy with two other children to realize the girl was about to do a back flip onto the pavement.

Cole smoothly scooped up the child as she began to fall. It would have been a total *aww* moment except for the way he then held her out at arm's length as if she were a grenade about to go off, his expression a mixture of discomfort and uncertainty. The way he was looking at her, you'd think he was holding a sewer rat by the tail instead of a pigtailed child.

The father took the girl from him, thanking him profusely. The whole incident had only taken seconds, but it was long enough for me to realize something.

I didn't want to sully Cole's aura. He was perfect just the way he was.

I felt like the rope in tug of war. I wanted Cole to stay true to himself, but I also wanted him safe. If there was another way to save him, I was too stupid to see it, and it was only a matter of time before his luck would run out.

My choices sucked. A dead Cole, or a changed Cole? I didn't want either of those.

But it wasn't about what I wanted. It was about keeping him safe, keeping him alive.

He was a good person, despite being rough around the edges. I hated myself for what I was doing. Or what I was going to attempt to do anyway. I still hadn't figured it out yet.

That was the pisser. Cole might hate me when it was over, and it might not even save his life.

But I had to try.

WE PICKED UP LUNCH AND headed back to the hotel. I was so sick of fast food and take out. I'd ordered a salad, but it was exactly what I expected from a fast food salad a month before winter. Limp, pale lettuce with tomatoes that were barely ripened, a sad shade of pink. I picked at it.

Cole crumbled up his burger wrapper and tossed it in the trash. "The gang found the guy who stripped their cars."

I looked up. "Oh, yeah?"

"Bill said the guy barely survived the beating. He's in the hospital right now under guard. Once he's well enough, he'll stand trial for all the car thefts."

"So that's it?"

He shrugged. "Yeah, I mean, we should lie low for a while just to be on the safe side, but they shouldn't mess with us again."

"But I did hit the one guy with a truck," I said skeptically.

"Yeah, but he was the one who messed up by going after the wrong guy. And Bill got it all on the surveillance camera, so I don't think we'll have much trouble with him."

I nodded but still felt unsure about the whole thing.

"Anyway," Cole continued, "we can go home after we see my brother tonight."

I nodded again, sighing and pushing the salad away.

"What's wrong?" He nudged me with his foot. "This is good news. You should be happy."

How could I be happy when Cole was in just as much

danger as he was when we left home?

"The Reapers are still after you," I said quietly.

He sighed.

I looked up sharply. "You don't believe me."

"No, I don't," he admitted. "You might be able to convince me of angels and all that other stuff, but me as angel material?" He laughed. "That's where you lose me."

"It's true, Cole," I said. "I don't know how else to convince you. I put a freaking gun to my head."

"About that." Cole rubbed his neck.

"Do you think I made it up?" I asked.

"You'd just had a shock. I figured, you know, with your death wish antics and all..." he trailed off.

"First of all, I don't have a death wish." I stood and put my hands on my hips. "Second of all, why would I make up something like that? I know how crazy it sounds."

"Like I said, there might be angels, but I'll never be one of them."

"I'm not crazy, Cole. This isn't something I'd just make up."

"Look, Ava." Cole stood and crossed over to me, putting his hands on my shoulders. "I'm not calling you a liar." His tone was one that a person might take with a toddler. "But you have to know how hard your story is to believe."

I jerked away from his touch. "It's not a story. It's my life."

I should have known he wouldn't believe me. I had known it. But I'd had to try.

I sat on the floor cross-legged and took some cleansing breaths, like I'd done with my mom when we were on a yoga kick a few years ago. Yoga had always relaxed me, so I went through the movements, did a few poses.

Cole huffed and sat on the edge of the bed, his hands clasped in front of him. Obviously he thought he was humoring me. He wasn't humoring me. Soon he'd find out this shit was for real.

I'd never tried to show anyone my aura before. I'd been taught to hide this ability from everyone, especially Xavier. My aura projections usually happened when I slept, and even then, not always. I'd been so stressed lately I hadn't even been concerned about it happening and Cole seeing it. But now I needed to force myself to de-stress and take control. I'd never tried to do it before, never had reason to, but I certainly had a reason now.

"What the hell are you doing?" he asked.

I ignored him and continued with a few basic poses—cobra, warrior, tree, sunbird. I repeated them all several times. The physical stress of the last few days left my body. Now I just had to deal with the mental.

I returned to my cross-legged pose and closed my eyes. I breathed in and out, imagining all of my troubles leaving my body with every exhale.

I prayed like I'd never prayed before, not to anyone in particular, but to whoever was listening, whoever would heed my plea. *Please let me show him. Please let him see.*

I slowly let my guards down but kept my eyes closed. I focused my attention to that little place inside me that burned slightly whenever I looked at auras and imagined forcing it up out of my body and into the room.

I pictured it as a breath of air. All I had to do was open up and release it.

The burning sensation slid through my body, spreading out and then lessening.

"Holy shit." Cole's voice was shocked, awed, disbelieving.

I opened my eyes and held up my hands. They were engulfed in a mist of purples, pinks, reds, and blues.

I smiled, sweat beading up on my forehead. I did it.

I looked over at Cole, wanting to see his reaction.

It was my turn to have a *holy shit* moment.

Cole's aura was showing. He had his arms held out and was looking at the soft white glow emanating from them in disbelief, his eyes wide. His gazed shifted back and forth between himself and me.

"Holy fucking shit," he whispered.

I struggled to maintain it but could only hold it for about ten seconds.

Abruptly, the glow ceased, and I gasped for breath, panting at the exertion this exhibition had taken.

I collapsed on my back on the floor and Cole jumped off the bed to kneel beside me.

"Are you okay?" he asked, putting his arm under me to help me sit up.

This worked out better than I could have ever hoped. Someone had not only heard my prayer but had answered it and then some.

Hope. For the first time since I spoke Cole's name to Xavier, I felt real hope.

I looked up into Cole's concerned eyes. "Do you believe me now?"

CHAPTER 21

WE WERE MEETING KYLE AT McDonald's again, but a different one that was close to the metro. No more *borrowing* cars until we had to.

This time Kyle wasn't alone. He and another guy, a much more sinister looking guy, were sitting on a bench in the parking lot waiting for us. I didn't have to check the guy's aura to know he was bad news. His neck tattoos, black baggy clothing, and hardened expression said enough.

Cole jerked his head at the guy. "Who's this?"

"Reggie," Kyle replied.

"What's up, man?" Reggie said in greeting.

Cole turned back to his brother. "Why'd you bring him?"

"Don't be like that, man," Reggie said, taking a step forward. "Kyle here's my boy."

Cole gave a scathing look. "Kyle's nobody's boy." He turned to his brother. "What, you can't speak for yourself now?"

"Reggie's a good guy," Kyle said lamely. "You don't got to be an ass."

The power dynamic between Kyle and Reggie was clear. Reggie looked to be a few years older than Kyle, and it was obvious Kyle wanted to impress him. So why he brought him to a meeting with Cole was beyond me. Cole had no mercy when it came to calling out someone who he thought was acting like an idiot. And Kyle was clearly acting like an idiot.

"So, man, I hear you work with cars," Reggie said.

Cole's eyes narrowed. "Excuse us," he said, grabbing his brother by his arm and dragging him a few feet away.

That left me with Reggie.

A slow grin spread on his face that reminded me of Xavier. It sent chills down my spine. I wrapped my arms around myself.

He pulled out a joint. "Cool?" he asked.

I supposed that was something. He asked permission before lighting up.

I shrugged. I hoped we wouldn't be there much longer. I looked over my shoulder to see Cole laying into his brother. Kyle's face was like stone. Whatever Cole was saying, it wasn't getting through.

Reggie offered me a hit—once again, how polite of him to offer me a hit of an illegal substance in public—but I declined.

"Your loss," he said, putting the joint to his lips and leaning against the fence. "This shit is the good shit. You probably never had anything like it."

I could confidently say *no* to that as I'd never smoked anything, much less a joint from a sketchy guy I'd just met five minutes ago.

"What's up with that guy?" Reggie looked over my shoulder to Cole and Kyle.

"Cole?" I frowned. "He's Kyle's brother."

"He's a douche."

"He's just worried about Kyle. That's all." Cole was far from a douche. Sometimes an asshole, but never a douche. I didn't think this guy would understand the difference, though. Plus, it probably wasn't in my best interests to engage in a debate with this possible gang member. My last encounter with a gang member didn't end so well.

"He ain't cared before now. Kyle's my boy. This is the first time Cole's been around. Don't seem like he cares to me."

I didn't have a response for that. I hadn't even known Cole had a brother until a few days ago, and I'd even explicitly asked him about it.

"Are you with him?" Reggie asked.

"Not like that," I said, getting a face full of smoke. "We're friends."

He took a step closer, taking another drag. "That's good to hear, chica."

I stiffened and tried to take a step back, but he had blocked me into a corner made by a wooden fence at the edge of the parking lot and the brick wall of the neighboring building.

"You should come party with us later." He put his hand on my hip. "Or now. You could ditch your friend."

"No, thanks," I said firmly, getting ready to step away.

"You won't regret it." Another hand found its way to my thigh while the first one snaked around to my butt.

Now he'd crossed the line. I was willing to play along with his Casanova routine so as to not make waves while Cole was talking to his brother, but after all the shit I'd faced the last few days, I was not going to stand for this punk putting his hands on me.

I grabbed his hand, preparing to shove him away, but before I could, he was roughly pulled away by Cole.

Reggie spread his arms wide, like he'd been wronged. "What the fuck, bro? She said she ain't your girl."

Cole repositioned himself so I was behind him. "Fuck off."

Reggie looked back at Kyle, who had witnessed the exchange in silence. Kyle's expression was unreadable. Reggie chuckled. "Man, Kyle, your brother has serious problems. I'd be hitting that bitch. Fucking cock blocker."

Cole grabbed Reggie by the front of his shirt and shoved him up against the fence so that his back was pressed to the splintering wood. "You're nothing but a little fuck wad, you know that?"

Reggie struggled a little to get himself free, but Cole just pushed him harder against the fence. If I were him, I wouldn't struggle so much. I'd be worried about getting splinters in the back of my neck.

"Man, this is my territory," Reggie said, trying to assert his dominance, which was laughable considering he was being manhandled by Cole. "You're the one who needs to fuck off."

"I don't give a shit about your territory. You stay away from her, and you stay away from my brother. Got that, hombre?"

Reggie sneered. Instead of replying, he spat in Cole's face.

Cole reared back and punched the guy so hard and so quick I almost missed it. He let go of Reggie's shirt and Reggie fell to the ground. Cole dragged his forearm across his face to wipe off the spit.

"Why'd you do that, man?" Kyle said, going over to his friend.

I grabbed Cole's arm and tried to pull him away, but it was like trying to pull a parked car. The wrath was coming off him in waves. I could feel it tingling in the air.

"Let's go," I said quietly. "Let it go, Cole, just let it go."

Cole looked down to me and when his eyes met mine, they focused and became less wild.

"Your boy's not so tough now, huh, Kyle? Are you sure that's who you want at your back?" Cole said before turning and walking away. "Remember what I said."

We quickly walked away from the parking lot. Behind us, Reggie yelled, "I'm going to fucking kill you, man! You're dead!"

I glanced over my shoulder at him, and I believed him. If he had the opportunity to take Cole out, he would. He'd have to get in line. I thanked God the Reapers hadn't found us here. Their influence combined with Reggie's existing rage would be a dangerous combination.

The air still tingled around us, causing my arm hairs to stand on end. It almost felt like tiny electric shocks were zapping me all over my body. This was a new sensation for me. I'd always seen auras, but if I wasn't mistaken, I was feeling Cole's aura.

Excitement filled me. Maybe the wrath pouring off him was enough to sully his aura.

I let down my guards, hoping this time it would be different, that Cole had finally tipped his aura into being colored.

Exhilaration filled me as I saw touches of red mixed in with the white. I smiled, relief crashing over me.

Then the white slowly engulfed the red, taking it over, absorbing it. Within seconds, the red had disappeared completely. If I hadn't checked his aura at that exact moment, I never would have seen it.

Just as quickly as the relief had washed over me, waves of dread slammed into me.

Despite his wrath that was so strong it filled the air, his aura had had only a momentary blip of red. He'd maintained his pure aura.

I didn't understand. Wrath was a deadly sin, and Cole's intentions this time were not good. He had honestly wanted to pummel that guy, and he might have if I hadn't intervened. Maybe his wanting to defend me and keep his brother out of trouble excused his thirst for violence.

Either way, his aura was white. My insides tightened.

Cole was going to die, and there didn't seem to be anything I could do to stop it.

"I'M SORRY," COLE SAID. HIS voice sounded lost, empty.

I looked up. We were the only ones in our metro car on the way back to the hotel. Before he spoke, the only sound was the *chug chug* rhythm of the car on the tracks.

"For what?"

He leaned his forehead on the glass. "I shouldn't have flipped out on that guy back there. I shouldn't have brought you here. I shouldn't have...I'm just sorry. For all of it."

"Hey," I said, squeezing his hand. "It's not your fault. And thanks for, you know, defending me." I waited a beat. "Thanks to you, my honor is intact."

My attempt at lightening the mood fell flat. My heart wasn't in it, and Cole wasn't in the mood.

He might survive this whole thing, but he wouldn't be unaffected by it. His forlorn expression when he was normally so steady was a sucker punch to my gut.

Cole nodded and looked back out the window. I reached over and held his hand. He squeezed mine back.

We rode the rest of the way in silence, both of us lost in our own thoughts.

Cole would bounce back from this. He'd been involved in some bad stuff before he met me, and he'd managed to turn himself around. Pulling me out of traffic that day had been his only mistake on his path to a better life.

I felt myself begin to tumble into the chasm of self-pity, but I yanked myself away from the ledge. My pity party over my lot in life was done. There was no point to it, and it had accomplished nothing.

Instead, I tried to think positive thoughts. There was power in positive thinking, right?

Sure, I was upset Cole's aura had returned white, but I needed to focus on the important part here—his aura had changed. This was the first time since I'd known him his aura had any color at all. That was progress. I had to think of it that way. I had to. I couldn't give up.

Cole's life depended on it.

"SO WHY COULDN'T WE HAVE borrowed a car days ago?" We were standing in a sea of cars in the same commuter lot we had fled from following the minivan incident.

Cole gave me a sidelong look. "We did."

I shook my head. "No we *borrowed* a car, your definition of borrow. This is a legitimate loaner, right?"

"It belongs to a friend of Bill's." Cole knelt next to the rear tire of a two door coupe and felt around in the wheel well for the hide-a-key.

And yes—I now knew the difference between a sedan and a coupe. I'd actually learned something from this internship.

"Right," I huffed, getting into the car. "So why didn't we borrow it days ago?"

He shrugged. "We've got it now."

I buckled my seatbelt, sighing and shaking my head. I was still floored by how nonchalant Cole was when it came to stealing cars.

As we were getting on the ramp for the interstate, Cole's phone chimed from where it sat on the console between us.

He glanced down at it. "Can you check that?"

I smiled to myself. It was a small victory that Cole now seemed to trust me implicitly.

The text was from Bill, and it nearly made my heart stop. I gasped and put a hand over my mouth. "No, no, no, no."

Alarm shone in Cole's eyes. "What is it?"

"It's my mom. She's in the hospital."

His grip on the steering wheel tightened. "What happened?"

"Bill...he didn't say. He just said she'd been hurt. The hospital called the shop looking for me when I wasn't at school."

I frantically texted back wanting more details, but my fingers were so clumsy I could barely get the text out.

I should have followed up when she didn't respond to

my email. That wasn't like her, but I was too busy worrying about the here and now to worry about what was happening back home.

Bill didn't respond right away, and I shook the cell phone in frustration, as if shaking it would make it chime with a text.

But I didn't need his response to know who was responsible.

Xavier.

Nightmares ran through my mind. Boiling blood. Suffocation. Who knew what other tricks he had up his sleeve?

I hadn't thought about him lately, but I was thinking about him now. I should have known he was too quiet, that he was building up to something. Xavier was the type of enemy you wanted to keep in your sights. When he slithered under the surface, that's when he could do his worst.

Closing my eyes, I leaned my head back against the headrest. Numbness set in. I couldn't imagine a world without my mom. She'd been the one constant throughout my carousel of a life. I refused to accept it was a real possibility she could be taken from me. I tucked everything deep inside a vault within me—all the fear and distress and anguish. Acknowledgment would only feed it, and I would succumb to inertia.

Cole reached over and took my hand in his. "It'll be okay," he said. "We're on our way. We'll be there soon."

I clasped my other hand on top of his, grateful. It was then I knew for certain I couldn't do it. I couldn't sully Cole's aura. Let me fix that—I *wouldn't* sully his aura. I didn't even know if it were possible, but if it were, I wouldn't do it. There was no way I could turn this person who meant so much to me into something he wasn't just to save him. That wouldn't be saving him, not really. It would be twisting him into someone unrecognizable.

No more trying to beat the system or trying to find a

loophole.

It was time I dealt with Xavier head on.

CHAPTER 22

WE WENT STRAIGHT TO THE hospital. During the drive, Bill had texted back with my mom's room number. I was still getting used to the constant surprises where Bill was concerned. He was turning out to be really handy to have around.

I hurried up to the fourth floor while Cole parked the car, skipping the elevator to charge up the stairs two at a time. When I got to room 408, I stopped, afraid of what I would find.

I took a deep breath, said a quick prayer, and pushed open the door.

My mom was hooked up to several machines. Her skin was pale, almost the same shade as the institutionalized white sheets. Her lips were barely a shade darker than her skin, with only a hint of pink. Even her hair seemed to have lost its color. White bandages covered her exposed arms.

She didn't stir when I entered the room, so I quietly shut the door behind me and sat next to her bed. I reached out and held her hand, afraid I would disturb the tubes flowing into her arm, but needing to touch her and feel the warmth of her skin. She looked like death.

"What have I done?" I whispered.

Xavier might have been the one to put my mom in the

hospital, but I was the reason for it. He'd never touched my mom before I tried to beat the system, his system.

Yet, even while staring at my mom in the hospital bed, I didn't regret it. I regretted it put her here, but I didn't regret trying to save a good person by turning in Joey Huslander's name instead.

I didn't regret protecting Cole.

I was like the thief who wasn't sorry she stole but was damn sorry she got caught.

I massaged my mom's hand a little, causing her to stir. Her eyes fluttered and she turned her head to face me.

"Ava," she whispered.

I nearly cried at the sound of her voice, even though it was hoarse and barely recognizable. The lock on my emotions loosened a little before I got them under control again. I wanted to weep in both joy and grief, but I couldn't indulge in that luxury. I needed to stay strong for both of us.

"Shh," I shushed her. "I'm here, Mom. I'm here now. You don't have to talk."

"Xavier—"

My face hardened at the mention of his name. "I know. He did this."

She nodded and licked her dry lips. "He did what he did to you that one time."

"Why aren't you healing?" I whispered, more to myself than to her. Seekers' rapid healing should have kicked in by now. The sores on her arms should not still be oozing blood.

"I...I don't know." She was having trouble speaking. I stood and ran my hand over her forehead, shushing her. Her skin was warm. She was still running a fever, like her blood was still hotter than normal.

Her breathing evened and I knew she was asleep again. I sat with her for a while longer, then slipped out before my presence would disturb her anymore.

Cole was waiting on a hard plastic chair just outside

her room. He stood when he caught sight of me.

"How is she?"

My chin quivered. He opened his arms and I walked into them. I lay my head against his chest, my tears soaking his t-shirt.

I spoke with the doctor and learned the official word was that she had some sort of infection, which was causing her fever. The doctors didn't know what to make of the open sores on her arms. Right now their course of action was treating the symptoms rather than the cause.

I would treat the cause.

Xavier was going to pay for this.

I SAT ALONE IN OUR apartment, my tears long since dried up. My sadness and heartache had been replaced by anger, a burning rage that set my blood on fire in a much different way. I now understood what it meant to "see red."

It'd been an hour, and the apartment was silent. The only sounds were the residual noises from the neighbor's TV.

Xavier was bound to show sooner or later, but I was willing to bet on sooner.

It'd been a week since the first attempt on Cole's life. Xavier had to be wound tighter than a rubber band by this point.

His actions were stupid, impulsive. I didn't know who he answered to, but I knew there was a hierarchy. My mom wouldn't be able to find pure auras while she was out of commission in the hospital, and I hadn't exactly been cooperative, so I was sure he knew better than to count on me. He wouldn't be able to pass any names along, which couldn't bode well for him.

His actions showed he was losing control. Xavier had always seemed so polished, so perfectly in control, but that was just an act, an illusion. I could see through it now.

Our front door squeaked open, then closed with a click.

Cinnamon.

I took a deep breath and said a quick prayer.

This is it.

"Xavier, how nice of you to join me," I called. My voice shook through the first few words, but was strong and sure by the end of my sentence.

"Come join me," I said, doing my best to make my tone commanding. Inside I was terrified, but I wasn't above using some smoke and mirrors of my own.

He still hadn't spoken, which was a bit surprising to me. I didn't know exactly what to expect, but silence wasn't it.

When he entered the dark room, I turned on the lamp sitting next to me. I'd purposefully chosen to sit on our couch where he normally sat.

He stood in the shadows across the room. He still wore his black suit, though the red tie was absent. In its place was a black one that was slightly loosened around his neck.

The first chink in his armor.

I smiled. "How've you been since I've been gone?"

He sneered. "Have you visited your mother?"

"She sends her best." I struggled to keep the anger out of my voice, to keep my tone indifferent. It took everything I had not to jump across the room and claw the sneer off his face with my bare hands.

His eyes bore into mine, but I didn't flinch, instead returning his hard stare with my own.

"You can't save him indefinitely."

"That may be true," I said. I crossed my legs slowly, much the same as I'd seen him do countless times before. "But if he dies, he'll be the last pure aura you ever get from me."

"You don't know what you're dealing with, girl."

I looked at him evenly. "I know exactly what I'm dealing with. People's lives. There is no greater tender."

He crossed the room swiftly and leaned down, pointing a bony finger in my face. "You'll do as I say."

"Why?" I asked. "Who do you answer to? I know this goes beyond you."

He stepped back and ran his hands through his hair, mussing it up.

"Make me understand," I said quietly. "Make me understand why I have to do this."

"It's what you were born to do."

Something clicked within me, and I cocked my head. "You need me." I laughed. I couldn't believe I didn't realize this until now. "You need me and my mom. There's a reason seekers can't die. Because *you* need *me*."

Xavier's eyes narrowed.

"But I don't need you," I whispered.

And I didn't. There was nothing about my ability and my existence that depended on him, but it seemed that everything in his existence depended on me.

"But you need me," I said slowly. "Don't you?"

Xavier didn't answer. He cracked his knuckles ominously, which once upon a time would have unnerved me. For the first time, I noticed the absence of his cigar, which had been just another part of his act. Smoke and mirrors. That's all it had been.

He knew it, and now he knew that I knew it, too.

"Tell me. Explain it to me," I demanded. "How does the system work?"

He remained silent.

I chuckled. "That's how this works now. It's give and take. You can't just keep taking."

"That's how the system works."

"Not anymore," I said firmly. "I'll give you two more. Two more in exchange for Cole's life. Then that's it. My mom and I are walking away."

"Aren't you forgetting something?"

Before I could answer, I was crippled with a blinding pain. It felt like nails were being hammered into my shin bones. I screamed, grabbing at my legs and collapsing on the floor. I screamed again as the hammers moved up into my thighs, then my ribs, and finally my arms. Soon all I could do was writhe on the floor in pain.

"It...doesn't...matter," I choked out. Sweat streamed down my spine at the exertion it took to get those words out. I had gotten cocky, a mistake I was now paying the price for.

Xavier knelt down next to me while I panted. "What was that there, dear? I couldn't hear you."

"Do what you want," I said through gritted teeth. "You'll get no more names from me."

He chuckled, a little of the old Xavier sparking back to life. "Think you can stand a lifetime of this? Because I have nothing but time. Believe me when I say this, Ava. You'll never walk away from me. And your boy is as good as dead."

He stepped over me with one foot, then with the second foot he stepped on my wrist.

I didn't know what was louder, the sound of my cry or the sickening sound of the crack of my wrist as it broke.

He looked down at me and buttoned his jacket. "You'll want to get that looked at." Then mercifully, he left.

The pain dissipated slowly until all I was left with was the sharp, stabbing throbs of pain in my wrist. I'd naively talked myself into believing I would be able to walk away tonight, free and clear. *Stupid.* He wasn't going to make this easy for me. But he had another thing coming if he thought I was going to give up. He may have won this round, but the fight wasn't over.

I crawled over to the coffee table, cradling my wrist. I used my good hand to grab my phone and call Cole.

"I need you," I managed to get out before everything went black.

CHAPTER 23

I WOKE TO FIND MYSELF being carried down the stairs. A sudden jostling banged my wrist, and I moaned, clutching it.

"Sorry," Cole said. "Just hang on. I'll take care of you."

I turned my face in to Cole's t-shirt and inhaled his familiar scent, which immediately had a calming effect. I loved being in Cole's arms. It'd be nice to be there for once without it being preempted by some sort of disaster.

"I'm sorry if I hurt you," he said, leaning awkwardly. "I have to unlock the door."

I twisted my head to see the Rustinator. I'd never been so happy to see that stupid car in my whole life.

"What?" I joked weakly. "No new car today?"

Cole chuckled. "Not today. My larceny days are over once again." He set me gently in the passenger seat and even leaned across me to buckle me in. If not for the shooting pain in my wrist, this could have been a romantic moment.

When he got into the driver's seat, I told him, "Go to the Urgent Care Center."

"Why not the emergency room?"

I shook my head. "No insurance. This will be cheaper."

Cole nodded and changed directions.

The awkward angle of my wrist got me into a room immediately, but then the nurse left me lying on the examination table with nothing but ice to dull the pain in my wrist. Judging from the bustling noise coming from the hallway, I was in for a wait.

Cole sat in a hard plastic chair, his elbows resting on his knees. "What happened?"

I sighed. "Xavier." I wished I didn't have to tell him. I didn't even like to say Xavier's name around Cole. Logically, I knew it couldn't hurt him, but the more separate I could keep the two of them, even in my mind, the better.

But I'd had no one else to call.

So I told Cole the whole story, pausing only when the nurse came in to check on me.

Cole paced the whole time. Finally, I said, "Please sit. You're making me nervous." The irony of how the tables had turned wasn't lost on me.

The look in Cole's eyes was murderous. "I'm going to kill him."

I sighed. "You can't kill him. He's...I don't know what he is, but I don't think you can kill him."

"Everyone...*everything* can die." The muscle in Cole's jaw worked.

"Don't, Cole," I pleaded. "This is my problem. Let me solve it."

"It's my problem, now."

"No, it isn't," I insisted. "It's not."

Cole flexed and unflexed his fists. "Isn't this the guy who's after me?"

I stilled, and Cole noticed my reaction immediately.

"That makes this my problem. It's me he wants."

I shook my head and struggled to sit up on the examining table. "No. I made this problem. Now let me fix it."

I let down my guards to peek at his aura. Swirls of red were mingling in the white.

Shit.

I should have known better than to involve Cole. He protected what was his. When there was even the possibility that the gang member had seen me and might go after me, he whisked me out of town. When Reggie put his hands on me, Cole pummeled him. What made me think he'd be rational when someone broke my wrist?

I was his now, for better or for worse. His savage expression and lethal tone confirmed it. I had to stop him from putting himself in more danger on my account.

"Cole, remember that thing with the gun?" I asked. "I have a certain amount of protection. I'll heal quickly."

I wouldn't have even sought out medical attention, but I was worried about the bone healing crooked. I knew it would heal on its own, but I didn't know enough about our healing abilities to know what would happen if the bone wasn't straight when it started to grow together.

And after seeing my mom at the hospital, I wasn't taking any chances. She should have healed by now. What if my shenanigans from the past few days had prompted the powers that be to somehow revoke our healing abilities?

A harried looking nurse came in. "The doctor is ready to take you back." She looked at Cole. "Are you family?"

He shook his head.

"You can wait in the waiting room. It'll be an hour, two tops."

The nurse pointed to a wheel chair and I hobbled into it, careful not jar my wrist. Even though my wrist was the only bone that was broken, the rest of my bones didn't feel great, making movement painful.

"Cole, remember what I said, okay?"

He stonily looked at the floor, his hands still clenched into fists.

"Cole?" I pleaded as the nurse began to wheel me down the hall.

"I'll be here when you're done," he said, finally

meeting my gaze. Then he turned on his heel and strode to the waiting room.

WHEN I CAME OUT OF having my wrist set, I searched anxiously around the waiting room, a black Sharpie clutched in my hand. I was going to ask Cole to be the first to sign my lavender cast.

But he was nowhere to be found.

The Sharpie slid soundlessly from my fingers as dread settled in my gut.

Cole didn't know much about Xavier, so where would he have gone to find him?

Think, Ava, think. What had I told him? Not much. I'd done that purposefully, figuring the less Cole knew, the better. And I didn't even know how to find Xavier. He always just kind of showed up at my apartment.

"Do you have someone to take you home?" the nurse asked.

I looked around the waiting room. "Um, the guy I was with. Did he say anything before he left?"

The nurse sighed and tapped on the glass separating the receptionist from the waiting room. "Bev, did that young man say anything to you before he left? The one who was with her."

Bev shook her head and slid the glass closed.

"It's okay," I said. "I'll call a cab."

The nurse pursed her lips in disapproval, but I slipped out the front door with a little wave before she could say anything.

I held my phone in my good hand and tried to search for the number of a cab company using that same hand. It was ridiculously difficult. Six weeks with this cast was going to be trying. Hopefully my super healing would kick in and shorten the time.

I found the number for the cab, but my thumb

hovered over the send button. Where would I tell it to take me? I had limited cash, so I couldn't afford to have the cab take me all around looking for Cole. I probably only had enough money for one destination.

My apartment or the shop? I was waffling between the two when the Rustinator pulled into the parking lot. My shoulders dropped in relief, and I let out a long breath, thanking the powers that be for small miracles.

Cole pulled to a stop in front of me and hopped out. "Sorry," he said, coming around to my side of the car to open the door. "The nurse said you'd be another twenty minutes, so I left to get you some hot chocolate. It took a little longer than I expected." His mouth tilted in a crooked grin.

Sure enough there was a steaming to-go cup in the passenger side cup holder.

I touched his arm, wanting to do more, but knowing I shouldn't. "Thanks."

He smiled. "No problem."

He opened the passenger side door for me, guiding me in, but I stopped him, putting my hand on his chest.

His taking care of me was too much. It did me in.

"Cole, I—" I broke off. I...*what?* What was I going to say to him?

I've never felt like this for anyone before.

I can't imagine my life without you.

I love you.

Cole looked into my eyes. "Ava, are you okay?" He put his arm around me to steady me, probably afraid I was going to faint or something.

I took a shaky breath and smiled. "I'm glad you're here."

He gave a lopsided grin, his eyes tender. "Where else would I be?"

He shut the door after helping me get buckled, and my chin began to quiver. My hands shook.

I could never say those things to Cole. Once I was sure

he was safe, I needed to put distance between us. I'd brought nothing but trouble to his life, a life he was trying to turn around. Even if I managed to ward off Xavier, something told me that wouldn't be the end of it. I would always be a seeker, whether I practiced or not, and along with that came inherent risks. How could I ever ask anyone to expose themselves to that just for being in my presence?

The cost was too great. My mom had the right idea. Detachment was the only way to go.

I clutched the hot chocolate in my hand so tightly the cup started to crumple and a tiny bit of the hot liquid splashed on my finger. I loosened my grip.

As I brought the cup to my lips, I looked over at Cole with his dark hair, serious demeanor, and those eyes I could lose myself in.

I looked out the window, praying for the strength to let go of Cole.

COLE WRAPPED HIS ARM AROUND me, helping me up the stairs to my apartment. The way he was supporting me you'd think I broke my ankle instead of my wrist, but I wasn't complaining. I was going to soak this up while I could. The timer was counting down on my time with Cole. I hoped. I wanted him to be safe, and as soon as he was, then that was my cue to leave.

Cole went to the kitchen to get me some water so I could take the next round of pain meds. I went into the living room and clicked on the light. My gaze immediately gravitated to Xavier's favored spot on the couch, where I'd been sitting before he broke my wrist.

I couldn't sit on that couch anymore. If we still lived in the country, I'd want to take it out to a field and start a bonfire with it. I could barely stand to be in this room. The smell of cinnamon lingered like mold and made me sick to my stomach.

I turned off the light and turned my back on the room to see Cole walking toward me with the water. I awkwardly tried to hold the pill container with my fingers that were protruding out of the cast and open it with the other hand, but it had one of those child safety tops.

Cole took it out of my hand and handed me the water. He popped the lid off with little effort—*show-off*—and handed me two pills.

"Do you want to lie on the couch and watch TV?" he asked.

I shook my head. "I'm gonna go straight to bed." It was late, and today had been the day from hell. I was ready for it to be over.

He nodded. "I'll be on the couch then if you need anything."

"Okay—wait, what?" My brain was running slow.

"I swung by my apartment and picked up clean clothes while I was out getting the hot chocolate. You're not staying here alone."

Tingling spread through my chest until my heart swelled. "Thanks, but you don't need to. I'll just be sleeping."

He stepped into the living room and stretched out on the couch, putting his hands behind his head. "Then you won't even notice I'm here." The couch was about a foot too short for him, so his feet were dangling off one end, perilously close to kicking over the lamp. I recognized the determined look in his face, though, so I didn't bother trying to dissuade him again. Choose your battles and all that.

"I'll get you a pillow and blanket," I said, crossing to the trunk we kept in the corner of the living room for things like that. As I walked further into the room, I caught the smell of cinnamon again and my stomach heaved.

I stopped in my tracks.

"What's wrong?"

"I, uh, I..." I sniffed the air frantically, but the smell didn't get any stronger. I relaxed a bit. It was just the same lingering smell from earlier.

But the smell reminded me that it wasn't safe for Cole here. Of all places, my apartment was the most likely place for Xavier to rear his serpent-like face.

"Ava?" Cole asked, bringing himself to a sitting position, his eyes on me.

"Just...having a flashback from earlier," I lied. I needed to get him out of here. He seemed to want to take care of all my problems these days, so I hoped I could use that.

"Oh." He frowned.

"I feel weird being here right now," I continued. "Do you think maybe we could stay some place else tonight? Like a hotel?"

I cringed as that came out of my mouth. Under other circumstances, that sentence would make me sound like a floozy. Even though I knew Cole understood after everything we'd been through in the last week, I still was aware of the implication.

Oh, well. I had bigger concerns than coming off like a floozy.

"We could stay at my place," he said. "It'll be a little cramped, but my bed's comfortable."

I blushed, my mind still in the gutter. He noticed immediately and amended himself. "For just you. I'll sleep on the futon."

His place wasn't a much better choice since Xavier no doubt knew where he lived, but I didn't want to take the time to hash out the exact arrangements right now. Once we were in the car and away from here, we could figure it out.

We shuffled back to my room to gather a few things. Cole insisted on me telling him what to pack, and he packed it for me. His pampering made me feel warm and fuzzy, but I drew the line at him packing my underwear.

I was in the bathroom getting my toiletries when I noticed the scent of cinnamon wafting in the air. I stopped and sniffed. That was weird. It'd never lingered in the bathroom before, usually just in the living room where he spent his time.

I stepped into the hallway, and it was like walking into a vat of cinnamon.

Oh, shit.

My brain wasn't firing on all cylinders, costing us valuable time when we should have been getting out. Xavier would be here within moments.

"Cole!" I rushed back into my bedroom. "We've got to go."

"Did you get everything you need?"

"Yes. We've got to go. Now."

Cole stopped mid-stride. "It's him, isn't it?"

I nodded. "He might already be in the parking lot. We've got to hurry."

Cole reached behind him and pulled his gun from where he must have had it tucked at the small of his back.

That was bad, very bad. He'd brought a gun to a super-charged demon-powered fight.

I grabbed his arm. "Cole, no, you don't understand."

"This needs to end, Ava. He can't keep terrorizing you like this."

"I agree, Cole, but not now. Please not now." I would have said anything to get him to listen to me, but nothing came to mind.

The sound of the front door opening made my pleas useless. My fear pulsed through the air and mixed with the cinnamon.

Xavier was here.

CHAPTER 24

THE OMINOUS CLICK OF THE front door closing sealed our fate. There was no escaping.

It was time to face Xavier.

"Stay here," I hissed to Cole.

He shook his head, so I grabbed his arm. "Remember, he can hurt me, but he can't kill me. Stay here. Please. Let me get rid of him."

Cole's eyes searched my face.

"Please," I said again. "Trust me."

Something in my expression or my voice must have convinced him. He nodded and pulled me into him, kissing my forehead. "If he hurts you, I'm shooting him." Then he let me go.

I squared my shoulders and stepped out into the hallway, leaving my bedroom door cracked so Cole could at least hear what was going on. If he could hear that I had everything under control, then maybe he'd stay put.

Now I just had to figure out how to keep things under control. My track record wasn't promising.

Xavier's eyes went straight to my cast, and they filled with a joyful gleam.

"Purple? Really? I would have figured you for a hot pink kind of girl."

"It's lavender," I said evenly. "And that just goes to

show how much you don't know about me."

He sat in his spot on the couch where Cole had been lying just ten minutes earlier. He pulled a cigar out of his jacket pocket and lit it.

His clothing was more in order, though not quite as pristine as normal. He'd lost that maniacal look in his eyes, and he looked more in control. I didn't know if that boded well for me or not. I'm sure he felt he had the upper hand again.

And right now, he definitely did. Cole was fifteen feet away with nothing but me and my bedroom door between him and Xavier. I'd give my life to protect him.

"In any event, I'm glad to see you're all patched up," Xavier said. "I hate seeing my girls hurt."

My nostrils flared, but somehow I managed to keep myself in check. We weren't his girls. We'd *never* be his girls.

"The doctor said I need rest," I said, trying to sound both pitiful and subservient. Smart ass comments weren't going to help my cause. "I was about to go to bed."

"Then I see I got here just in time." He twirled the cigar between two fingers. "We're behind on our quota, my dear. You're going to have to hurry to get caught up. The Reapers don't like being idle."

"I have to rest," I repeated. "I can't go back to school until the doctor clears me." It was all a lie, but I figured what did he know about modern medicine? It wasn't like he'd ever used it. "I can't find any auras until I'm back at school. That's where all the teenagers are."

He leaned forward, his eyes narrowing. "How stupid do you think I am?" he asked. "There are teenagers everywhere. Go to the mall, the local hangouts. Once upon a time, it was the arcade or the corner soda shop. Certainly you know where to find teenagers outside of school. You are one, after all."

"I need some time to heal," I repeated. "You really messed me up this time." I paused, a contrite look on my face, as if it pained me to admit this. "Give me a week and I should be better."

Xavier sighed and put out his cigar on the sole of his shoe. "You have a broken wrist. It's not the end of the world."

"Have you ever had a broken wrist?" I asked.

His response was a laugh.

"Then how do you know how it feels?" I took a deep breath, using the moment to remind myself to keep my mouth in check. "It really hurts. I can't focus on auras when I'm in this much pain. And the pain meds also mess with my ability."

Xavier stood and crossed the room to lean down in my face. "Don't be so dramatic." Then he swept my feet out from under me and I crashed to the floor, banging my elbow and jarring my broken wrist. I bit my lip to keep from crying out in pain.

He crouched next to me. "I hope the meds are strong enough."

Instead of fire running through my veins this time, it was ice. It started in my chest. I could hear the crackling as the ice spread through my body. I convulsed on the floor and stared at my fingertips as they started to swell.

It hurt. It hurt so bad. It felt like every inch of me, inside and out, was coated in a layer of ice. I couldn't breathe. Panic filled me as my fingers began to turn a pale shade of gray.

"You see that? That's frostbite. I suspect your toes look about the same. Soon they'll turn black. Frostbite really is quite a nasty phenomenon."

I couldn't speak because of my chattering teeth. I curled in a ball, trying to conserve what little warmth I had left.

Just as quickly as the cold set in, it stopped, but the shivering remained as my blood slowly warmed and started to return my body to normal temperature.

I looked up from my spot on the floor to see why

Xavier had abruptly stopped. He was grinning, looking past me. I turned my head to see Cole in the hallway with his gun raised.

"Ava, you were holding out on me," Xavier said. "You had a white aura stashed in your bedroom this whole time. Shame on you, naughty girl."

It was then I realized I'd fallen right into his trap. He knew I'd turn to Cole for help with my broken wrist. After all, who else did I have with my mother incapacitated? He'd set a trap and I'd walked blindly into it.

I'd delivered Cole right to him.

"Ava, get some blankets and warm yourself," Cole said, keeping his eyes on Xavier. "It's important for you to get warm."

I continued to shiver on the ground and tried to pull myself into a sitting position, but my limbs were too stiff.

"I-I-I c-c-can't," I stuttered.

Cole circled around the living room, grabbed a blanket from the trunk, and tossed it over me, all without taking his eyes or his gun off Xavier.

"That's so sweet," Xavier said, clasping his hands.

I needed to think, but if I wasn't firing on all cylinders before, my Popsicle brain certainly wasn't helping.

I was so stupid. Why hadn't I taken a weapon with me to face Xavier? Why hadn't I taken Cole's gun? I had my doubts that Xavier could be killed, but a gun might slow him down at least. I had been so eager to keep Cole hidden that I hadn't thought ahead.

I should have brought a weapon.

I should have made Cole leave my apartment immediately.

I should never have given Cole's name in the first place.

All of these *should haves* ran through my mind.

Then it hit me.

"Xavier, check his aura." I twisted to lie on my back so I could see Cole better. "It's not white. He's full of wrath.

There's red there."

I couldn't check his aura. I was in too much pain to focus enough, but I would bet my life that there was red there. I could just barely feel the electricity in the air that I felt the last time Cole's aura was stained with red.

But it was the wrong thing to say, a mocking thing to say.

Xavier's nostrils flared slightly. He couldn't check Cole's aura. That was the reason he needed me, the whole reason I was in this predicament.

Damn it! I couldn't believe I'd just done that—taunted the demon.

This was about to get worse.

"She's right." Cole sneered. "I'm full of wrath."

I saw his trigger finger flex right as Xavier began to suffocate me.

I gasped sharply, which was just enough distraction to make Cole hit Xavier's shoulder instead of his chest where he'd originally been aiming.

Air rushed back into my lungs as I saw a flash. Then Cole went down.

I saw it in slow motion. The burst of red on his chest, the shock in his eyes, his knees hitting the floor, followed by the rest of his body.

"No," I said, crawling over to him. Blood began to spread over his chest, soaking his t-shirt.

"I hit his heart," Xavier said, a small silver gun in his hand, "which is where I suspect he was trying to hit me. It's too bad for him you distracted him."

I took the blanket and pressed it to his chest, applying pressure with my good hand. "Stay with me, Cole." Was he already getting paler?

The blanket was saturated in no time. Cole's eyes became glassy.

Xavier put his gun back into the holster hidden under his jacket.

He knelt down next to me. "He's losing a lot of blood."

He looked up and around. "Reapers are coming. No, won't be long now."

"His aura's not white," I whispered. "He shouldn't have to die."

And now that he was dying without a pure aura, he stood no chance of becoming an angel. I'd damned him twice over. First for his death, and second I'd taken his chance of being an angel.

"I don't care about that," Xavier said. "Consider this a lesson."

He stood and walked away.

I grabbed Cole's gun and pointed it at Xavier, screaming as I pulled the trigger. My shot went wide, taking out the lamp. I squeezed again, this time hitting him in the back of the thigh.

I turned back to Cole. His eyes were closed, and he was definitely paler.

Oh God, oh God, oh God. It wasn't supposed to happen this way.

"Open your eyes," I pleaded. "Look at me."

Where was my phone? I needed to call for help, but I had no idea where it was. I felt in Cole's pocket for his phone and yanked it out.

Xavier laughed. "It's too late."

"No," I sobbed. I put my hands on Cole's cheeks, then his chest, and felt his breaths were shallow, his heartbeat erratic. "Cole? Cole, stay with me."

Xavier simply laughed.

I wanted to rip his throat out, rip that laugh right out of his body, but that would mean leaving Cole's side. Nothing was worth that.

CPR whispered the voice of reason inside my head.

"I'm going to fix you, Cole. Don't worry," I choked out the words, trying to remember what I'd learned in the first aid portion of health class. "I'm going to fix it."

I put my hand on his chest, felt it was no longer rising and falling. I was too late.

"No!" My cry was frantic. "No, Cole, no! You can't leave me. You can't—"

I lay over his chest, stroking his cheek, touching his hair, kissing his lips.

He was gone...gone...gone.

Ashes to ashes, dust to dust...

Nothing mattered anymore.

I was void inside. There was nothing.

I suddenly became re-aware of Xavier's presence, and the void filled with rage, wrath, anger.

Hatred.

It was as if the void was a black hole that swallowed all the red auras that existed in the world. If I could see my aura, it would be deep red, the color of blood.

Grayness filled the room, like shadows swirling around us.

I picked up the gun again and turned it on Xavier.

"Go ahead," he said. "I can hurt you faster than you can pull that trigger."

I squeezed it anyway, and as my finger applied the last bit of pressure, my insides started burning. I screamed in agony as the first drops of blood started seeping out of my pores.

Xavier limped toward me. If I'd had the capacity to feel anything but agony at that point, I would have been glad Xavier was limping. At least I'd done some damage.

Then he stopped abruptly and stilled, looking up and around as if he could see or sense something I couldn't.

I'd never seen Xavier look terrified, but his eyes filled with sheer horror.

My pain stopped as a white glow filled the room.

Xavier took off running, taking the smell of cinnamon with him. It was replaced by the scent of sugary sweetness.

The light filled the room, but it wasn't blinding light like a white aura. It was warm, comforting, cozy. It was like being embraced by all things good in the world.

A form materialized in front of me.

It was an angel.

THE AIR AROUND ME SWIRLED with electricity so that the hairs on my arms stood on end. I leaned over Cole, protecting him from the current, refusing to accept he no longer needed my protection.

Gray shapes swooped above us. One by one they left, but where they went I didn't know. One second they were there, and the next they were gone.

I hugged Cole's body—

Cole's body.

A sob escaped my lips, and I pulled Cole into my lap, holding him close, not caring about the smears of his blood that were staining my clothes.

The angel observed quietly, like a passive mourner at a funeral. But this was no funeral. This was my life.

It had been Cole's life until it was taken from him.

"Why?" I screamed at the angel. "Why did you take him?"

The angel cocked his head. He looked like a normal man, except there was a shimmer surrounding him, like he was iridescent. He was dressed in all white with a fair complexion and pale blond hair. There was no halo or wings or anything like that. He could pass as a human if not for the shimmer.

Well, that and his grand entrance.

"This work was not mine," he said reverently.

"Wasn't it though?" I said bitterly. "He was taken so he could join you. So he could be an angel."

Except he couldn't now. But still I hoped. All I could do was hope he was in a better place.

The angel stared at me, a sad expression on his face.

"Is he..." My voice shook. "Is he going to be an angel?"

"I don't know."

I ran my hands over Cole's hair and leaned down to

kiss his forehead. "Why are you here?"

He sighed. "I'm breaking many rules by being here."

"Then go. I don't care about your rules. Just go and leave us." I stroked Cole's cheek with my fingertips. His skin was already growing cool.

"You're the first I've appeared to since my fall."

"Your fall?" I looked up. "So what, you're like a fallen angel?"

He shrugged. "Some might have considered me that at one time. I've been redeemed. Saved. I want to tell you a story."

He knelt in front of me.

"Once upon a time there was an angel. This angel was very unhappy and sought happiness in the Earthly realm. For he loved people, you see. One person in particular. A woman."

He paused for a moment, a pained look in his eyes as his gaze settled on me.

"The angel loved the woman more than anything else. You can see how that might be problematic for an angel. He forsook everything to be with this woman. There was a child. The child was wanted and loved more than any child ever was or would be, I'm sure of that. However, it was not to last. Tragedy struck and the woman perished."

Tears unabashedly streamed down his cheeks. His telling was different from the story I'd heard, but the emotion of his face left me no doubt his version was true.

"Did the Reapers take her?" I asked.

"Every time someone dies the Reapers take them. But if you're asking if she was slated to be an angel, then no, I don't think so. She had her faults, like most humans do."

He smiled, lost in some memory for a moment. The he stood and paced. "Without her, I was lost. I couldn't remain on Earth without her, not even for the sake of the child. I begged to come home, and I was a favorite, so it was permitted. There was a price, though, and it was a price I was willing to pay, a price I was honored to pay, for it meant my legacy would contribute to the greater good. The results were so pleasing, in fact, that others were baptized to perform the same service. It seemed my folly had turned out to be rather fortuitous. It wasn't until later that I realized the true weight of this price on those who would have to pay it."

He was talking in circles, and I was having trouble following. "What was the price?"

"My child and all children after her became seekers."

I took a minute to process what he said.

"So you're like my great grandfather or something?" I said slowly.

He nodded. "Several times great, but yes."

I fisted my hands on Cole's shirt, trying to control my anger. "This is all your fault, then. Because of you, my life and my mom's life are a living hell. I'm responsible for people dying. Do you have any idea what that's like? For your entire existence to be centered on choosing people to die?"

"No, I don't. I imagine it must be..." he trailed off, struggling to find the right word, "difficult."

"Difficult," I repeated. "Difficult?" The decibel of my voice was raising to near shriek level. "Look around you! Look at this. Look at him." I looked down at Cole. "Difficult doesn't begin to cover it. He died because of me."

"Ah, yes," my angel ancestor said. "So that's him."

I looked at him, a question in my eyes. "You know him?"

"I look in on you from time to time, though I'm not supposed to. I was there that day he pulled you out of traffic."

"Did you slow it down?" I whispered.

He nodded. "Yes. You would have survived. The Reapers would have seen to that, but it would have been painful."

"What about when I pulled the gun on myself?"

He nodded again. "That was me as well. You would

have survived. Once again, the Reapers would have taken care of that. I couldn't bear to see you hurt so severely though. I can sense when my lineage is in danger. I saved your mother as well."

"My mother?"

"Yes, the night she almost died. She was already pregnant with you. Not far along, yet." Noticing the look on my face, he stopped. "Oh, it appears I've spoken out of turn. I thought you knew about that."

I shook my head, trying to absorb the fact that my mother and I had an angel looking out for us. He'd saved us both now. I wanted to ask for more details, but now wasn't the time. And she deserved to tell that story herself. I forced myself to believe she'd have the chance.

"It's forbidden for me to intervene," he continued, "but when I look at you both, it's like looking at my Elizabeth all over again..."

He cleared his throat. "Anyway—the boy. I'm not supposed to see you, and it's inevitable I will get caught eventually. When he stepped in to save you, I found a solution. He could be your guardian angel."

I closed my eyes. "Is that why his aura is white? Did you make his aura white?"

He shrugged. "It's not that straightforward. There is lingering darkness because of his past. He has natural goodness in him, and when he's with you, the goodness is amplified. You bring it out in him. It's his instinct to protect you. He would be the perfect guardian angel for you, so if you came to be in danger when I could not be there—"

"You marked him?" I was flabbergasted. "You marked him for death so he could become my guardian angel?"

A hollowness filled me. The minute Cole showed kindness toward me his death had been determined. I really was bad for him. I'd just had no idea how deep it ran.

"I see I've upset you." He sighed. "I only meant to

keep you safe. The connection you have with the boy—"

"His name is Cole. He has a name."

The angel nodded, looking sad. "I'm sorry."

"Where is his soul?"

He looked troubled.

"Where is it? Did the Reapers take it already?"

"The Reapers left when I arrived. They actually can't stand to be in the presence of angels."

That explained the gray shapes swirling around us that disappeared when the angel came.

"Are Reapers angels?"

He chuckled. "No. Reapers perform different functions. One of their functions is to collect the souls of the departed, both pure and evil souls and all in between. The other function is to arrange the deaths of those whose time has come. That takes a certain detachment or coldness, if you will, so no, they are not angels."

He knelt down next to me again and took my blood-stained hand in his. I resisted, not wanting to take my hand away from Cole's, but as soon as my skin touched the angel's, a sense of calm settled over me.

"Angels are harbingers of light and life, not death."

"What does that mean?" I whispered. He was telling me something important, but in my grief, I wasn't understanding.

"That means I can bring him back. His soul still lingers."

My eyes widened. Cole could come back to me. I would give anything, *anything*, to bring him back.

"It is not without consequences," the angel said quickly. "I will have to share my blood with him, which will make him part of my line."

"So that means..." I had figured it out, but I needed to hear it.

"He will become a seeker, like you."

I recoiled from the angel. I looked down at Cole's face, at his long lashes. Could I do that to him? Could I damn him to my same fate?

"What happens if I decide not to seek anymore?"

"You will most certainly die. The Reapers will no longer have a use for you. It is forbidden for angels to procreate with humans, and the only reason my descendants are allowed to live is to serve the purpose of seeking."

"And Cole?"

"He is already gone. This is the best I can offer you. I'm sorry."

I traced my fingers on Cole's face. What would he do? If our roles were reversed, would he save me with the condition I'd become a seeker?

I didn't know. All I knew was a part of me died when he did.

"You have to decide, Ava. I can't stay much longer."

I closed my eyes and sent a prayer off into the universe.

"Save him."

CHAPTER 25

THE ANGEL NODDED, AND I gently slid Cole off my lap and scooted back to give the angel room to work. I couldn't bear to be separated from him, so I reached over and held his hand.

So many things ran through my mind. What was going to happen to him? Was this a mistake? Would he want this? What had I condemned him to?

Before I could ask for clarification, the angel reached into his pocket and took out a dagger sheathed in a leather case. He cut the end of his finger, deep enough to produce a steady stream of blood, and held it over Cole's wound, letting the blood drip into it.

Nothing happened at first. Then his skin shimmered, and the wound began to heal, slowly at first, then quicker until it completely closed. All that remained beneath the blood was a whitened scar.

I gasped.

The angel continued his work by tilting Cole's neck back and breathing into his mouth, like he was giving CPR. He was literally breathing life back into Cole. The rise and fall of Cole's chest made my heart soar. I squeezed his hand, hoping Cole would miraculously squeeze it back.

That didn't happen. Nothing happened. I couldn't stop the sinking of my heart, and I hung my head. Maybe it was too late. Cole had been de—I couldn't say it, even in my mind. He had stopped breathing minutes ago. Maybe we waited too long.

But when the angel sat back, Cole's chest began to rise and fall on its own. I lay across him so I could feel it.

"He's breathing," I said in disbelief.

The angel smiled softly. "Yes. He'll need a few days to completely heal. I'm sorry I couldn't bring him back to full strength right away, but I am not as powerful as some."

I crossed around Cole and threw myself into the angel's arms.

I squeezed my eyes shut, tears streaming down my face. "Thank you."

He hesitated for a moment, perhaps lost in memories of his beloved Elizabeth, before embracing me back. "You're welcome."

I stepped away from him to tend to Cole, dropping down and placing my hand on his chest once again to ensure he was still breathing. With every breath, a new thrill shot through me. I would never grow tired of that feeling.

"I have to go. I've already stayed too long." He retreated a few steps.

"Wait, what about Xavier?" I asked. "What if he comes back?"

The angel's face hardened, the first time anger had graced his expression since I'd been in his presence. "I'll make sure you get a new handler. Xavier should have no reason to contact you again."

I nodded.

There were so many questions I still wanted to ask, but he was already becoming more iridescent, finally completely fading from view. I wondered if I would ever see him again. He'd given me the greatest gift I could ask for, and for that I'd be eternally grateful.

I looked down at my gift.

Cole's eyes fluttered, and a soft moan escaped his lips.

"Cole, come back to me." I put my hands on his cheeks.

His eyes opened briefly, then closed again. "Ava," he whispered.

"I'm here, Cole." I wiped the tears from my cheeks with the back of my hand. "I'm here."

"I'm sorry," Cole whispered. "I'm sorry I couldn't protect you." His voice broke at the end.

He'd died. Cole had died, and his first thought was of me.

The game had changed because Cole would now be a seeker, but even if the game remained the same, I knew I wouldn't be able to keep my vow of walking away. I wasn't strong enough to walk away from him.

And maybe that wasn't such a bad thing.

"Shh," I said. "Save your strength."

"When I knew he was hurting you, I couldn't—"

"It's okay."

"I couldn't stay away. I had to get to you."

"You've got me now." I took his hand in mine and squeezed.

His eyes closed, but not before he squeezed my hand back.

"You've got me, too."

EPILOGUE

"YOU HAVE TO GO OR you'll be late."

Cole's hand snaked under my shirt to my bare stomach, and I pushed it away. "I'm serious." I said this with a smile, though, negating its effectiveness.

Cole smiled and leaned down to kiss me, returning his hand to my stomach. This time I let him, putting my hand over his beating heart.

Cole was always doing that now—making contact with my skin. Whether we were at school, like now, or in the shop or just hanging out, he always had to be touching me. It turned out Cole and I actually were one of those couples. And I couldn't say I minded.

The angel was true to his word, and it had taken Cole several days to regain his strength. I guessed dying wasn't something you came back from overnight. But now he was back to normal.

Cole ran his thumb over my cheek, tucking a stray hair behind my ear.

Well, a new normal, anyway.

Once again, I wasn't complaining.

The warning bell rang, telling me I had one minute to get to class. I pulled away from him. "Bell," I said meaningfully. "Me, class. You, Bill's."

Cole snuck in another kiss, then rested his forehead

on mine. "You're coming after school, right?"

I nodded. The internship was technically over. We had gotten an A on our project. Ms. Green was especially impressed by all the extra time we'd devoted by going on the "business trip" with Bill.

If she only knew.

Cole's dark eyes found mine and my breath stuck in my throat.

"I'll see you later," he said.

I stepped just inside the classroom door and watched him walk away, checking his aura as I always did. It was a mash-up of colors. Most people's auras leaned dominantly toward one color, but Cole's was a veritable rainbow.

If I projected my own aura right now, it would be laced with guilt. Cole still didn't know the bargain I had made with the angel in exchange for his life. He hadn't started seeing auras yet, and there weren't any other indications of his new role as a seeker. It was going to be the shock of his life when the abilities finally did kick in. I couldn't gauge how he was going to react. I chose not to think about it.

He hadn't asked a lot of questions about what happened, and I hadn't offered any explanations. He seemed happy we were both okay, and I was content to let him be. I'd have to tell him the whole story eventually, but it could wait. I was too busy living in the moment and enjoying our new normal.

My mom was home from the hospital, but she wasn't one hundred percent. The doctors still hadn't figured out what the problem was—and they never would—but they were convinced that given her current trajectory, she'd make a full recovery.

So far we hadn't seen Xavier, nor the new handler the angel promised me. He had said Xavier should have no reason to contact me, but I could think of a few. He didn't know Xavier as well as I did. Xavier wasn't going to let this go, and neither was I. He'd killed Cole. He'd almost killed my mom.

Forgiveness wasn't an option.

But for the time being, life was good. If I'd learned anything these past few weeks, it was to enjoy small blessings and not borrow trouble. It was a hard lesson, and I wasn't taking it for granted.

Right now I had no new seeking assignments, my mom was on the mend, and most importantly, I had Cole. Cole, with his delicious lips, sultry eyes, and roaming hands.

What more could a girl want?

Thank you for reading *Birthright*! I hope you enjoyed it. If you did, please help other readers find this book by telling your friends and leaving a review on Amazon, Goodreads, or your favorite book retailer. Word of mouth and reviews help authors more than you know!

ACKNOWLEDGEMENTS

Writing is a solitary endeavor, but no author does it alone.

A special thank you to my biggest champion, my husband. Sometimes I think you believe in my dreams more than I do.

To my children—you inspire me every day. Your pride in me and my books warms my heart.

To my agent, Sarah Younger—Thank you for supporting and believing in me. I've learned so much from you.

To my writer friends—Marnee, Terri, the Dreamweavers, the NAC, #TeamSarah, and countless others I'm forgetting—your friendship means so much to me. There are no words.

ABOUT THE AUTHOR

Jessica lives in Virginia with her college-sweetheart husband, two rambunctious sons, and two rowdy but lovable rescue dogs. Since her house is overflowing with testosterone, it's a good thing she has a healthy appreciation for Marvel movies, Nerf guns, and football.

To learn more about Jessica, visit her website jessicaruddick.com. Connect with her on Twitter at @JessicaMRuddick or on Facebook at facebook.com/AuthorJessicaRuddick.

Other Books by Jessica Ruddick

Letting Go (Love on Campus #1)
Wanting More (Love on Campus #2)

Made in the USA
Middletown, DE
27 January 2017